# MAD
# ABOUT BEES

# Candida Crewe

# MAD
# ABOUT BEES

HEINEMANN : LONDON

William Heinemann Ltd
Michelin House, 81 Fulham Road,
London SW3 6RB
LONDON   MELBOURNE   AUCKLAND

First published 1991
Copyright © Candida Crewe 1991

A CIP catalogue record for this title
is held by the British Library
ISBN 0 434 14338 3

Typesetting by
Deltatype Ltd, Ellesmere Port
Printed and bound in Great Britain
by Clays Ltd, St Ives plc

For Pierre Hodgson
and Alastair Bruton

Love is either the shrinking remnant
of something which was once enormous;
or else it is part of something which
will grow in the future into something
enormous. But in the present it does
not satisfy. It gives much less than
one expects.

Chekhov

# ACKNOWLEDGEMENTS

Many thanks to Professor Marks of the Maudsley Hospital, London; and George Else of the Natural History Museum, London, for their kind help and attention. Special thanks, also, to my editor, Laura Longrigg, for her unstinting patience and generous encouragement.

# CHAPTER
## 1

Out Patients.

The white lettering on the blue board was plain.

Out Patients. For patients out of their minds, thought Samuel Sorrell.

He began to stroll across the hospital car-park towards the notice and the entrance. His heels tapped on the stone steps as he jogged up to the double swing doors. At the top, he paused for a moment and held on to the railing. It was like a scaffolding pole, cold and hard.

He braced himself by inhaling steadily, then walked inside. For a minute or two he stood under the long loud yawn of hot air issuing from the blow heater above the door.

The large room, with dreary gruel paint, was bleak. The flesh-coloured strip lights were poor substitutes for windows. To one side there was a formica reception desk. A nurse with bare arms sat protected by its black panels. Some small ageing posters were pinned up behind her. On a torn orange one were two matter-of-fact questions: 'Are you a junkie? Why not seek advice from Narcotics Anonymous, South London's self-help group? We think of you as a person.'

Opposite the desk was an enclosed kiosk, sulky green, above which was written 'Refreshments'. A young girl was handing a bearded customer a cup of tea. She had a white paper hat shaped like an upturned toy boat. It was anchored to her hair by a kirby-grip.

With reluctant deliberation Samuel moved to the middle of the room. There were five rows of plastic chairs like those

1

on a Channel ferry. Most of them were occupied. But he found a free one. Before sitting down, he looked at it and hesitated.

To sit down was to take a big step. To sit down was to shake off the possibility in the minds of anybody watching that he might be a plainclothes psychiatrist. To sit down was to make a public acknowledgement for the first time that he was on the other side of the fence. He held on to the chair's arm and sat down.

Now I, too, am an out-patient, out of my mind, he said to himself, starting to watch his fellow madmen.

The woman next to me is holding a stump of a cigarette to her lips between her thumb and forefinger. She's inhaling so intensely it's as if smoke is as crucial to her existence as oxygen. One bare leg is resting on a low table in front of her. She doesn't appear to be in possession of an ankle. But there are plenty of varicose veins curling on the surface of her flesh. Sandworms on a wet beach.

What's she here for? Which psychiatric disorder is it that afflicts her so? She has a mad look. Something to do with the shape of the leg, in a funny sort of way. And so tangible, her misery. Can almost smell it. Feel concern. Is that patronising? Is it? But feel more than concern. Urge to help, flapping like a bird inside me. Powerless. Should have been a doctor. No. No good. Couldn't have been a doctor. I am mad. Mad doctors are not much in demand.

Samuel smiled at this thought, and shifted in his chair. His trousers made a jagged squeak on the seat. Quickly he moved again, trying to repeat the noise.

Just to make sure they don't think I'm farting like a madman.

Out of the corner of my eye there's a small peculiar movement. Surreptitious glance at the end of the row. A grey-haired man in a buff-coloured anorak. Remarkable for his ordinariness. Except for one thing: he's got his thumb pushed into his cheek very hard, as if pressing a button into a pin cushion. The fingers, splayed out, appear to be indulging in some sort of avant-garde dance, continually rotating and jumping in a circular motion. Now his hand's making a dive between his knees. A rest? I can't make it out. Hang on, the fingers are starting their lively performance at his face again.

I mustn't stare.

A couple of chairs along from Samuel was a girl with an evident liking for lime green: lime green polo-neck, lime green mackintosh, lime green sandals. She was reading an old magazine.

Nothing unusual there, but for the fact that she's crossing and uncrossing her legs at the rate of twenty or so times a minute. What could that mean? A mental disturbance brought on by lack of physical affection as a child, perhaps, or severe sexual frustration? Or is that a completely crass diagnosis, wildly off the mark? She has a nice face.

There were so many faces.

Young, old. Some apparently sane. What's the matter with them all?

*Us* all. Am I really one of them? Are they speculating about me, wondering wherein, precisely, lies my particular madness? Can they possibly guess? Is there something in my appearance or behaviour which gives it away?

Samuel felt the urge to cross his legs. But in view of the conclusions he had drawn about the lime green lady, he thought better of it.

Dark Shetland jersey, tatty corduroy jacket. My clothes seem sober enough. A canny observer might gather a superficial thing or two from them, but they don't give much away.

I expect people could gain a pretty good idea of what I do. Country vet. Or a local politician, possibly. God forbid. Countenance not supercilious enough. At least, I hope it isn't! Perhaps I could pass for a picture restorer. I'd like that. Wonder if they see me in a little room in the basement of some gallery or museum? Pervading smell of dust, glue, oils. Specialist instruments, laid out in perfect rows. Magnifying glass in hand. Utterly absorbed by one square inch of canvas. A tiny part of a beautiful painting. Da Vinci? My sole responsibility to repair shotgun wound to the oil and fibres. Damage by some complete madman . . .

Well, no, maybe not. They'd only have to spot the chalk dust on my elbow and they'd know. Bloody stuff, chalk dust. Ubiquitous. Found it in my socks before now.

Yes, a teacher. Obvious really. Science. By default, mind you. Should have been history. Too late now, of course, mid thirties, to change.

Samuel shook his head.

Such scope for regret. Already, in so little time. Regret within regret, even. Wish I wasn't teaching science, wish I wasn't teaching full stop. Being in education, as bad as being in the National Health. Christ, here I am in both!

I must be mad.

Oh, the wit. Very funny, Samuel Sorrell. Give it all up, pack it all in, why not? And go into comedy.

What? And not see Miss Hardcastle again? Not share break duty with her every other morning? Not be able happily to cover for her when she's off sick? Not watch her through the window in the door of Hall, taking hymn practice, Thursday afternoons? Not giggle with her in the staffroom when she reads Sally Payne's dotty essays out to me?

Christ, what's that noise?

Samuel looked up sharply. A greasy-looking man was drumming the reception desk with a child's rattle.

'I want a san witch! I want a san witch!' he said, wheezing. Then he turned to face everyone and began beating the rattle against his raincoat.

He was so tall and thin his legs were like stilts inside his trousers. As he limped up and down between the rows of chairs, it seemed as if at any moment he might fall from his own great height.

Everyone ignored him.

'I want a san witch, I want a san witch,' he repeated.

4

Samuel, too, affected to ignore him, but felt troubled by the man's menacing air.

What does he want? Why is no one helping him?

'I said I want a bloody san witch,' the man cried out more urgently.

He stopped in front of the lime green girl, loomed over her, and aggressively tapped her magazine.

'Can yer hear me, gel? A bloody san witch!'

She did not look up.


Desmond Sprout was a revolting man.

The whites of his eyes, like the whites of raw eggs, were yellow and clammy.

Nell John stared at his face. The complexion was as if covered in a thin layer of strawberry jam. His light beard was encrusted with small flakes of dead skin.

Desmond sat down. He had a cream leather sofa and pale loafers to match. Both the padded upholstery and the shoes had about their seams puckers like wrinkles on the pursed upper lip of an old lady.

'Thing is, Nell,' he said, 'I'd prefer it if you could stop Jagger making scatological references on the front doorstep. Offends Sylvie's sensibilities as well as her stilettos.'

Sylvie was Desmond's wife, Jagger his dog. He described them as 'the two most important people in my life – in the opposite order.' It was his notion of a *bon mot*.

There was a photograph of Sylvie on his desk. She was sitting beneath a turquoise Mediterranean sky. Topless. Her brown breasts had the flattened look of old leather shoes at a jumble sale, her nipples resembled toecaps.

'Discipline, all right? That's what's needed.' Desmond sniffed.

Nell watched as his fingertip then manoeuvred maggot-like into his nostril.

'Otherwise everything seems to be working out fine,' he went on. 'I think Jagger enjoys his walks with you.'

'Good,' said Nell flatly. She looked at the mean animal at

5

Desmond's feet. Its purple mouth was split open like the skin of a rotten fig. Its tongue oozed out obscenely from between its teeth.

She hated dogs; she hated being employed by Desmond Sprout as a dog-walker. She had been working for him for some weeks now, taking Jagger out for an hour's exercise in the afternoons. Desmond paid her because he claimed he was too busy to go out walking himself. But it was not so much lack of time that prevented him as lack of inclination, for he was a lazy man. Daily business lunches had, over the years, rendered him sluggish. It was a convex path his ties now made over his stomach. And, anyway, walking was boring in his book. If man was meant to walk, Desmond reasoned, he would not have invented the car.

No, his energies were entirely devoted to the exercise of amassing huge sums of money. In this he had succeeded. He was a television producer of considerable distinction. He had won awards for his talent, and he had won enemies for his unpleasantness. He was brilliant and nasty.

So it was he could afford to live in a manner of such extreme luxury and such unimaginative vulgarity.

'Any jobs lined up?' he asked. He took a duty-free cigarette with a white filter from a long box, and lit it with a lighter as blatantly gold as the sequins on a showgirl's bra. He didn't offer one to Nell.

'Possibly. Quite a lot of auditions recently,' she replied with deliberate courtesy. It was quite hard to be polite to Desmond. She had to resort to acting. 'I'm waiting to hear.'

'Got that Granada serial?'

'Don't know yet.'

'You said David Green was producing it, didn't you? Old mate. Why don't I have a word in his ear, tell him my dog-walker's a cracking little actress?'

'No. Thank you,' Nell said quickly, alarmed. She did not want 'help' from anybody, let alone Desmond. And inside she was responding violently to the notion that she was a 'cracking little actress'.

6

'There's gratitude for you,' Desmond remarked, not angry. 'It's foolish to be proud in this business. A bit of string-pulling never harms. And frankly you're hardly in a position to be snooty about these things.'

The words made Nell's flesh quiver, as if it was being brushed with gorse. 'Things are beginning to look up, in fact,' she said, icily calm.

'Fancy,' Desmond declared, with a patronising smile as he folded his arms. He turned in his seat and stretched his stumpy legs out on the sofa cushions.

'As it happens, I think I'm going to have to turn down your kind invitation to discipline Jagger. It was nice of you to offer, all the same.'

'It wasn't an offer, darling. More of an order,' Desmond told her, laughing. 'I can't keep buying Sylvie new shoes for ever, you know.'

'Whatever. Thing is, I'm not going to be able to take him for walks any more.'

'Oh? Why ever not? I thought you were out of work, needed the cash.' Incredulous.

'I do. But I've other commitments coming up, and I wouldn't want to let you down.'

'I'd have thought it was rather a useful way of earning yourself a bit extra. Still, if you wish to be grand, I can't stop you. Have you got any friends who don't have "other commitments"?'

'I doubt it,' Nell answered.

'That's really boring of you, you realise,' Desmond observed. 'Who do you suppose is going to walk Jagger now? I have to say you've let me down badly. Very inconvenient. Dog-walkers don't grow on trees, you know. And I'm an extremely busy man.' He paused, sat up straight and turned to face Nell directly. In a deliberate gesture he placed his fingertips together, like a minor bureaucrat keen to demonstrate his earnest importance.

'I was under the impression we had quite a good little

working relationship, you and me. Can't I persuade you to carry on?'

Nell shook her head and stood up to leave. 'Sorry,' she said brightly, glancing at the shiny plant in the corner. She mischievously wondered if Desmond, with his concern for smart labels, watered it with Perrier.

'Pity,' he remarked hastily, standing and following her to the door. Jagger followed him. 'Hang on a minute. Before you go . . .'

She looked at him with an enquiring expression, unable to imagine what more there was to be said.

Desmond took her hand as if to shake it. His palm was sticky. 'Don't I get to exercise my *droit de seigneur* before you go?' he asked in a cajoling, playful voice, his thumb stroking her knuckles. His puffy face leaned towards hers, enabling her to view at leisure his detailed complexion, and the thick purple lips. They were glazed with spit.

'We could do it on the sofa. A quickie now, why not? Sylvie would never know,' he whispered reassuringly. Jagger then barked encouragingly at her, like a voyeuristic pimp.

Nell would have paid to die rather than be fucked by the revolting Desmond Sprout on his anaemic leather sofa.

He pressed her against the door, closing his eyes. The mouth was open. His tongue rested on his lower lip, plumply expectant, and edged with a frill of saliva bubbles. Through his lightweight Dior trousers his erection dug into her thigh.

Nell calmly pushed at Desmond's chest with her palms.

Surprised, he opened his eyes.

'I bet I can make love to you like no one's ever made love to you before,' he boasted. 'You want it, I know you do.'

She bit her lip and tried to grab the door handle. But Desmond clasped her wrist.

'You're reaching for the wrong knob, love.' He thrust her hand between his legs. His breath was damp and like the odour of feet emerging from sweaty gym shoes. Nell jerked her arm from his grip, opened the door and made her way downstairs, saying nothing. She could hear Jagger snarling.

Outside, the October air chilled her face. Walking along the pavement, Nell put her fingers to her cheeks. The flesh already felt taut with cold, but it was a relief to be out of Desmond's stifling house, away from his invading fingers. She drew in a deep breath. The sharp air rasped the inside of her chest.

Reaching the Fulham Road by the Queen Elm pub and an expensive flower stall, she crossed over to the other side. Her pace was urgent. She wanted to leave the area as quickly as possible, but there was no sign of a bus.

She decided to walk on to the next stop and passed a cluster of small shops. In the window of a gloomy funeral parlour, she glimpsed her reflection and was relieved to see she did not have the air of a girl who, minutes before, had been manhandled. Surprisingly self-possessed, not remotely hysterical. Taking it in her stride. These things happen. Forget about it.

She caught the number 14 in Sydney Place and felt pleased to be turning her back on Chelsea and Desmond Sprout. The bus's progress to the West End was characteristically relaxed. But Nell was in no particular hurry. Because she had not gone to the park with Jagger she would arrive at the theatre earlier than necessary.

The stagedoor of the theatre in Shaftesbury Avenue was in a Soho back street. There were urine stains, like dark ribbons, on the pavement outside it. They let off a stomach-curdling stench. Nell pushed herself against the door and stepped inside. The air was thickly warm. A man inside the glass booth was on the telephone. He smiled, waved at her and mouthed 'no messages'. She moved towards the wooden stairs. They were worn and grey, wearied by years of exposure to heavy feet and damp mops. The glossy paint on the walls, loo-paper orange, was chipped. As she went up, Nell pondered upon the nature of theatrical glamour,

9

and decided it could be summed up with a single adjective: elusive.

The cramped dressing-room was cold. As Nell closed the door a floral crêpe dress, which had been hanging limply on a metal hanger, fell to the floor and appeared to shiver as it settled into a heap. She switched on the blow heater and the kettle. The one teabag, already used, squatted fatly on a saucer. It reminded Nell of one of Jagger's 'scatological references', as her former employer had put it so primly. She decided against tea.

She made some coffee, stood in front of the mirror, stared at herself. She was wearing a black skirt of floppy material which brushed her ankles. Beneath it dark tights, loosely wrinkled. Her rust-coloured old cardigan was thick and gathered like a smock. It might have been worn by a gypsy or a fisherman as a protection against the wind. Nell took off her shoes and sat down in front of the bright bulbs. They bleached her complexion, but her eyes still looked dark. Two pebbles pressed into the face of a snowman. Callous lighting, she thought. Could her twenty-seven years bear up to such scrutiny? Doubtful. She did not dare peer too closely. As it happened, if there were any early signs of age, she would have no really legitimate excuse to resort to greasepaint to conceal them.

She was only an understudy after all. Use of stage make-up was therefore superfluous. Chance of actually having to perform as unlikely as falling for Desmond Sprout.

Horrific idea. Nell hastily opened her bag and took out her book and began reading.

A while later Jodie Welles, the girl with whom she shared the dressing room, appeared with her usual flourish of sartorial brightness and cheerful melodrama. She undressed, put on a towelling robe and went over to the table. Then she sat down beside Nell and began to tell her about her frustrating day. Some friend had let her down. She slapped white cream on her face and, talking all the while, started rubbing it in with a vigour which complemented the vigour of her indignation.

10

A short while later there was a knock on the door. A voice behind it said, 'Fifteen minutes.'

Jodie swore and looked at her watch. 'Damn, I'm not nearly ready. Robert will be furious if I'm late again. Can you believe I did that? I've never missed my entrance before. How could I? Sweetie, pass me my dress, would you? Thanks.'

Some moments later, the door burst open and two actors stumbled in. Their faces were almost orange, their eyebrows artificially black. They were laughing.

'We came to make sure you were going to make it tonight,' the older one said cheerfully. 'Always keen to avert murder wherever possible.'

'Is Robert still cross?' Jodie was leaning into the mirror painting her lips. Nell was trying to do up an uncooperative zip for her. 'I can't bear it if he is. I've apologised enough.'

'Come on, you hopeless creature. We're on any second now,' the other man urged. 'You all right, Nell?'

Jodie grabbed her bag and was practically bundled out of the room. Nell could hear their exuberant voices recede along the corridor. A distant fire door banged with a deadening thud. Silence.

Nell, alone, sat down and picked up her book.

It was an odd sort of job, she thought. What it actually boiled down to was being paid to spend many hours indulging a great pleasure. There had been rehearsals, of course, which were proper work, but they had taken place months ago. All the same it was hard to regard sitting in a room reading every evening as professionally taxing and fulfilling, enjoyable though it was otherwise.

She longed to be busy, mind stimulated by activity and challenge. To have a part, however insignificant, one which at least entailed real *work*.

But unlike many actors, Nell did not harbour fantasies. She did not sit in the wings fruitlessly dreaming. Her aspirations were modest: simply to act, preferably in something she liked and felt was good.

There were a number of auditions lined up over the next few weeks. Maybe she would get something. It was important never to raise her hopes. If one disciplined oneself, Nell reflected, it was possible to keep them in check. She had chosen a profession where elevated expectations were nothing but a foolish diversion from reality.

She opened her book.

In the interval, Jodie returned to change.

'I can hardly believe it,' she remarked, 'I've only got to say those lines seven more times, and that includes the matinee on Wednesday. George Parker might be a great playwright but even his words lose their impact if one has to speak them every night for almost a year.'

'Perhaps you'll miss saying them when you haven't got to any more,' Nell suggested.

'In some ways, but I don't think I'll do a play again for a while. Need a rest.' Jodie stepped out of her dress and put on a skirt for the next scene, and an ugly hat. 'Think, I'll never have to wear this again!' She lit a cigarette.

'Listen, I've heard something that might interest you. I was talking to Gaby just before we went on for the drinking scene. Oh, don't say I've lost my shoes – '

Nell leaned down, brought them out from under the chair, and passed them to her.

'Thanks, love. What would I do without – ?' she began, but her mind wandered as she put on the shoes. She looked down at her small ankles sticking out above the skyscraper heels. 'It's a wonder I haven't fallen off the stage.'

'Don't speak too soon. You've still got another seven performances to go.'

'True. Anyway, Gaby said her agent had put her up for this new production of a Chekhov scheduled for the spring. *The Cherry Orchard*, she said she thought it was. Heard about it?'

'No.'

'That Russian director who put on the Dostoevsky at the Lyric last year. What was his name? Anyway, it's him doing it.'

12

'Belinsky? He's wonderful.'

'Exactly. Anyway, I think you should go up for it.'

'Belinsky? Are you joking?'

'No. If I wasn't contracted to do this TV series I'd be there like a shot. What have you got to lose?'

'I'd like to do some Chekhov,' Nell admitted.

'Well, ring Annie then. I'm surprised she hasn't told you about it already.'

'I'll think about it.'

'Not good enough, Nell. If you don't, I will.'

'All right. I'll ring her.'

'I'm the one who should be your agent. What's Annie's problem?'

'She's very good.'

'Then make sure she arranges for you to go to the audition. I'm being bossy, but I'm serious.'

Jodie stubbed out her cigarette, hitched her skirt to her hips, and pulled up her tights.

Making for the door, she looked at her watch. 'Now, listen, I'll be back in precisely fifty-three minutes, fifty-one if I speed up the regret speech and kick Ian up the bum when he takes his bow. So you've got a bit of time to think about the audition. Promise?'

Nell promised, and Jodie disappeared to the stage in time for the start of Act Two.

Samuel went into the empty staffroom and wondered, as he often did, about the person responsible for the lurid covers on the various chairs scattered about. What had possessed whoever it was to choose that particular orange? Inspired by a sunset, perhaps? Even he could have told him or her that sunset orange is never quite as good when translated on to a chair cover.

He dumped a pile of exercise books on to the table and looked at the bakelite clock hanging between the two huge windows. Lesson three would be over in five minutes, and

13

then it would be lunch for which he had no time. He had to mark fifth form homework.

He needed a boost of caffeine before he began. Samuel crossed the large sunny room to the pompously named Hot Drinks Dispenser in the corner and placed a white polystyrene cup in the small alcove. He pressed a button and an anaemic brown liquid posing as *café au lait* gushed out tidily.

He sniffed it, glanced at the door to make sure no one was coming, and quickly tapped his head twenty-four times before taking the first sip.

In the corridor outside, a shrill bell sounded. A second's silence followed like the sharp intake of breath before the clattering cough: two thousand feet let loose from the classrooms, banging doors, excited voices.

The staffroom door opened and Samuel's colleagues straggled in, weary. Weighed down by books, they plumped themselves on to the sunset upholstery and sighed.

'I've had it with Madeleine Good,' said one. 'Takes all my self-control not to clip her round the ears. She offered me a cigarette bang in the middle of the causes of the Thirty Years War.'

'She's third form isn't she,' said another. 'I thought she was becoming less difficult than she used to be.'

'Apparently not,' the history teacher replied. 'What gets to me is her cheek. It's a well aimed dart. Straight for the weak point. She knows I'm trying desperately to give up. So I say, feebly, "No cigarettes on school premises, Madeleine, as you're well aware." "Oh yes, Mr Crawford?" she comes back immediately, full of innuendo, and I could shoot her, I really could.'

'A trouble-maker, that's for sure,' someone remarked sympathetically.

'So I confiscated them of course. And she said, "Don't go and smoke them all yourself now, Mr Crawford, will you?" ' He brought the packet out of his pocket and looked at them wistfully. 'And the bugger of it is that's probably precisely what I will do.' He frowned, and Samuel smiled.

'Not coming along for lunch, Sam?'

'Marking,' came the resigned response, accompanied by a shake of the head.

'Me too, but it's Monday today,' Tim Crawford pointed out, 'which means rhubarb crumble and custard. And if I'm going to resist Madeleine Good's cigarettes, I'm certainly not going to try to resist rhubarb crumble and custard as well. Won't be long,' he added, and left the room with the others. Only Rachel English, the new young French teacher, stayed behind quietly working.

Samuel opened an exercise book – three down, twenty-four more to go – to find a pupil's badly drawn illustration of the previous week's experiment. He wrote 'Very careless' beside it.

I should have been a history teacher, he thought. Tim has the Thirty Years War on his syllabus. And what am I stuck with? Rats' intestines. And the sex life of bloody buttercups.

He leaned back in his chair, unconsciously chewing the lid of his red biro. 'Thank God I'm not a bloody buttercup,' he said out loud, 'Vulgar yellow, and sexually frustrated to boot.'

'What was that, Sam?'

Rachel was still there. He had forgotten he was not alone, and hiccuped with embarrassment.

'Just muttering. Nothing important,' he told her, flustered.

Rachel English was in love with him, he was almost sure of it. Perhaps it was conceited, such an assumption, but Samuel was not a man of conceit. There had been signs. She learned very quickly he didn't take sugar in his coffee. Battleaxe Barbara (head of the language department) still didn't know, and she had been at the school for three years. Not that he was a chauvinist. It wasn't to do with sexual roles, him assuming his female colleagues ought to know his sugar requirements. He often got the round of coffees, and he had been careful to learn people's likes and dislikes, out of courtesy more than anything else.

15

Rachel English always remembered. She also always offered to go to the stationery store for him.

'Can I get you anything, Sam?' she would say. 'Need more chalk? Paper?'

It was hard to decline: going to the stationery store was a trial – all the way over in E Block, and no way of avoiding that Cynthia who ran it. Cynthia had moles on her wrists and dollops of bitterness in her heart. Thwarted aspirations. Namely, the lab loan cupboard. She had been self-important in charge of pencils and A4 pads long enough; she wanted to be self-important in charge of something that really merited it – the science equipment. But she was not a technician, so it was never to be.

'A new box of chalk would be lovely, yes. Thanks Rachel,' Samuel would tell her. Thinking about Cynthia enabled him to give in to her kind offer. 'And another Bic, please. Blue.'

'You like the ones with the transparent barrels, don't you?'

Rachel's memory was admirable in all matters to do with himself.

'Are you going to be taking part in Lucy Hardcastle's play?' she asked lightly, still bent over her books.

Samuel slapped shut the exercise book with the bad illustration, and picked up the next.

'Sorry?' he said, biding his time, allowing the information to sink in. 'What play?'

'Haven't you seen the noticeboard? Lucy's producing the end of term play for Christmas.'

Samuel admitted he had not.

'She pinned it up in break this morning when you were at the doctor's. Caused a riot in here,' Rachel laughed.

Samuel stood up and went over to see for himself. Amongst the clutter of notices haphazardly pinned up on the large board was a small poster headed 'A Midsummer Night's Dream' in beautiful lettering, pale watercolour pink.

'A staff and sixth form production,' he read out loud. 'Rehearsals start in November. Actors, designers, musicians,

16

costumiers wanted. Please contact Lucy Hardcastle in the staffroom.'

'You'd make a great Puck, Sam,' Rachel remarked, affectionately teasing.

'When did she decide to do this, then?' he asked, distracted. 'I hadn't heard about it. She kept it pretty quiet.'

'You sound almost cross.'

'Surprised.' Samuel's eyes darted about the room, revealing an innocent confusion which Rachel found charming.

'Well, I hope you'll be in it. I've never acted in my life, but I thought I might give it a go, audition.'

'Audition?' Samuel's voice almost screeched in consternation. 'It doesn't say anything about auditions on the poster!'

'Well, of course we'll have to audition, so she can see what we're like, cast us appropriately.'

'I reckon that's a bit steep, isn't it?' he suggested, and was instantly worried that Rachel might think him pompous. Such an eventful day, he thought. First the hospital, and now this. It was all very troubling.

'It makes sense, Sam. I mean Battleaxe Barbara might harbour secret ambitions to play Titania, for all we know. At least if she auditions, Lucy can tactfully put her in another role,' she paused. 'Bottom,' she added mischievously, a moment later, and giggled.

Samuel looked at her. With the back of her hand over her mouth, giggling, she reminded him of a third former. She had a plait, tied with a velvet ribbon. And she had rather grown-up nipples beneath an expensive thin jersey of a smart sand colour. Not quite a third former, then.

'Barbara as Bottom. Brilliant!' Rachel declared through more giggles.

Samuel smiled. It would be an inspired bit of casting, he had to admit.

'Think you'll audition, then? Go on, Sam, it'll be fun.'

'I might,' he replied gloomily. He sensed impending humiliation. But he wanted to be involved in Miss Hardcastle's play.

17

He returned to his pile of books on the desk, and resumed the business of marking them.

His progress was systematic and steady. But all the while he was aware of niggles inside him. They were darting about fretfully, like a school of minnows disturbed by a predatory pike.

When the last lesson of the afternoon ended at ten to four, Samuel felt exhausted. Three of the Bunsen burners in the lab had been faulty, which had caused havoc with the class. He had planned to finish the experiment so that he could move on to a new topic next week. But no. Another equipment failure, which meant another chemistry practical wasted, another setback. He would have to have a word with the technicians. It was time some new apparatus was provided. But government cutbacks would probably see to it that that particular necessity remained ignored. If Battleaxe Barbara hadn't had any luck with language tapes and textbooks, then he could hardly expect the miraculous appearance of new Bunsen burners. It didn't matter that he had a case. Having a case meant nothing. Bugger all. Just gut-rotting frustration.

The children clambered from their stools the moment the bell rang, and cleared the benches of files, books and pencil cases. They did so with an amazing speed. Samuel would have admired such conscientious efficiency had they been able to redirect it a little and apply it to their work.

'Bye, Mr Sorrell,' they cried, dashing from the room as if being freed from a torture chamber. Admittedly, the lab did look pretty sinister: long high desks of dark wood fitted with dusty, old-fashioned appliances; looming glass cases filled with stones, skulls, strange specimens in bottles. But was he such an unattractive figure that they felt compelled to be released from his presence as quickly as they possibly could? Were his lessons so dull they resembled a form of mind-numbing purgatory?

How to be a good teacher? How to prompt enthusiasm to

learn and also bring pleasure? How to encourage them to enjoy the subject, whip up genuine interest in it, love for it? How to make it fun for them, stimulating?

One of Samuel's greatest desires was to be what people term an inspired teacher. And he wanted so much to inspire. He devoted a lot of time and energy to this end.

'Have you got a moment, Mr Sorrell?' one of the children asked as he was clearing up. 'The thing is, with this experiment, there's something I don't quite understand.'

Samuel smiled, and sat down patiently and happily to explain it. As he did so, he became very animated, talked very fast.

Much later, as he was driving home, he suddenly remembered that he had made the pupil laugh. Laugh about the curious behaviour of molecules. And immediately he felt uplifted. So much so, in fact, that he made an on-the-spot decision, just like that.

He would definitely audition for Miss Hardcastle's production of *A Midsummer Night's Dream*.

It might positively be fun, he thought.

What was more, as he opened his front door he realised – to his complete astonishment – that he was even excited by the prospect.

Stepping inside, Samuel wiped his feet on the doormat. Four times each foot, as always.

He took a deep breath. The smell – damp, clean washing, French cigarettes – was familiar, welcoming. It imbued him with a sense of wellbeing which, though modest, never failed to alert him to the pleasures of arriving home.

The small, scruffy house was in a quiet street behind Shepherds Bush Green. It belonged to Liza, his wife, who had bought it shortly after they married. She came from an old Scottish family which was much grander than his.

Samuel's background was more humble. His mother was a solicitor's daughter. His father was a vicar in the village near Stoke-on-Trent where Samuel had been brought up.

19

His father could not afford a car, but rode a bicycle instead. A man bent on neatness and order, he wore white bicycle clips because they matched his dog-collar.

Samuel and his older brother William went to the local grammar school. Life revolved round the parish. Samuel sang in the choir and helped decorate the church on important occasions. His favourite was Harvest Festival.

Every night he, his father and William would sit round the wireless together and listen to the news. Their mother went out most evenings after cooking supper, though their father never mentioned the fact. She would return late. Even in his sleep, Samuel could smell her breath when she came to kiss him goodnight. It was warm but bitter. Occasionally in the day he would catch a whiff of her breath. Sometimes, more often than not when she was angry with him and shouting, it would smell the same as it did at night, and remind him of his dreams.

The rectory was dark and draughty. Its bricks, like those used in most Staffordshire buildings, were the colour of dried blood. The sky only varied from smoke grey to charcoal grey.

'They don't call it the Black Country for nothing,' his mother would say. She came from near Bath. 'It's green, the West Country, all green.'

Once his father heard her. 'It's always greener the other side of the fence,' he said with an indulgent smile.

Samuel had stared through the kitchen window and past the washing-line to the wall at the end of the garden. Beyond it was a field with hedges and a railway track, but there was not a fence in sight. The following Sunday his father had used the phrase again, in his sermon, but Samuel still couldn't work out what he was talking about.

It was only when he was a teenager that he began to understand it. His brother returned home one weekend for a visit. He had a job in London. He also had flowing hair, flowing trousers and shoes like tower blocks. He was well informed about the music in the Hit Parade as he called it, and told Samuel about drugs and girls with long fringes, shiny boots up to their thighs and pale pink lipstick.

Suddenly the attractions of the small village began to dim. Samuel wanted to get out. 'You can, son,' his father told him, 'if you work hard and earn yourself a place at college.'

Samuel earned himself a place at Manchester University. He did his teacher's training at Kingston Polytechnic. He stayed at his first job, at a school in north London, for some years. He lived with friends who had been to drama school and were trying to become actors. They rented a flat together in Belsize Park. He was still there when he went to work at Parsons Green School, and when he met his wife.

Samuel's mother died of drink a year after he married Liza. At the funeral his father told him, 'With the possible exception of a certain house in Shepherds Bush, I think there's only one place that really is greener the other side of the fence.' They had both laughed. Then he added, quieter, 'I only hope that your mother's found it now, at last.' There was a tear in the old man's eye. Samuel remembered he had felt the urge to put his arm around his shoulder.

He bent down and picked up a large red toy bus which had crashed into the skirting board and was lying, upturned, on the rush matting. Putting it on the hall table, he glanced through the open door at the end of the short passage.

He could see Liza sitting at the kitchen table.

She was working away in that scatty style he found so winning. Papers, manuscripts, dictionaries had grown up around her like a miniature building site. And she was settled in the middle of it all, unfazed by her self-made chaos. Between her lips a cigarette had been left to its own devices, while she concentrated on tapping at her manual type-writer. One finger was going at the keys with the frenzy of a woodpecker's beak laying into a bit of bark.

She had not heard him come in. Samuel stood silently for some moments in the hall, watching. Watching her with affection and pride.

His mother had approved of Liza for the wrong reasons.

21

But at the same ime she had resented her for her wealth and what she referred to as her 'connections'.

'Married to your father, I was never going to have either,' she told Samuel drunkenly when he said he was getting engaged. 'You've bettered yourself, just as he did.'

But neither he nor his father had married to better themselves. Samuel found it hard to forgive his mother for failing to see how much his father loved her, and for being blind to those qualities in Liza which had nothing to do with class or money. His father did recognise Liza's modesty, generosity of spirit and lack of pretension or ostentation, but his mother had gone to her grave untouched by her daughter-in-law's warmth and sense of humour.

Samuel shook himself from his thoughts. He was momentarily anxious that, because Liza was unaware of his presence, he was spying. But to witness her thus, from the perspective of intruder, was strange. He realised he had stumbled upon a very private world. While he looked on at the scene in front of him, he became suddenly alarmed. Even Liza, whom he loved so much and knew better than anybody, had a whole vibrant existence of which he had no part.

She loved him completely, apparently, yet every day she was committing a kind of infidelity, wantonly, with her Smith Corona.

'How does the idea of one of my special whiskies grab you?' he asked quietly.

Liza jumped, then laughed. 'You gave me a real fright,' she told him. 'How long have you been standing there?'

'A few minutes,' he said. 'Do you mind?'

'No, silly.'

Samuel, having moved from the door to the table, leaned over to kiss her.

'So, what about one of my special whiskies then?'

He went to the cluttered dresser. A large bottle of Scotch nestled among the rough pottery mugs, the children's drawings, old newspapers, postcards, gatherings of plugs, fuses, Sellotape, bits of string. Samuel took down two glasses. They were large and solid. A friend had once said that drinking from them was like drinking from a fish tank. Samuel had liked that. It implied he was a man who was not mean with drink.

He poured out two big slugs and joined Liza at the table.

'Ought to do some work. The thought of it,' he murmured, his eyes dulled by fatigue. 'I'm disturbing you,' he added.

Liza was wearing one of his old shirts. The material was soft and crumpled. The sleeves were rolled up, the neck was undone. Her dark hair was tied back in a child's red butterfly clip, her vivacious eyes darkened by mascara.

She looks so good, Samuel mused. Sexy. Beautiful hands, with those elegant knuckles and mysterious veins. The skin as smooth and warm as newly spilt candlewax.

He wanted to touch it, but bloody buttercups beckoned. 'I'm sorry I'm so late. Are Nancy and Max in their room?'

'Reading.'

'I'll go and say hello, then put in an hour or so's work upstairs. Forgive me, sweetie. Piles of it.' He pulled a gloomy face.

Later, at supper, Samuel asked after her work.

Liza was employed by a number of publishers in a freelance capacity. She compiled indexes, mainly of biographies and history books. It was the perfect job for her. She could do it at home, and take on as many or as few titles as she chose. In the school holidays (her children's and her husband's) she would cut down considerably. The pay was pretty paltry, but she was not poor. Liza's father, Angus John, after years of financial struggle, had died a rich man.

He had been born in a small castle in Argyllshire, but his family had fallen on hard times and within a year moved into a bleak farmhouse nearby. Angus was not sent away to public school in England but educated locally instead. He apprenticed as a bookbinder in Oban, but wanted to write. He moved to London and found a job in the editorial department of an established publishing house.

23

Angus, who just missed having to fight in the war, arrived in the south, a direct and plain-speaking man in his twenties with a faint accent and a beard. He found lodgings in Bloomsbury. He did not possess a suit. Rationing was still in force, and he applied the same principle to the consumption of whisky that a camel does to water – drink as much as possible to stock up in case supplies run dry.

Angus made no allowances for those niceties of London society which had survived the war. Unprepared to wait till old age to behave exactly as he liked, he spoke his mind and openly declared his contempt for all that he found pretentious and insincere. He quickly earned the reputation for being a dangerous figure who could not be relied upon to conform. But far from alienating him from other people, this drew them to him. They appreciated his singular wit and intelligence. His style was original, deliciously shocking, and all the more compelling for being unconsciously so. Ironically, the more he pilloried people's affections – maybe precisely because he did – the more they embraced him.

A greater number of people made friends with Angus than he made with them. Many were keen that his fashionable roughness might rub off on them, while he was keen that none of their London ludicrousness should rub off on him.

There was a handful of writers and painters though, whom he respected and liked very much. One of them, some years older than himself and to whom he became especially close, was the Irish poet Cillian O' Neill.

O' Neill came from Dublin, and at that time rented a flat in Chelsea. He liked to wear yellow socks. In fact, he wore yellow socks every day. He had a theory that they detracted from the bright colour of his ears, a worrying purple. His eyes were an affecting blue, in his own words, 'like frigging sapphires.' He acknowledged that they helped him seduce women, but said that he would have been happier with 'non-fancy ones, just plain brown, like Guinness.'

They were considered to be a wild pair but likeable. They

24

drank heavily, chased a lot of women and regularly went to the Chelsea Arts Club. At the Gargoyle Club in Soho they came across the likes of Cyril Connolly and Lucien Freud, and danced to the music of Benny Goodman and Artie Shaw.

They somehow managed to work hard too.

Cillian urged Angus to start writing in his free time 'when you get back from the office, before you go to the pub'.

'At that rate I'd still be on my first book well into my eighties,' Angus pointed out.

'So, write a short story,' came the practical reply.

Angus had laughed, but later when he thought about the suggestion more seriously, it occurred to him it was not such a bad idea.

A few weeks later he summoned up the courage to show Cillian his first effort. O'Neill was impressed, and in turn showed it to a friend of his, the editor of a monthly literary magazine.

Angus had been living in London for a couple of years and had moved into Cillian's basement flat by the time the story was published.

Their local newsagent had two copies of the issue in which 'The Loch' appeared. Angus bought them both so he could send one to his father. They cost a few shillings, almost as much as the sum he was paid for his contribution. But seeing the story in print gave him the confidence to start writing his first novel, which later led to a second, and greater fortune.

By the time he died, over thirty years later, Angus John was a distinguished and highly regarded author with nineteen novels, six collections of short stories and considerably more than a few shillings to his name.

He had met his wife Jocasta at one of Cillian's parties which took place in their flat in Glebe Place. She was a painter and had just returned from America. She was unusually well travelled for a girl of her age and privileged background. She had spent a year or so in Paris, mostly in cafés and living on a shoestring with friends, before taking off across the Atlantic to travel round the States in a Greyhound bus. She had ended up in New York for nine months. Angus was transported by her descriptions of a jazz club where she used to go, called the Metropolitan.

While the other girls at the party were wearing twin-sets or circular felt skirts with wide elastic belts, Jocasta had more of a gypsy look. Angus admired her droopy, loose clothes which he supposed she had probably bought in the Portobello market. She wore an old black sweater; an ankle-length jersey skirt which was russet-coloured and uneven at the bottom; and bright beads round her neck. She had long dark hair. Her shoes were flat and worn, her tiny ankles rather grubby. Her shyness prevented her from speaking in anything but a whisper. But it was a whisper made alluring by the considerable amount of red Algerian wine which she drank and the numerous cigarettes which she smoked. Although she coughed like a consumptive, she looked healthy. Her skin had been made radiant by the American sun. She told Angus about the week in New York when she had been particularly broke and had to sleep in Grand Central Station. During the day she had sketched waiting passengers and sold the drawings to them in order to afford some lunch.

They married ten months later, shortly before Angus's first novel (which was not a success) was published. The Johns' first two children, Daniel and Liza, were born in London. Then, following the death of his father, Angus returned with his family to the Scottish farmhouse where he had lived as a child. He had no money. Cillian, a frequent visitor, would arrive bearing wine and books for his friends. He was staying with them when Nell was born, and joyfully drank and sang with her father all night long. He promised Angus and Jocasta that she would bring them luck.

A matter of weeks later Angus's second novel came out. It was that book which made his name.

'This book seems to be taking longer than most,' Liza said in answer to her husband's question concerning her work.

'Every paragraph, practically, has at least ten new references, all of which have to be included.'

'Index'll be as long as the text if you're not careful,' Samuel remarked.

'Very likely.'

'You're too conscientious. Maybe you don't have to log absolutely everything.'

Liza smiled. 'Don't you worry, I'm very selective. But even so the whole thing takes for ever.' She stood up to clear the plates and poured them each another drink. 'I pray to God I'll have finished by Saturday. It's the last night of Nell's play and Conrad's asked a few of us round to celebrate.'

'That's nice of him,' Samuel replied enthusiastically. 'Bet Nellie'll be pleased when it's all over. I can't imagine the boredom and frustration of sitting about night after night, backstage, never once going on. Must be the most soul-destroying thing.'

'She never moans about it though.'

'I know. She's very admirable, your sister. 'I know I'd go mad.'

He put down his glass and picked up his cigarettes. He lit one of them and stared at the sparky flame of the match as it devoured the pink head. Then he threw the curled black stick into the ashtray.

Leaning back in his chair, Samuel crossed his legs. 'Of course, that's a silly thing to say, because I'm not an understudy, never will be.' He paused, then in a heavier voice, devoid of humour, he added, 'And I've gone mad anyway.' As he said the words his eyes began to sting. He swallowed.

'I wanted to ask,' Liza ventured gently. 'How did it go this morning?'

'Fine,' came the unexpectedly abrupt reply. He knew from her tone that she could sense his pain.

'What was he like, the doctor? Can he help you? What did he say?'

'This and that.' Samuel shrugged and took a deep puff of

his cigarette. But his apparent nonchalance disguised a certain shame. He knew it was irrational. All the same, he found he was suddenly unable to look his wife in the eye. He could not cope with himself, or with her heartfelt concern.

Precisely what had gone on at the hospital between him and the shrink was a subject he did not wish to talk about with Liza. Of all people. It would be like talking to his parents about sex. Out of the question.

She did not pursue it.

Instead, she stood up and opened the washing-up machine. She started to load it, clunking the plates in the racks and dropping the knives and forks in the white plastic basket. Another man might have thought the clatter she was making was a deliberate show of displeasure, that she was cross with him for not being more forthcoming. Samuel, though, knew she was not angry, merely a bit carefree with china.

'Will you watch that film with me?' she asked with a sweetness which confirmed to him her lack of reproach. 'Starts at ten. We've got a couple of minutes.'

'Love to.'

He began to clear some more things from the table and piled them by the sink.

'Let me do this,' said Liza. 'Go next door, turn the telly on. I'll be in in a moment.'

'Sure you don't want any help?'

'Go on. I'll make some coffee.'

Samuel went through to the sitting-room.

Liza joined him a few minutes later.

The television was not on.

One dim lamp threw a gentle yellow light on to the buxom cushions of the small sofa by the fireplace. There was a soft sound of panting, like a breathless Pekinese.

In the semi-darkness Liza could see her husband crouched on the floor. He was on his knees, and bent over as if he had been kicked in the groin by a hobnailed boot. His arms were covering his head protectively, and he was slowly swaying.

Alarmed, and with tears welling, Liza put the hot mugs of coffee down on the low glass table, and rushed over to him. She put her arm round his shoulders and whispered in his ear. He was quivering like a child.

A desperate hand, flailing about for something comforting to hold on to found her calf and squeezed it: fear, embarrassment, affection.

'What was it? Was the plug out of the wall? One of the children must have taken it out. Don't say they left the switch on.'

He nodded.

'My God, Samuel. I should have looked before you came home. I'm so sorry.'

'No, it's me, it's me.' His face was close to the carpet so his sad voice was muffled. 'Oh, this is such a nightmare. What the hell's the matter with me? I know it's not really poisonous. I feel so fucking stupid – no, so fucking mad. Yet I know I'm not, I'm perfectly sane except for this absurd . . . absurd, what? Mania.'

'You're not mad,' she assured him.

'And yet what sane person, what *science teacher* believes that poisonous electricity can emanate from bloody plug-holes, for God's sake?'

'A lot of people have those fears.'

'No one in their right minds.'

There followed a silence. Hesitantly Samuel sat up. He took a deep, jerky breath. Liza looked at him sympathetically.

'I don't want to discuss it any more,' he murmured firmly, but not unkindly.

He slid himself up from the floor on to the sofa, like a hospital patient trying to prop himself up in bed, sapped of strength, dogged by dull pain. He lay back.

'Switch on the telly. Your film.'

'The film doesn't matter,' Liza told him.

'No, turn it on, I'd like to watch it.'

She did so, and sat down beside him. He held her hand and

29

squeezed it apologetically. She kissed him on the neck, and passed him his coffee.

Just before he took his first sip, he gently tapped his head twenty-four times, turned to Liza, shrugged, and smiled. She smiled back and then rested herself in a comfortable position against his chest.

Neither of them said another word as they turned their attentions to the television screen.

# CHAPTER

## 2

'I won't be able to nag you any more,' Jodie pointed out to Nell during the interval on the last night of the play. 'Today's Saturday. At the end of Monday's performance you promised me you'd call Annie.'

Nell put her book down. She was touched, not exasperated, by Jodie's persistence.

'I made you a cup of camomile tea.'

'I don't want tea. I'm bossy, not thirsty,' Jodie declared as she changed into her clothes for Act Two. 'I want you to ring your agent and make sure you get an audition.'

'I spoke to her today,' Nell said quietly.

'Why didn't you tell me? What did she say?'

'She said she knew about it.'

'Yes. And?'

'And that she would try and organise my going up for a part.'

'Quite right too,' Jodie said, looking down at her skirt. She hitched it up to examine the hem which had become unstitched and carried on talking. 'Now listen, you must stick around afterwards. You will join in the end-of-run celebrations, won't you? I know you don't really enjoy that sort of thing, but Ian told me Management have supplied some champagne. We've all got to take advantage of this burst of generosity.'

A bell rang in the corridor. Jodie flew from the room.

When she had gone, it was very quiet again in the dressing room except for the peaceful burr of the blow heater. Nell reflected upon the hours she had spent sitting there, listening to that sound, night after night for so many weeks. It was strange to think this was the last. A relief, really. She would miss Jodie, of course, and one or two other members of the company. But it would be interesting to be involved in something else, a different production, with different faces.

Nell read for a while. After about an hour, she was disturbed by screeching voices and shouts in the passage outside. The door opened and a small crowd danced through it, cheering. Jodie hugged Nell, laughing.

'I'm going to miss you so much,' she declared. Her eyes were pink. 'Oh, it's going to be awful. Ian, how am I going to manage without her?' She hugged him too. 'Without you? Quick, a drink, before I disintegrate.'

'Champagne!' A general cry went up. Someone opened a bottle and poured it into the coffee mugs. Nell, smiling, quietly watched the celebrations. Like the others, she felt both happy and sad. But she could not be moved to quite the same degree of theatrical exuberance.

'Come on, Nell, you can't call yourself an actress and not have champagne tonight, our last night,' an actor said, passing her a mug. She thanked him and took a swig.

A few minutes later the stagedoor man appeared. He beckoned to Nell and she squeezed her way over to him through the lively group. There was a strong smell of smoke, greasepaint, flowers and sweet aftershave.

'Conrad's here to give you a lift home, love. Shall I ask him to come up?'

'Thanks, Alan, but don't worry, I'll come down.' Quickly Nell gathered her belongings, kissed Jodie goodbye and promised to keep in touch. Nudging her way out, she vaguely waved to the others and escaped.

She went downstairs to find her boyfriend, Conrad Holland. He was leaning against the stagedoor kiosk, chatting to Alan while he waited. One foot rested on a metal camera case. He was wearing a short brown jacket. Its suede was limp and floppy with age. The zip was undone.

32

Underneath he had on a black V-neck jersey and a white T-shirt. On his feet, black lace-up shoes.

Conrad, who was in his early thirties, had a medieval face. Nell had seen figures like him in engravings and illuminated manuscripts of that period. The narrow eyes, high forehead, and widow's peak were all typical. His straight dark hair hung close to his long cheeks. If he moved his head violently it swung out like a skirt and revealed his ears. She had often fancied he might have looked more comfortable in a woollen doublet and hose, and poulaine shoes with bells.

'I hope I'm not dragging you away?' he asked when he saw her.

'Not at all. Thanks for coming.' Nell gave him a kiss.

'Of course, for your last night.' Conrad put his arm round her shoulders. 'It's all over at last. Well done.'

'I haven't done anything.'

'You have. Takes more character to be an actor who's understudying than an actor who's acting.' He picked up his case.

Nell said goodbye to Alan and they left the theatre and made their way to the car.

'You must be feeling guilty about something,' she said on their way back.

'Why?'

'Giving me the star treatment, coming to collect me. Who is she?'

Conrad put his hand on her knee, and they both laughed.

'She? They, you mean.' At a red light he turned to her and smiled. 'Christabel's holding the fort. Liza and Samuel hadn't arrived when I left.'

'Anybody else?'

'We're only seven altogether. It's not a big party, I'm afraid.'

'Well it's a real treat all the same.'

A few minutes later they turned off Ladbroke Grove into Oxford Gardens, where they shared a rented flat. It was on the first floor of a large house, the decrepit, unpainted facade of which looked like a partially burnt pie-crust.

They went inside and upstairs. Their door opened straight into the sitting-room. It was a big, square space with expansive windows overlooking the tree-lined street and had high ceilings. The white paint on the elegant central rose and the cornices was grubby. Bulky radiators squatted against the dusty walls. The grey hair-cord carpet was worn.

But the room was far from depressing. There was an assortment of clutter in the form of pictures, rugs, books. Nell had stuck colourful postcards round the frame of the old mirror above the fireplace. There was a hideous, kitsch cocktail cabinet behind the puffy sofa. One Saturday Conrad had gone off for breakfast with a friend to a café in the Portobello Road. Hours later he had returned from the market and given it to her as a spontaneous present. It was made of champagne-pink glass with a twee swirly inlay. It opened smoothly like the elaborate set of a musical, into a polished wooden stage with several levels. Its cast of bottles would rise up from its midst, like a troupe of exotic show-time girls.

When Nell and Conrad entered, they found the room lit only by a few candles. Three figures were sitting round the table in the window – Samuel, Liza and Nell's oldest friend Christabel Howard.

Liza stood up to kiss her hello. She was smaller than Nell. Her hair was held in a clip, loose strands falling about her neck. The sisters were alike. They were both simply dressed in old jeans. Liza's loose white sweatshirt, having met something red in the wash, had acquired a pink tinge. Nell's faded man's shirt had the crumpled look of a pyjama top. Liza's face, like Nell's, was heart-shaped and unlined, but, because she was two years older, it seemed more mature.

'Great relief that it's over,' she said. 'I except you're glad you'll never have to sit in that damp little dressing room again.'

Nell nodded.

34

'I felt for you,' her sister remarked.

'It wasn't bad. I got used to it.'

'But from now on – luxury – you can see us all before eleven o'clock at night,' Samuel pointed out.

'Ah, yes,' Christabel said, 'but from now on – misery – she has no excuse to stay in bed after eleven o'clock in the morning.'

'That's not fair,' Liza protested in Nell's defence. 'You're always up by nine, aren't you?' She took her sister's arm and sat her down. 'Conrad?'

'It's true.'

'Here, have a drink,' Liza said, handing Nell a glass. 'You probably need it.'

'Definitely.'

'The puritanical streak which gets her up in the morning,' Conrad said, 'isn't so stringent that it bans her from drinking. Thank God.' He kissed Nell on the head. 'It's not puritanism which gets you up at all. It's the thought of seeing Desmond Sprout, isn't it? Because, secretly, you're madly in love with him.' He laughed.

Nell smiled. 'Don't you sound so confident. How do you know I'm not?'

'This is a man,' Conrad explained to the others, 'who, only the other day, she said, made a wart hog look like an Adonis. I can't claim to be someone generally over-brimming with confidence, but I think in this case – '

'Ah, but you never know, she might've not been telling you the truth,' Christabel interrupted, 'to put you off the scent.'

'I think she was telling the truth,' he said, looking at Nell affectionately.

'I'm glad you're so sure of me,' Nell teased. 'Are we running out of wine or will Daniel bring some?'

Nell, who was extremely fond of her brother, was looking forward to his arrival. Daniel, a political journalist on a Sunday newspaper, was a busy man. He was as protective of Liza and Nell as he had been since they were children, but

35

the nature of his work and his stressful way of life meant he could not see them as often as they would have liked.

'He's not coming,' Liza told her. 'He rang to say he was very sorry but he couldn't make it.'

'Work?' Nell asked.

'That's what he said,' her sister replied.

Nell raised her eyebrows as if to imply it was not what he meant. Daniel's life was always complicated by more than one girl at any given time. Whereas Liza often complained that he managed to find time for all of them but not for his sisters, Nell was not so resentful. Sometimes her tolerance exasperated Liza.

'Well maybe Hilary'll bring some,' was all Nell said. Her sister sighed.

At that moment Hilary Black – an old friend of Nell's and Christabel's – arrived with a bottle and settled down at the table next to the others. He helped himself to a drink, and nibbled at the French bread and cheese which had been laid out by way of a snack supper.

Hilary's surname was very fitting. He had black hair, black stubble and black clothes. His friends had often told him he looked like a funeral director.

Christabel nudged him. 'Pass me the wine,' she demanded. Her head bent forward to light a cigarette. The numerous auburn corkscrews that made up her mass of hair fell forward and covered her face. 'I have to get drunk tonight.' She did not look up.

Nell watched her friend and guessed that her sartorial brightness – red trousers, shocking pink cardigan – was in direct contrast to her mood.

Christabel was normally noisy. Everything about her was loud – her voice, her sense of colour, her taste in music, even the jangle of her brassy jewellery. Such was her ebullience and general enthusiasm for everything that people were drawn to her, hoping she would infect them and set them alight. She was incapable of boredom. Nell had seen her listen to long descriptions of strangers' dreams with genuine

36

interest. Christabel could hear about the inner workings of a lawnmower and want to know more.

The two of them had known each other since they were children.

Nell's childhood had been unsettled. Her father, a taciturn man, was rarely to be seen outside the dark room at the back of the farmhouse where he would write and drink. (Nell could still remember the fear she felt when she had to knock on the door of that sacred study and tell him that lunch was ready.)

Angus John was a tall, imposing figure who wore trews or kilts of his family's dark tartan. He smoked a pipe and had a habit of emptying it by knocking it on the side of his head. Much of the gritty ash would not reach the stone floor but would, instead, settle in his hair and on his shoulders.

Every morning he would eat plain porridge – made with just salt and water – for breakfast, and encourage his three children to do likewise, to prove they were really Scottish. It made them silently retch, but they wanted to please him. Sometimes, when he was not looking, their gentle mother would liven it up for them with a little brown sugar and milk or cream. Once, when he spotted her doing so, he stood up and kicked a wooden chair against the Aga until it broke and she cried.

Daniel was the fearless one. He stood up to his father, and protected his mother and two younger sisters. Angus seemed to admire that.

He used to take his son shooting. Nell envied her brother his attention. She believed her father was a kinder, less dour man beneath his formidable exterior, but he didn't often give her the opportunity to get close to him. Occasionally he would play cards with his daughters and allow Nell to make him laugh. When she did this, and knew she was the cause of his deep booming delight, she felt happier than she had thought it possible to be. But it had only happened to her a few times. She could recall each incident, even now, in vivid detail.

The time when she was seven was the best. She told him a funny story about her teacher at the local primary school and a fisherman. He laughed so much that when he picked her up in his arms to hug her, she could feel through the thick tweed of his jacket the vibrations going on in his ribs. Then, a few days later, when Cillian came to stay, he actually told her to repeat the story to his old friend. And, when she did, he laughed all over again.

Jocasta John, Nell's mother, had an extraordinary warmth about her. Angus, when he first met her at a party in the fifties, had found it compelling, beguiling, and continued to do so until he died. Her children, whom she loved unequivocally, found it comforting.

She smelt of woodsmoke and had lots of ethnic rings on her fingers. She liked to fill the house with heather. Daniel, Liza and Nell would go on to the moor to gather it for her. It pricked their hands, sometimes made them bleed. Little shiny dots of blood, like moneyspiders' bodies, would appear. But they did not mind: she would kiss them better; each wrist, each palm, each finger.

She painted wonderful pictures of the landscape, and spoke of the solitary travels she had made before she married, in Europe and in America. (Nell's favourite possession, on the white wall of her simple bedroom, was one of her mother's line drawings, in pencil, of an old man playing the piano. It was given to her on her eighth birthday; her mother told her stories about the old man, said he had been a friend in New York, a jazz-player.)

She was not like other mothers. They were old and had stiff skirts and frigid curls. But her clothes and her hair were long and flowing, and her laugh had a tinkling sound like a child's. She had full lips, and was beautiful and sad.

Late one summer's night, when Nell was nine, she awoke to hear the faint sound of her mother weeping. The next morning her father, who was completing a novel, did not appear at breakfast. He had gone into his study, early, to write. Joscasta gave the children toast and honey, and whispered that she was taking them away on an adventure.

She said they did not have to clear the table, adding that she was going to leave the washing up. Instead, she took them upstairs telling them not to make a squeak or breathe a word. 'Ssh,' she instructed with a greater urgency than usual. 'Papa's working.'

She helped them each pack a bag.

Minutes later, without saying goodbye to Angus – 'We mustn't disturb him,' she reasoned – she drove them away.

It was the longest journey Nell had ever made. They were in the car for hours and hours, heading south. They were going so far they even had to stop off two, maybe three times, for nights at roadside hotels along the way. They cried with fatigue and said they wanted to go home. But their mother was firm of purpose.

Blackwell Farm in Devon belonged to an old friend of Jocasta's, Rosie, who was married to a man called Bill Howard. They had three children. Christabel was Nell's age, and became an instant friend. It was a magical place.

The house had a television, carpets in all the rooms upstairs, radiators in the bathroom, and no packets of porridge in the larder. The young Howards had their own bicycles which they happily loaned to their new friends, and a hayloft in which they could play.

All the children were allowed to stay up late for dinner with the grown-ups. Afterwards, when everyone went back into the sitting-room, Bill and his cousin John would sit at the piano together. They would put Nell and Christabel on their laps and begin to play. The two men would sing funny, sometimes rude, old songs and, as they did so, their kind, gentle faces would appear to dance.

When they had finished Bill always clapped his hands with glee, and would hug his smiling wife.

During those evenings, John smoked thin cigars. Once, Nell saw him giving one to her mother, who giggled when he passed it to her and stroked her shoulder at the same time.

Her mother was wearing one of her father's old shirts. Nell watched John's hand on the familiar, frail silk, and knew it would be warm. While he was lighting the cigar, Jocasta closed her eyes and inhaled as if the smoke was fresh air. She seemed no longer sad.

Christabel's older brother, Ben, who was thirteen, smoked. One time he took Nell alone with him on a walk to show her the woods. He was as friendly and warm as the rest of his family. Garrulous, too. He showed her some mushrooms, but did not pick them: he might come back for them later, he said, they were magic. She did not ask him in what way or whether in fact he did ever remember to pick them.

Ben had his own hive of bees in the field in front of the kitchen window. After the walk to the woods, he took her to see it, and told her all about the bees. He gave her a present – her very own pot of honey, with a section of comb inside it. He drew a label specially with a picture of some of his bees and wrote the words 'To Nell, Love Ben'. She showed it to her mother and told her about Ben's hive. 'You're very lucky,' she told her. 'Aren't they amazing?' Her mother, who knew about all sorts of things, knew about bees. 'You and he must show me the hive sometime,' she said, 'because I love bees.'

For long days and nights, weeks, at Blackwell Farm, she felt that same rare elation she had only experienced when she had succeeded in making her father laugh. There was something about the Howards. Nell guessed, even then, that it was because they were happy.

After the summer she had to return to Scotland with her mother, brother and sister. Her own house appeared colourless and cold. Her father looked gaunt, and spoke even less than he had before they had gone away. He wrote more and more and smelt of whisky, though he never kicked a chair again.

Her mother made trips to the post office. She sent thick, handwritten letters but as far as Nell could see they were not the sort that required replies, for she received none at home

40

in return. A couple of times she picked them up directly from the post office. They were addressed to her and 'a man,' Liza told her, 'who is an old secret friend of Mama's, who we mustn't tell Papa about, who's French and called Poste Restante.'

Nell wrote endlessly to her new friend in Devon, and always received letters back. She felt guilty sometimes that Christabel proved to be a far better correspondent than the person her mother was writing to.

Over the years, her mother took her and Daniel and Liza back to Blackwell Farm two, maybe three, more times. The subsequent visits were as blissful as the first, and served to confirm in Nell's mind that the Howards had something that her family lacked.

When she was sixteen – two years before she and Christabel went up to Oxford together – she lost her virginity to Ben, in the hayloft. She was no longer in love with him, but she well remembered their walk in the woods, her joy at being shown his beehive. There could have been no better person to sleep with for the first time: Ben was a Howard and she loved all the Howards – him, his sisters, and his parents.

Looking back, Nell saw that her parents, although they had loved each other in their own way, had stayed together only 'for the sake of the children'.

Bill and Rosie – who were like a favourite aunt and uncle to her – had never needed any such excuse. Their three children had grown up and left home long ago, but that couple were still together, as happily as ever.

'Yes,' Christabel said as Hilary handed her the open bottle, 'I want to get really pissed tonight.' Little laugh. As she filled her glass, she looked at the wine as if it was a supply of blood. 'My parents,' she announced, 'told me some news today. They've been married for, what, over thirty-five years? And now they're getting divorced.'

Liza gasped. 'I don't believe it. Is it true?'

Christabel jutted her jaw out, gritted her teeth, and nodded.

41

'Oh, I'm so sorry,' Liza said.

'It is rather depressing.' Christabel looked at Nell.

Nell was sitting silently and completely still. Her face was devoid of expression. She was staring without blinking, at an ashtray on the table. It was a beautiful, cream-coloured shell that had turned very slightly rose-pink. A present from Conrad. She wondered how old it was, where it had originally come from. In her mind, she saw a beach, the sea, some rocks, but she could not guess where they might be.

'Nell?' Christabel's voice. 'Sorry, I've put rather a dampener on things. I didn't mean to blurt it out in the middle of your party,' she apologised.

While everyone hastily assured her it did not matter, Nell just shook her head. An imaginary fist was pounding her chest from the inside.

'I always mock Nell about that over-inflated cynicism of hers,' Christabel told the general company. 'Maybe there's something to be said for it.'

'No,' Liza and Conrad disagreed in unison.

'I suppose it's funny really. Well, quite funny.'

'What?' Samuel asked.

'The reason for the divorce. A bailiff.'

'How do you mean?' Samuel fiddled with some candle-wax, embarrassed by his inquisitiveness. 'Sorry, I don't mean to pry.'

'It's all right,' Christabel reassured him. 'There's this bailiff who's been after Mum's goods and chattels, and by that I don't mean her table and television.' Her voice was falsely bright.

Hilary laughed. The others, except Nell, smiled.

'He's been collecting them for quite a while as it turns out. Twenty-six years, to be precise.' Christabel faltered momentarily. 'It began just one year after I was born. Comforting thought.' Pause. 'Why the hell did it have to be a bloody bailiff?'

'They're bastards,' Liza remarked.

'You'd have thought Mum would've had better taste.'

Nell sighed, exhaling with controlled steadiness. Two pictures presented themselves in her head. First, the Howards' farm awash with sloppy mud, hay bales, heifers with grass-green knees; she could even smell the aromatic cowpats, the warm fresh milk, the hot, home-made bread. Second, the faces contorted with scorching laughter round the piano after dinner.

Misplaced nostalgia.

'Apparently he wears a bowler hat,' Christabel revealed with a giggle: nervous, brave.

'How do you know?' Hilary enquired.

'When Dad found them in bed, the man jumped up and covered his cock with it.'

Nell's memories began to discolour, like bruises.

'How did Bill react when he found out?' Liza asked.

'Oh, he knew all along apparently, just as she knew that he was screwing around all those years. It was an unspoken arrangement, practically from the beginning. What Dad couldn't take was having his nose rubbed in it, catching them at it. That's what upset the status quo. So,' she added, 'the idyllic childhood I had turns out not to have been so idyllic after all.'

'That can't ever change, despite what you now know,' Samuel told her.

'Even though the set-up was based on deception,' Christabel asked, 'and was entirely false all along?' She poured herself some more wine.

Nell looked pensive, bleak.

'But that doesn't mean that your happiness was any less real at the time,' Samuel reassured Christabel.

'Maybe.' Christabel, who had been slouching over the table, her head in her hands, sat up.

'Are you all right?' Conrad was concerned.

'Oh, yes. I'm okay.' Her spirits were beginning to lift. 'Bit of a blow, that's all.' She held up her glass to indicate the wine was doing her good. 'Don't worry about me.'

'I've always admired your stoicism,' Hilary told her gently.

43

'I remember it from the time we met,' Hilary went on. 'Our second term at Oxford, I think it was, when that boyfriend of yours, the one at Balliol, had just given you such a hard time. I was so impressed.'

'Thanks.' Christabel gave him an appreciative look. Then, 'I think I've depressed everyone for long enough. Come on,' she said with some of her usual enthusiasm back in her voice, 'let's change the subject, talk about something else, why not?'

'All right, if you like,' Hilary said. 'There is something, before I forget, which I've got to ask Samuel.' He turned to him.

'Oh yes?'

'In your capacity as a science teacher.'

'Oh God, Hilary,' Liza chuckled.

'What?'

'I can guess what's coming,' she said to him, though she was looking at her husband.

'Can you?' he asked. 'It's just I was in my studio today, trying to get on with a bad sculpture I'm doing at the moment, and I began staring out of the window, you know, unable to concentrate. Then I found myself asking all these questions.'

'Like why the sky's blue, for example?'

'Yes exactly that,' he replied, adding after a pause, 'Bloody hell, Liza, how did you know?'

Samuel laughed. 'It's a family joke,' he explained. 'Everyone asks me that. Occupational hazard.'

'Like when doctors reveal what they do,' his wife said, 'no one can resist burdening them with details of their medical histories and demanding cocktail party diagnoses of the pain they've been having recently in their shoulder.'

'People ask me what make of camera they should buy,' Conrad said with a grin, 'as if I'm some walking copy of *Which*?'

'Well, I don't see it's so unreasonable to want to ask,' Hilary said, defending himself from their teasing. 'The sky

44

was very blue today, you have to admit. I just thought, why? That's all. Why blue, for heaven's sake, not green?'

Samuel laughed again.

'And another thing,' Hilary went on, 'I had to go out later. It was so bright I took my glasses, the kind that go dark in the sun.'

'How the hell do they do that? you asked yourself.' The science teacher pre-empted the sculptor's question.

'Quite. I'm sorry I'm so predictable. But are there microscopic chameleon-type animals trapped in the lenses or what? The fact is, I really don't know these things. It's awful. Basic chemistry.'

'Physics,' Samuel corrected.

'There you are, then, you see. Just tell me, am I right about the sunglasses?'

'Nearly. Molecules, though, not animals.'

'Ah ha!' Hilary burst out, clapping his hands. 'I shall have to tell Jo. She said I was being ridiculous.'

'Who's Jo?' Christabel wondered out loud.

Hilary shrugged. 'Friend.'

'Really?' His interrogator's tone was sceptical. 'You've practically gone the colour of the wine. Who is she? Come on.'

Hilary looked to Samuel and Conrad for support. His host poured him some more wine.

'Was it her who prompted all this staring out of the window?' Christabel went on.

'You're so inquisitive,' Hilary remarked, beginning to fiddle with a button on the sleeve of his shirt.

'Do I know her?'

'No. You might have met her. Nell has.'

'I don't know anyone called Jo.'

'You've just spent the last however many months sharing a dressing room with her.' Hilary was now twisting his shirt button, challenging the threads to hold. 'Jodie.'

'Jodie. How do you know her?' Nell asked, surprised.

'I only met her the other day. Party.'

'She's lovely.' Nell smiled.

'Are you in love with her?' Christabel probed.

The cotton threads on Hilary's shirt gave up the will to fight any longer, and the button came off in his hand.

'I take it by your silence you mean yes?'

'Exhausting, you are.' Pause. 'Probably.'

Christabel laughed with excited pleasure. Nell nodded and smiled again.

'I think you can depend on their approval,' Conrad whispered to Hilary, standing up to go and make some coffee. It was getting late.

The table was by now a desolate landscape of stubby candles on the point of suicide, empty bottles, scattered breadcrumbs. A smell of smoke, thick and stinging, hung above it like a hostile mist.

Conrad came back from the kitchen with a tray. He filled the first cup with coffee and passed it round with some cream and sugar. Hilary clunked a rocky brown lump into the brown liquid.

Samuel shivered, growing anxious. Liza glanced at him, understanding. Conrad gave her a cup to give to Samuel. Holding it in her hand, she raised her eyebrows by way of a private question. Did he want it?

There was no law which dictated that he had to accept a cup of coffee. But he had made a rule to himself.

He could of course, give up drinking coffee altogether. That would seem the simple solution to his problem, which was the irresistible urge to tap his head a specific number of times before he could take the initial sip. Yet that was not an option, for various reasons. For a start he loved coffee; he was a caffeine fiend. But more important, his psychiatrist had told him that the tapping could in time be eliminated but not by turning down offers of cups of coffee when he wanted them. Far from solving his problem, to do that would be to make it much worse.

Samuel knew that would be the beginning of the end. Looking at his wife's outstretched arm, he reminded himself that then there would be no looking back.

I want a cup of coffee.

'Samuel?' Liza prompted in a whisper.

Accept that cup of coffee.

'Please,' he said at last, without enthusiasm. He took the cup from Liza and put it down in front of him.

'Will you tell us about it?' Nell asked Hilary. Her questioning was gentler than Christabel's.

'Not much to tell. I met her at this party. Awful party. Private view at some fashionable gallery. Everyone sour-faced and dressed in black — '

'Including you,' Liza pointed out.

'Including me,' Hilary admitted. 'I was sour-faced, too, but that was because I was having a horrible time, not because I think it's fashionable.'

Everyone smiled at this, except Samuel. He had not heard. He was staring at the coffee in front of him. Distracted. Troubled.

'I was just leaving,' Hilary continued, 'when in came this flourish of a figure. I can't describe how affecting it was — such colour amidst all that mourning.'

Samuel still stared at his coffee. He needed to tap his head twenty-four times before he could drink it.

He needed to because, if he didn't, his children would be run over by a bus.

In his rational mind he knew it was a crackpot notion but, irrationally, it made sense. For as long as he had been tapping his head that number of times before drinking cups of coffee, Max and Nancy had always come home safely, thereby proving his theory. What could possibly persuade him to reject the ritual?

Yet how could he do it, now, without everyone noticing and thinking him mad?

Silent dilemma.

A wrestling match, divertingly fierce, going on inside his head between the rational and the irrational. As usual, the latter beating the shit out of the former. Heavyweight against featherweight.

47

'Violet eyes, violet dress, made of this really lovely material I'd never felt, all soft, I don't know what it was.'

'Nell, have you ever heard him notice girls' *clothes* before?' Christabel asked.

Nell shook her head.

'And so alive, her face,' Hilary went on. 'I couldn't stop staring at her. It's so wonderful, isn't it, Nellie, Jodie's vivacity? And she just didn't seem to care that everyone else was boot-faced. It seemed she was laughing all the time. I love her laugh.'

Try to forget it just this once. Samuel.

You bloody fool, and needlessly put your children's lives at risk? For the sake of avoiding social embarrassment; attracting a few odd looks from old friends?

Do you honestly think if you don't tap your head, Max and Nancy will die tomorrow under a bus? What are you on, eh? You're a man of considerable intelligence and a sense of reason. What's this with bloody tapping?

Could you ever forgive yourself? Let's just say they *were* involved in a fatal accident, it would be your fault and all because you were worried about what a few drunken people round a table would think. You would deserve to die yourself of guilt. Tap your head, you ass. Nobody will notice, they're all too far gone.

An entirely private madness.

No one was aware of it. Except Liza, and even she only to a certain extent.

His coffee was getting cold.

'Hilary, it sounds to me like you're in love with this girl,' Christabel was saying. 'I've never heard you speak like this about anyone.'

'Don't embarrass him,' Nell whispered kindly, inwardly acknowledging to herself that Christabel had a point.

'Well, has anything happened?' Christabel quizzed. 'That night? Since then? My God.'

'I'm not saying another word,' Hilary declared. He looked at his watch. It was very late. 'I really must go home.' He leant to kiss Christabel and Liza goodbye, and stood up. 'Conrad, lovely evening, thank you. Nellie, I'll ring you.' He gave her a hug, and whispered, 'I might have to have a word about our mutual friend.'

She smiled, sensing his elation.

He turned to Samuel. 'Will I be able to persuade you next time to explain why the sky's blue?'

'I expect so.' He managed a half laugh.

'You haven't drunk your coffee,' Hilary noticed, shrugging his arms into his coat. 'Mind if I have a sip? Keep me awake on my way home.'

'It's cold I'm afraid.'

'Doesn't worry me.'

'Are you sure?'

'Unless I'm depriving you?'

'Not at all,' Samuel said, pushing the cup towards Hilary. 'You'll be having the first sip, then I can finish it,' he added, unguarded in his relief. He smiled for no apparent reason.

'Er, yes,' Hilary agreed.

His puzzled look did not pass Samuel by. He was convinced Hilary thought him odd. He flinched. Yet he was so taken with gratitude he did somehow manage, through his embarrassment, to shake his hand. This was because Hilary, completely unwittingly and unexpectedly, had turned out to be his saviour.

# CHAPTER

## 3

Cillian O'Neill, in an old-fashioned red dressing-gown with cord piping, was sitting on a solitary chair in the middle of his bright kitchen. He was surrounded only by the uncluttered expanse of black and white lino tiles on the floor. He looked like a piece on a chess board: the triumphant but lonely king.

It was Tuesday morning.

The old man was drinking from a huge cup. Steam wafted about the surface of the coffee like that on a hot pool in a Turkish bath. A large bakelite wireless stood on the cream-coloured sideboard. Cillian was listening to *Yesterday in Parliament*. The volume was up high. He did not hear the click of the front door along the passage. But then he jolted his head upright, alert at the soft sound of light steps approaching. The kitchen door was almost closed. A figure moved behind the frosted glass.

Cillian, though, could not see it. He could not see a thing. He was blind; and his eyes were cloudy moonstones.

The door opened silently, and round it appeared a face which stared at him for a moment. It took in his sprigs of white hair; the purple veins pushing up between the translucent flesh of his gnarled hands; the baggy pale pink and yellow pyjama legs. His black slippers of leather and corduroy were grand, as was the smell about him of Trumpers lime cologne. But he looked hunched and vulnerable; possibly in pain.

'I know you're there,' he remarked after a few moments. The visitor stepped into the room.

'Cillian, I can't ever catch you out, however little noise I make.'

'Nell, my darling, you never believe me however much I tell you I'm really a bat.'

'If that was the case you wouldn't play your radio quite so loud. It'd deafen you,' came the cheerful response. 'That's better,' she declared, turning the volume down and then giving him a kiss.

'But I like noise,' he insisted. 'Lots of it. Quietness makes me feel old.'

'You are old. You're an old codger.'

He laughed. 'And you're not so young. Twenty-seven.' Cillian tutted with mock sympathy. 'Pushing on, old thing. On the shelf.'

'Cillian!' Nell protested, and smiled. 'Blind, *and* senile. We've had that conversation. A hundred times. And there's no more to be said.'

She poured herself some fresh coffee, and pulled the handle of the vast rounded fridge. A pint of milk stood on a turquoise moulded ridge on the inside of the door. It was in a big glass bottle with a gold foil top. Everything in Cillian's flat was dated. That was why Nell liked it so. Yet she did wonder how the hell he managed to obtain 1950-style milk bottles. She took a spoon of sugar from a blue and white striped tin. It stood in a row with others marked 'Rice' and 'Flour'.

She sat down on the kitchen table in the window and looked across the landscape of rooftops. It reminded her of a scene in *Mary Poppins*.

'Are you in a grump?' Cillian asked guiltily.

'Of course not. It's very sunny out there. I couldn't possibly be.'

'Even though I tell you you're old?'

'I don't mind the idea of being old. Not really. And I'm certainly not on any shelf quite yet. More coffee?'

Cillian held out his cup in the direction of her voice.

'I've got more important things to think about. Like the

fact that we finished *Our Mutual Friend* and you haven't said what you want now. More Dickens?'

'I hope when you say that you don't think I'm going to do a Mr Todd on you and keep you here in my Amazon jungle making you read Dickens to me forever? If it would make you feel any easier, I quite fancy a little Tolstoy. Haven't read *Anna Karenina* for years.'

'I don't feel remotely uneasy,' Nell told him fondly, passing him more coffee. 'I want to read whatever you like.'

'Ah, but I'm anxious that my reader should be as happy as myself in the choice of book. Let's go next door and have a look.'

Nell helped the old poet to his feet, and held him as he shuffled to the door. She intinctively felt that he might be in more pain than usual, but did not mention it. Cillian had a bad liver, having abused it almost since birth. He claimed to have been weaned on Guinness and Irish whiskey. He was not one, though, to complain. 'I can't be doing with illness,' Nell had often heard him say. 'All nonsense. Anyway, who wants to be sent off sober, for Christsake?'

So Nell did not nag him. Cillian had more than three ex-wives who made it their business to get at him about his unhealthy way of life. She loved him, but that was not her role.

Nell's role was to appear at Cillian's huge, messy flat in Belgravia twice a week to read to him. That was the arrangement, and he paid her by the hour. He was not poor. His collections of poems made a lot of money.

But their association was not limited simply to a formal financial arrangement. Nell liked, if she could, to visit him most days but refused to take money except for the specific reading hours. Despite the age gap, the old poet and his reader were exceptionally close. There were between them none of the complications or reservations that arise between parent and child. They confided in one another unrestrainedly. Nell thought Cillian wise and funny.

She knew that he, her father's greatest friend, had been

staying with her parents, at home, when she was born. She remembered his frequent visits to the house in Scotland. Her earliest memory of him, dating back to her early childhood was of a man with a regular, booming laugh, and yellow socks. He was especially popular with Daniel, Liza and Nell for appearing not to have noticed they were children. Although he was some years older than their father, he treated them like equals.

He used to read to Nell in the days before he went blind. Not children's books, but any one he happened to be reading himself. She could recall going on a walk alone with him and sitting on a rock by the loch for a rest. It was some time in the late 1960s or early 1970s. She was under ten. From the ripped pocket of his vast dark blue overcoat he produced a flask of whisky and a copy of a new novel by Patrick White. *The Vivisector*.

'It's about a little boy in Australia who becomes a painter,' was the only explanation she was given before he began. He read aloud for two hours that misty mauve morning on the rock. Nell fell in love with the fictional Hurtle Duffield who had scabs on his knees and was scared of pissing in his pants. She also fell for Cillian who shared a bit of his whisky with her, and carried her all the way home when it began to rain.

They went through to the drawing room. The paintwork was grubby, the drooping silk damask curtains had faded to the washed-out green of an old paper handkerchief. They were closed. When Nell opened them the sun alighted upon a crushed sofa and forlorn armchairs; a couple of glasses scummed with the dregs of last night's drinks; precariously high-rise blocks of books and loaded ashtrays. Cillian sniffed the air. Nell opened a window.

'Room's got a bit of a hangover, I'm afraid,' he observed. 'A friend and I were up late abusing it. Is there an awful mess, Nellie? Shall we choose a book and go back next door?'

She said it was fine.

'I suppose I ought to get dressed.'

53

'You do that, I'll take these through,' she told him, picking up an empty bottle or two, and the glasses.

'I'm a spoilt man,' he muttered, making his way to the door.

A while later the pair had settled on the sofa, Nell with a leather-bound copy of *Anna Karenina* in hand. Cillian had his feet, in yellow socks, resting on the low mahogany table in front of him. His eyes were closed and the expression on his face was one of utter contentment. The sound of Nell's voice billowed over him softly, like a linen sheet drying in a breeze.

After an hour or so, Nell broke off to make more coffee and fetch another packet of cigarettes from the kitchen.

When she returned, Cillian, still on the sofa, was thwacking the air with a rolled-up newspaper. He looked like a crazed conductor.

'Can't abide a wasp,' he remarked. 'Wretched bloody buzzing. Drive a fellow mad. Garotte the bugger for me, would you? I won't be able to enjoy *Anna Karenina*. Distracting.'

'Here, give me the paper.'

'Are you going to kill it? I hate wasps.'

'It's a bee.'

'Ahh!' Cillian shrieked excitedly. 'Stop, stop, you mustn't kill a bee.'

'I wasn't going to,' Nell said calmly, trying gently to nudge the whizzy insect towards the open window.

'Never squash a bee. Jake would kill me.'

Although Nell had come across most of Cillian's grandchildren, she had not met Jake O'Neill. Jake's father, Patrick, was a diplomat, so much of Jake's life had been spent abroad, mainly in Paris. 'His father's a pompous ass,' Cillian had told Nell more than once, 'but he's my favourite grandchild.' Recently Jake had returned to London to take up a job at the Natural History Museum as a bee expert. The old man, who spoke of him often, was enormously proud of him.

54

'They come in all different colours, he tells me. Not just your common or garden brown. He's described them to me so well I can picture them clearly. Beautiful creatures. You should go and see them.'

'I don't know much about bees,' Nell admitted. 'Ben showed me his hive at Blackwell Farm once, and I think I read a sinister Roald Dahl story about them. It was very detailed. Didn't a man consume so much royal jelly he turned into one?'

'I remember it, yes. Very creepy. But I think all the details about their lives were right. They're fascinating. I'll get Jake to tell you about them one day. I know you'd love to see them. He's got drawers and drawers of them at the museum. Thousands. Each individually laid out and labelled, apparently. Exotic ones from all over the world.'

With Nell's help, their bee managed to escape into the open.

'It's gone,' she told him.

'Free? Oh good, I'm so glad we didn't squash it. Now I can listen to the next chapter with an easy conscience.'

His companion picked up the book and once more began to read.

At midday she broke off again knowing it was time to give Cillian a drink.

'Will you join me?' he asked hopefully. 'Before you go back to that photographer friend of yours? Have I told you I don't approve of photographers?'

'You have, yes. Every day you tell me.'

'All that fashion stuff.'

'You know Conrad isn't a fashion photographer. Landscapes. Architecture.'

'I knew one once. A prick. But I suppose they're not all bad.'

'You liked Conrad when you met him,' Nell reminded him. 'You're just prejudiced because you didn't like this one man you met back in the fifties.'

'I'm old. It's the prerogative of the geriatric to hold prejudices.'

'His photographs are magnificent.'

'My darling, I don't doubt it. If I could see them, I'm sure I would agree. But that's all very well. When's he going to be helping you down off the shelf?'

'For one who's been described as unconventional in endless magazine and newspaper articles . . .'

'God I hate that . . .'

'You're remarkably conventional. He has tried, Cillian. But I don't want to be "helped down off the shelf" as you put it. Certainly not for the time being.'

The old man reached out for her hand.

'Give me that,' he said, 'and my drink. Now, why not?'

'Why?'

'It can be good. I should know. I've given, what, five women a helping hand.'

Nell told him that that was precisely the reason she wanted no such 'help'. 'I've seen you, Mum and Dad, and God knows how many others all make a mess of things. To believe in love and marriage after you lot I'd need to be either irredeemably unobservant or unforgiveably naive. Things don't last. That's all there is to it. Part of the human condition. Every association crumbles. Why draw out and exacerbate the inevitable alienations and partings with tedious religious and legal complications? Pointless.'

'Such cynicism in one so young,' Cillian remarked, but his tone was melancholy as opposed to patronising. 'That's another thing that should remain a prerogative of the old.'

'But I am old,' Nell replied.

'Ah, yes, of course. Makes sense then. I'm ancient, though, and I'm not entirely convinced that *all* partnerships are doomed. I can think of a lot that aren't.'

'Up until the other day, I could think of about two.'

'Oh really? Who?'

'Well, Liza and Sam, obviously. And the Howards. But I had to cross them off the list. Christabel told me Rosie's been having an affair with a bailiff for the past twenty-five years or so.'

56

'Ah yes, Bill, Rosie and the bailiff.'

'You knew?'

'Of course I knew. She told me, I think, or Bill did, I can't remember. Years ago.'

'But we've talked about them often and you've never mentioned it to me.'

'Times I've been tempted – to prove to you it's not only men who go in for infidelity.'

'Come on, I know women treat men badly too.'

Cillian grinned. 'But I haven't heard you say it too readily before now. I thought it was just men who were meant to be shits?'

'I've never said that.'

'By implication.'

'Well, I don't believe it, not necessarily.'

'As it happens,' Cillian said 'although Rosie was unfaithful, I don't think she treated Bill badly.'

'So why didn't you ever tell me?' Nell asked. 'I always thought their marriage was perfect, the ideal. Thought if I ever did get married, I'd like it to be like theirs. You let me go on thinking that, when all along there was this subtext. Proves how wrong one can be.'

'But, in fact, it didn't matter or make any difference. That's why I never told you. You'd have been disillusioned however much I tried to convince you they were actually happy.'

'Clearly delirious. Come on, how could they have been? It was all a farce, buoyed up only by deceit.'

Cillian shook his head. 'Bill knew, and the marriage worked well all the same. As you know. It only went wrong when he actually came across them *in flagrante*. Otherwise, it was as good as you thought it was. Christabel, the rest of the family, you, would never have known about the bailiff if Rosie hadn't been so daft as to take the silly man back and do it in the marital bed. It was an unspoken rule that that would never happen. Can't think why she did after all that time when they had been perfectly happy in his bed.'

57

Nell closed the book which lay on her knees. She stood to pour the old man another drink. There was a quiet swiftness about her movements. Although Cillian could not see her sad expression, he was able to sense she was upset.

'I know it's rather grim,' he murmured.

Nell, agreeing with him, picked up her bag. Then she said she had to go. 'Or I'll be late for an audition.'

'Oh,marvellous. You didn't tell me. What's this one for?'

'Another thing for telly. A play. I didn't get the Granada series. Letter this morning.'

'No matter. You might fare better this afternoon. What play?'

'A Simon Braine. A new one.'

'Goodness, darling, are you sure that's the thing? I never thought much of him even when he was still fashionable. Awful stuff, I recall, or am I quite wrong?'

'No, I think you're absolutely right.'

'Pretentious crap, isn't it? Full of meaningless meanings signifying nothing. Do you want the part?'

'Not especially, but I promised Annie I'd give it a go because she'd pulled out all the stops to get me an audition very late in the day for *The Cherry Orchard*. And she, like practically everyone except you and me, seems to think Braine's a great playwright. I'd really like to get the Chekhov, though. New production at the National.'

'I can quite see that, but there's no harm trying for the Braine, I suppose, as long as the productions don't coincide.'

'I'm unlikely to get either, let alone both! It's a dilemma I doubt I'll have to face,' Nell told him.

'Still, let me know how it goes. Ring tomorrow if you can't make it round here.'

'I will make it round here,' Nell assured him.

'I hope you brought a coat? You say it's sunny, but it's certainly not warm.'

'My thick black one. And the yellow scarf you gave me. Woolly yellow tights to match.'

'I suspect you look a bit like a bee?'

'A wasp. Bees are brown.'

'A bumble-bee then. You're so pernickety. Aren't they black and yellow? Whatever, I'm going to tell Jake my Nell's a bee.'

She asked if there was anything she could fetch for him. He shook his head so she gave him a kiss goodbye.

'Actually, before you go, my darling, just another half 'un?' Cillian gave her his glass, and with the forefinger and thumb of his other hand held a couple of inches apart he demonstrated to her his definition of a half 'un. 'Oh, and one other thing, probably no great shakes as a piece of information coming from an ancient bat like myself to a merely aged bee, but I might as well say it anyway. I honestly have come to the conclusion that fidelity isn't terribly important.' He took a gulp from his newly filled glass. 'Best of luck with this afternoon, I'll be thinking of you. But maybe give that one a thought while you're at it. I'm sure there's a lot of truth in it.'

An hour or so later, Nell found herself on a hard plastic chair staring at a wall of whitewashed bricks. Mind blank. She was in a basement in Soho, waiting in a dank passage to audition.

A woman with thin plaits and beads in her hair brought her a cup of coffee. The assistant producer. She had a friendly disposition devoid of the self-importance normally associated with such people. Not a trace of television sneer.

'Geoffrey won't be long. And don't worry, he's very friendly. Let me know if you want more coffee.'

Another girl was sitting beside Nell. A rival officially, but not one of those hard bitches with sinewy knees, razor eyes and a spiky voice, the kind that out-of-work actresses always come up against in predictable films about the road to stardom.

'My third audition today,' she said. 'Had one this morning for an ad. A new soap. They'd rigged up this mock shower, no water, in the middle of this plush office in Goodge Street, and got me to step in it with all my clothes on and pretend to wash. Feeling like a complete bloody fool, I did so for a couple of minutes, till they stopped me and said, "Listen, love, we want to see you *make love* to our soap," so I told them where to put it. I didn't get the job, of course. But they claimed it was because I hadn't been able to make them *hear* the water! I didn't want to be in their crummy ad anyway.'

Nell laughed.

'I wouldn't mind a part in this play, though, even if the Beeb isn't into big salaries. Who cares, if one keeps hold of one's integrity? Mind you, it's all a bit beyond me.'

At that moment, the beaded assistant producer reappeared and asked Nell to follow her along the passage. When she stood up, the girl wished her luck.

The audition room was hot and dark, the black-painted floor scratched like an old record.

The director was sitting with a couple of other people at a small table. He was wearing jeans, a collarless shirt and heavy-duty sneakers that went up to his ankles. Uneven teeth like a miniature African necklace.

'Call me Geoff,' he said, standing up and leaning over to shake Nell's hand. 'This is Jean, our casting director. You've met before?'

Jean, whose choice of shirt was ruched peach, nodded.

'And Tony, our producer.' Tony had an alarming pallor, the yellow of the sole of an old person's foot. 'Don't mind him, he's got a bit of a hang-over.' A little humour to put Nell at her ease. 'Lovely, now, what can I tell you, Nell? You know Si's work I expect?'

'Yes, I do.'

'Great, super, fantastic. Well, this new one, and I think the others will agree, is probably the best. That's not to say his previous stuff isn't marvellous, too, of course. Anyway, we're testing today for the part of Persephone. A truly lovely character. I think you'll like her. Great part. Perhaps you'd read a bit for us? I've chosen a really nice little speech which I think you'll be able to get your teeth into. All good meaty stuff.'

Geoffrey handed her a few pages of tyepescript. 'Do you

60

want to have a quick glance over it first, for a few mo's? The scene all takes place in a bowl of pot-pourri, you see, which is by way of a kind of really clever, I think, allegory, of . . . of a microcosm of the petty bourgeois ideal. Okay, right. Take your time, start when you're ready, Nell, okay? No hurry, and most important, enjoy.'

After she had read the speech there was a moment's respectful silence while the effusive director stroked his chin, studiedly pensive.

'Great, love, you read well. Thank you. Sexy speech, isn't it? I really think it's going to translate well on to the screen. You know, I've been in this business quite some years now, done a lot of good stuff in my time, but I reckon I've never worked with better words. Poetry.'

Nell wondered, as Geoffrey took a swig of beer from a can on the table and lit a cigarette, precisely which poetry he was referring to.

'So, anyway, we've still got a minute or two, so tell us a little about yourself, Nell. What do you enjoy in your spare time? What are your hobbies, other than boyfriends?' A little laugh.

It was a bad moment in a bad afternoon.

Nell told Geoffrey that what she most enjoyed doing in her spare time was playing hide-and-seek.

He hesitated a moment before responding. Enthusiastic.

'That's a very profound statement you just made there, and one which I think I can truly relate to. I know exactly what you're saying, Nell. It's what life's all about, really, isn't it? One big game of hide-and-seek. Trying to untangle illusion and reality; getting to the bottom of perception. I would say, in fact, that that is much of what this play's about. I mean, as I see it – correct me if I'm wrong, Jean, Tony – ' Geoffrey paused and raised a humble eyebrow. Jean and Tony nodded. 'And I reckon you've cottoned on to that factor with tremendous speed and accuracy; got the essence of the meaning from that one speech. Jolly good. You're an intelligent woman, Nell. Well done. Marvellous. Thank you, Nell, very much.'

Geoffrey stood and shook her hand again with a hospitable firmness as if he was in a drawing room.

'Jean will give you a call in a few days, all right? Let you know. Take care, now, and mind how you go.'

Nell thanked them and made her way to the door without looking back.

On Samuel's second visit to the hospital, the lime green girl was in Out Patients again, but she had changed to shocking pink.

Sitting down on one of the plastic chairs, Samuel thought that maybe she saw herself as a fluorescent highlighter pen.

It was Monday morning, and, perhaps for that reason, there was a hot air of gloom in the room, a strip-lit look of resignation on all the faces of the waiting patients. Except Samuel's. His expression was one of gentle anticipation; he was looking forward to an hour with the psychiatrist.

The first session, a week earlier, had gone well. Dr Oak had proved to be a thoroughly agreeable man; warm and sympathetic. He had worn neither a white coat nor a supercilious expression. Samuel had faith in him.

The treatment, he was told, would go on for as long or as short a time as necessary. The weekly meetings would concentrate not on trying to discover possible causes of his problem, but on a direct cure for the symptoms. Dr Oak had explained it was an old school of psychiatry which believed in examining life histories, reconstructing childhood incidents. Samuel was relieved, keen to have practical help, unkeen to delve into his past, blame his parents, feel laden with guilt.

He had always been a fastidious character, someone who felt faintly uneasy if he did not use up the last tiny sliver of soap, or if a picture hung slightly askew. Each night he used to turn off the television by the switch at the wall. It was a small precaution, hardly very inconvenient, because he had read somewhere that sets had been known spontaneously to combust.

62

These were all harmless quirks, not abnormal, and ones which did not disrupt his life.

But things had begun gradually to alter about seven years ago. He had been married to Liza for about a year, when he began noticing that some of his habits were starting to trespass on his consciousness, like squatters over whom a landlord has no control.

Sometimes he would find himself lying in bed worrying that he had not turned off the television switch, though he knew, really, he had and that he was just being ridiculous. But then it reached a point where he was unable to sleep unless he got up and went downstairs to make sure.

A while later he was appalled to discover that when he went to check the switch, he was first checking his slippers to see if they were insulated. He would look many times at the soles before he dared risk electrocution by putting his fingers on it.

No one knew what was going through his mind. Such was the humiliation he felt at his own increasing anguish that he was unable to confide in a soul. He was a science teacher after all. Although he did not usually teach it, his knowledge of physics if nothing else told him that his fears were imaginary and wholly without reason. But this only made him feel worse, as ridiculous as an arachnologist with a phobia for spiders.

Liza noticed his neuroses, of course; she could barely have failed to for long, especially when he began regularly to leap out of bed just as they were about to go to sleep.

'What are you up to?' she asked at first, tolerant but curious.

'Er, just forgotten something downstairs. Won't be a minute,' he would reply.

After a while she questioned him further. 'Can I ask you something?'

Samuel had bit his lip. 'Um?'

'What is it downstairs you keep forgetting, my love?'

'Oh, you know. Just checking.'

'Checking what?'

'Lights and stuff.'

'But we switched them all off together.'

'Front door,' he added, desperate. 'Not sure I remembered to lock it.'

'Oh.' She sounded more puzzled than impatient.

Then one night it was particularly awful.

'I've checked everything, Samuel,' she announced triumphantly when they were lying in each other's arms. 'Door, lights, windows. No need for you to go down.'

His reaction terrified him. Liza's announcement had literally caused him to shake.

'What's the matter?' She took his hand and felt that it was sweaty; his brow hot. 'Samuel, don't you feel well? Have you got a temperature?'

Samuel found it hard to speak but he somehow plucked up courage to explain. 'If you just let me check, I'll be all right,' he whispered. 'Just got quickly to check, just to make sure.'

'But, my love, that's daft. I did that for you before we came up, specially so you wouldn't have to get out of bed.'

'I know, I know,' he replied, kissing her, staring into her eyes, willing her to understand without further explanation. He had then gently manoeuvred himself from her embrace, laid the bedclothes aside, and stood up, a tentative figure, milky-white in the blue dark.

'You mad fellow,' Liza said, laughing.

It was a shocking moment.

Never before then had the notion that he was mad entered his head. He had managed to stave it off.

During the course of the following weeks he told himself to pull himself together.

In vain.

Thus the ritual continued.

And others began to appear.

There was the coffee one which began soon after the children were born. It cropped up as if from nowhere and

Samuel found it not only perplexing but also disturbing, because it also affected him away from home. Strangely, his fear of electricity was limited to the confines of his own house. In other places he was fine. He thanked God he was not afflicted by it at school, otherwise life would have become completely impossible, especially in the labs. It was a terrifying thought, that one day he might have a panic attack, not in the privacy of his own bed, but in a class full of pupils. Fortunately, that horror had not yet occurred, but he was petrified it might not be far off, since he was now having to tap his head in the staffroom before drinking coffee in breaktimes. Was this an early indication that he was well on the slippery slope?

At one point he quietly went off and tried hypnosis. It was a practice for which he had considerable scepticism, but because he was desperate, he tried to contrive faith in it.

It did not work.

He found out the name of a psychotherapist and made an appointment to see her. She lived in St John's Wood, and had a neck like a tortoise. Around it she had hung an exaggerated number of brassy necklaces. Doubtless this was because she had a self-destructive urge and unconsciously wished to hang herself. Samuel could see why. Her plush house had remote control curtains and a green carpet of such a luxuriant pile it reminded him of alfalfa grass. Imagine wading through that with a hangover, he thought.

She charged intolerable sums of money – £40 for a session that was not even an hour. Psychotherapists were a rule unto themselves, Samuel discovered, when it came to defining an hour. She also seemed unkeen to speak. To be fair, she did occasionally break her vow (probably more out of boredom than anything else) but then only to repeat verbatim exactly what he had told her or to voice interpretations remarkable for their crassness.

'It might be construed that your fear of electricity stems, perhaps, from your fear of your mother who, I think it would be fair to deduce from what you say, had a very, well, *electric* nature.'

65

Samuel had managed to resist the benefit of her professional opinion more than once. He did not book a date to see her a second time.

In the end, although he had been reluctant to do so, Samuel went to his GP. He finally made himself recognise that he needed proper help, to be referred to a psychiatrist.

He loathed the prospect. There was a puritan streak in him which dictated that to go to such meausures was a shameful, undignified weakness. It had felt absurd sitting and talking to a complete stranger who charged a fortune, had the insight of a goldfish, and couldn't have given a fuck about him. But here he was contemplating it again, just with a different type of shrink. Weren't they all the same?

Yet seven years had passed, and although he had really tried, his neuroses had not subsided. If anything, they had become more urgent. Perhaps a proper medically qualified shrink was the answer. It would probably cost a lot of money, and although Liza was generous, he couldn't agree to let her pay for him. Unfortunately, he himself did not have a lot of money. In fact, he had very little money: he was a state school teacher. But he could no longer bear being trapped, imprisoned by his obsessions. Sometimes his rational mind was so burdened by the weight of them that he was propelled into a sickening, terrifying despair.

On such occasions he wanted to be dead.

He did need help.

It was a painful admission.

But Dr Dunn had been kind. He had asked questions, taken notes, and suggested he be referred as an out-patient to the relevant department at a psychiatric hospital in South London. 'The unit there is run by a Dr Oak, who specialises in this field and will definitely be able to help,' he had informed him.

For the first time in years, Samuel had felt a jitter of hope, a rousing of the spirits.

Before he went to his introductory appointment, he was asked to fill in a long questionnaire relating to his particular condition, so that Dr Oak could form an initial impression, make the foundation of an assessment.

The first meeting had been a success. They had covered a great deal of ground. Samuel asked if he would have to take drugs. Dr Oak told him that clomipramine was sometimes used. 'It's useful for relieving anxiety and depression,' he said, 'but doesn't cure obsessional symptoms. The best, most up-to-date treatment is one whereby we help you to become your own therapist and devise your own self-help programme,' the doctor explained. 'For example, I can come up with a series of exposure exercises for you, but you're at liberty to reject them and to suggest some others.'

The remark made Samuel smile. Dr Oak's words were comforting.

Moreover, at the end of two whole hours, he had told Samuel he had no need to fear self-indulgence. 'You are a case that needs to be treated,' he said, 'and far too hard on yourself to have supposed you could have done it alone. That's what I'm here for.'

The relief, on hearing those words from the expert, was almost magical.

'Can you come once a week?' the doctor had asked.

Samuel had nodded joyously.

'Same time, Monday mornings? Not difficult to get off school?'

'I've got two study periods now, so I'm not meant to be teaching at the moment anyway. I can easily get up earlier to make up for the hour or so lost.'

'That's settled then. Lovely. I'll see you next week, Mr Sorrell.' Dr Oak had shook his hand warmly. 'And I promise, together we'll crack this one.'

Samuel had thanked him. Then he had added, 'Tell me one thing before I go. Do you think I'm mad?'

Dr Oak had smiled. 'We all feel anxious, you know, to greater or lesser degrees, especially these days, modern life being so taxing. Most people are a bundle of neuroses. Some face them very pragmatically, while others don't even know they have them, but some people suppress them brilliantly and find they manifest themselves in different ways. Their worries are translated into all manner of rituals, obsessions, phobias, addictions.

'Howard Hughes was preoccupied with germs, you know,' he went on, 'and Samuel Johnson suffered in his own way. Boswell pointed out that he used to touch every post along the street or road as he walked. According to Sir Joshua Reynolds' wife, Johnson had this peculiar method of entering houses. Before he went through the door, he'd start these funny hand gestures and then suddenly he'd spring across the threshold in a flying leap.'

Samuel had even managed to laugh.

'Of course,' Dr Oak had said, 'everyone is affected in different ways. It might be fear of flying, or the compulsive desire to spend money, or the need to drink twenty litres of water a day, or agoraphobia, whatever. It doesn't mean the sufferers are mad, Mr Sorrell. I can assure you, you're by no means mad.'

It was one of those rare moments in Samuel's life when he found himself wanting to cry.

Little wonder, then, that he had returned to the hospital, the following week, full of excitement, and was now sitting without the air of resignation which uniformly hovered over the faces of his fellow patients. He could not wait to see the reassuring Dr Oak again. Dr Oak was going to be his saviour.

He settled to await the moment he would be called.

There was a man of about thirty-five sitting beside him. He was wearing a baggy blue suit, rather elegant, but no socks. He had a salmon-pink plaster on one of his ankles and invitingly friendly eyes. He looked as though he might have worked in television. One of his sleeves had been pushed up almost to the elbow, the cuff of his mauve shirt splayed back. The man, as far as Samuel could make out, was scratching his arm. Scratching and scratching.

Probably been abroad, Samuel thought – mosquito bites. But then he noticed the man was picking at the skin very intently, and with the concentrated deliberation of a monkey extracting fleas from its fur.

Without looking up from the task in hand, he suddenly began to speak to Samuel. He found himself oddly pleased that the man, perfectly naturally, had just started talking.

'I've got all these bugs, you see. Don't worry, you won't catch them, but you'll forgive me if we don't shake hands, just in case.' He had a Scottish accent. 'They're real little buggers, jump all over the place, itch like mad. I'm Eddie McLean, by the way. Nice to meet you.' He stopped and turned to Samuel. 'Though it's hardly your average spot to make social introductions, an asylum. Not exactly the pub, is it?'

Samuel laughed.

'What're you in for?' Eddie asked.

'I think it's called Obsessive-Compulsive Disorder.'

'Oh, you're one of them. Count the number of letters on every street sign you see, do you? Wash your hands a hundred and sixty-three times a day?'

'That sort of thing,' Samuel replied, smiling, enjoying Eddie's frankness.

'You're a daft dingbat, know that? Mind you, you wouldn't be here if you weren't, so that's fair enough,' the Scotsman remarked, nodding. He carried on flicking his forearm.

'How about you?'

'Well, I've got this infestation of bugs, you see. Crawling with them.'

Samuel was puzzled. 'Where did you get them from?'

'My house. Dust and that. Fucking pain in the neck. They get everywhere.'

'But can't you just buy some sort of stuff to get rid of them? And some cream from your doctor for you?'

'No good, any of that. Persistent little fuckers,' Eddie told him. Suddenly he put his hand up level to his ear. 'Hang on a sec.' Then he slapped the side of his head, rather hard, as if it was a tiresome child's wrist. Samuel was a little alarmed.

69

'Got you, you bastard,' Eddie exclaimed, examining his palm. 'Serve you right.' He held out his hand for Samuel to look at.

Samuel could see nothing.

'They must be very small,' he observed innocently. 'I can't see anything.'

'Yes, they're very small, and very irritating.'

Samuel wondered what sort of insects they might be, and asked Eddie as much.

'I don't know, they won't tell me. Some sort of flea, I guess. God, if I had half their energy, bloody jumping about all the time, I'd be a fit man.'

'But I don't see why you're here for something physical. I thought this was purely a psychiatric hospital.'

'It is. But they've got this crackpot theory that I haven't got any bugs, and they've slapped some posh name on my so-called disorder to prove it. But if there weren't any rotten bugs, I wouldn't be itching the whole rotten time, would I?'

'What do they call it?'

'Delusory parasitosis,' came the reply. 'They can label it Delusory-whatever-they-damn-well-like, but I've got bugs all right, that's all there is to it. I don't care what those wankers think. They think I'm a nutter.'

Eddie could not have looked less like a nutter. Indeed, Samuel knew he wasn't a nutter, any more than he himself was. He liked Eddie, felt him to be intelligent and good-humoured. He had been wrong on his first visit to assume that all those around him in Out Patients were loonies. Some might have been, but not all of them. It was unspeakable to brand them, himself included, in one lump and call them mad.

It was time to go along to Dr Oak's room. He stood up. 'Will you be here next week?' he asked the Scotsman.

'Oh yes, I'm here every week.'

'I didn't see you last Monday,' Samuel remarked.

'I was a bit late last Monday. Itching so much I had to change my clothes just before I came out. What's your name, mate?'

'Samuel Sorrell.'

'Nice to meet you.' Eddie put out his hand automatically, and then retracted it. 'Sorry, you won't be wanting to shake it in the light of what I've told you.'

'Yes I do,' Samuel assured him, smiling.

'Oh, very good.' Eddie held out his hand again to meet Samuel's, pleased that someone was prepared to ignore the risk involved in touching him. 'We must have a drink sometime.'

Samuel agreed enthusiastically, before saying goodbye. Then he walked along the row of chairs and made his way to his second appointment with Dr Oak.

The pollination of the buttercup was a second-year topic which, if not hugely exciting, was at least straightforward. Teaching human sexual reproduction, however, to a bunch of fourteen-year-olds was a less certain business.

Samuel was sitting in the staffroom having just returned from the hospital, and was preparing that afternoon's lessons.

It was one thing, he thought, talking about bees and their part in the continuation of the buttercup race, but it was quite another talking about the coming together of homo sapien gametes.

He knew he shouldn't be embarrassed, but he was. Couldn't help it. It just *was* embarrassing standing up there in front of a giggling crowd of horny adolescents, chucking about words like scrotum and vulva and trying casually to sound as though they were describing nothing more erotic than a dustpan and brush.

And the video, so helpfully provided by the education authority, hardly made his life any easier. Full colour computer diagrams; a commentary in a voice as bright as that of the television narrator for Thomas the Tank Engine; and, inevitably, its excruciatingly graphic climax.

Samuel, feeling low at the prospect of another afternoon with the subject, opened his canvas briefcase and started

71

sorting papers for the relevant worksheet. As he did so, his mind meandered from human sexual reproduction to Miss Hardcastle: a thought progression which was not entirely *non sequitur*.

He looked at his watch. Five past eleven. Ten minutes till break.

She would be in soon. Radiant, doubtless. Possibly with chalk dust on her neck. He had seen it there before, like the merest wisp of talcum powder, and had wanted softly to stroke it away . . .

The worksheet needed to be photocopied. Samuel glanced at the cumbersome machine in the corner, then stood up and went over to it. It was humming. He lifted the lid, placed the paper on the glass surface, closed the lid. His finger hovered, not consciously, for a split second before pushing the square 'operate' button.

The machine began to wheeze, to blink, and to burp out copies. They spurted and spluttered on to the side tray.

Samuel took a small step back. As he waited for all the copies to appear, he looked out of the window.

Apparently it was bad for the eyes to watch a photocopier's flashing light. At any rate, that was what he had heard.

A bell rang to indicate the end of the second lesson. Commotion in the corridor.

Tim Crawford and Rachel English were the first to appear, followed by Battleaxe Barbara in a bright yellow suited neither to her fading Lucozade colouring nor, Samuel noted to his secret and gleeful delight, to her temperament. (He happened to know, because Tim had told him, that she was terrified of bees. Thus decked out, like a big blowsy buttercup, she was the perfect target for their attentions.)

A few more of his colleagues wandered in and over to the coffee machine, chatting. The usual sort of stuff. Madeleine Good causing Tim yet more angst, Rachel appalled by the low standard of some boy's French dictation.

The English teacher came in a minute or two after the others. She, like Samuel, was in her mid-thirties. She had long dark hair, very straight, with a fringe. Her face was as white as a woman in an Elizabethan portrait, and she wore tulip-red lipstick. She walked to the table on which was a kettle and a short row of Pyrex cups and saucers. These were laid out for those who liked herb teas or powdered soups, luxuries the Hot Drinks Dispenser was unable to provide.

Samuel watched as Miss Hardcastle took a packet of her own teabags from her basket which hung by a thin rope over her shoulder. She was keen on rosehip. She smelt of rosehip. Very faintly on her breath. He had often noticed it when they talked together close to.

She made herself a cup of tea, and put two biscuits on her saucer from the square red tin, then looked up and caught Samuel's eye. He smiled. She moved towards him and sat down on one of the dilapidated orange chairs.

'You look a bit anxious, Lucy,' he observed. (She remained Miss Hardcastle in his mind only, a bid to keep his thoughts about her as professional as possible: a considerable struggle.)

I feel it,' she replied, leaning down to put the pile of mustard-coloured exercise books in her arms on to the floor. Samuel held her tea for her as she did so.

She had chosen a chocolate bourbon and a Nice. He always picked the custard creams. Maybe it was time for a change. She was inspirational on so many levels, Miss Hardcastle, even the most mundane.

'Thanks,' she said, sitting upright again and taking back her cup and saucer. 'No, it's just I went in to see Mr Cliff earlier this morning to ask for more copies of *Far From the Madding Crowd* for the fifth form. He said, "Isn't one between two sufficient?" I told him, "I dare say we could manage on that if we had one between two, but we don't".'

Samuel nodded knowingly, sympathetic.

'We have precisely three copies for a class of thirty-three,' Lucy went on. 'I mean, how am I supposed – ?' She broke off

73

and sighed. 'I'm sorry, how often do we have this conversation? But sometimes, you know, I feel so frustrated, I long to buy copies for them myself. I would, too, if I could afford it.'

'By the time I've photocopied the relevant pages of the one textbook available to me for my third year, it must be costing more than buying them all brand new ones.'

'Why don't we just pack it in, eh?' Lucy asked, not seriously. 'I don't know what's worse – this or the NHS.' Her upper lip dabbled upon the red, hot surface of her rosehip tea. 'I feel sorrier for the nurses in a way. I suppose they stick it out because they're as mad as we are and love what they're doing.'

'The government relies on our madness for its survival,' Samuel said.

'I can feel the frustration inside me like nausea, you know, but I guess it doesn't do me any real harm.'

Samuel, who liked Lucy's stoicism, shook his head. He wondered if she could possibly guess at the kind of frustrations to which he was daily subjected, quite apart from those provided by the Minister for Education.

'Or rather, that's the way we've got to see it,' Lucy added, 'otherwise we really would give up. Secretly I think about it more and more. The school play has helped a bit though. Seeing them all get so excited about it, funnily enough, reminds me why I go on.'

'It's certainly an achievement to muster their enthusiasm for Shakespeare,' Samuel observed. Had it been his place to feel it, his tone might have been one of pride.

He regretted that he had probably failed to inspire pupils likewise. How could he excite them with science?

How could he excite Miss Hardcastle as long as he taught a subject which concerned itself with nitrates? It didn't matter how well-read he was, how literary his bent, or how many hours the two of them spent discussing books together. The bottom line was that while she was teaching the poetry behind *Measure for Measure*, he was teaching the physics behind a bar of soap.

74

And for that reason, although she was nice to him and they got on well, she could never feel more than that, could she?

For Christ's sake, Samuel, he berated himself, what are you thinking of? What would it be to you anyway, even if she did? You're a happily married man.

'Have you decided to audition for it, Samuel, by the way?'

Lucy received a nervous half-cough by way of reply.

'I do hope you have.'

Why does she hope I have? Could it be she wants an excuse, if I got a part, for extra hours together at rehearsals?

God, you ask yourself stupid questions sometimes.

'I'm still thinking about it,' he told her out loud, although he had really already decided.

'Come on, it's going to be great fun,' she urged.

All this encouragement. Very affecting.

'Well, I suppose I could come round to the idea. But I doubt I'd get a part.'

'Don't be silly. Anyway, I've never known you be flummoxed by a challenge. I won't forget you as goalie at last year's end of term football match for a long time.'

Won't forget? Define 'for a long time', Miss Hardcastle.

She stood up suddenly. 'Bell's about to go,' she said, 'and I've got this lesson right the way over in E Block. I hope I've persuaded you?'

Miss Hardcastle was wearing a drill cotton skirt, black, knee-length. She had a flat stomach but her legs were not very good. They were shapeless, like the bodies of sausage dogs. Endearing, nonetheless.

'I expect so.'

'That's great. Listen, I'd better go. See you later. And you can let me know for certain, okay?'

The winning smile, and she was gone.

Just before lesson five, which started at ten to three, Samuel wheeled the television and video recorder into the lab.

Leaning down he held the plug near the socket, but as he did so the nerves in his arm tingled.

75

He looked at the socket, and was alarmed to discover that he was unable to bring himself either to push the plug in or to touch the switch. His hand began to shake.

Fortunately, at that moment, the bell went and he leapt up. The third year pupils started arriving for his class. There were nearly thirty of them.

Some were wearing their white regulation polyester shirts, sleeves rolled up. Others had on their V-neck jerseys too, grey and uniformly holey. All their ties, once shiny navy blue with pale blue stripes, were darkened by ink stains or grease. The rubber soles of hi-tech training shoes squeaked on the wooden floor.

As they gathered round the television, they dropped their various bags, satchels, books and pencil cases on to the floor and desks. Noisy and boisterous as ever, but excited too.

'Calm down you lot,' Samuel shouted above them. 'Come on, now, hurry up and settle down.'

'Yeah we don't want to miss the end, not today,' declared one teenage boy. 'Best bit, eh?'

Huge laughter all round.

'I appreciate your enthusiasm, Mark, I just hope you're not going to be disappointed, that's all.'

'How can a porn video be disappointing, Mr Sorrell?'

Wolf whistles, and the odd clap.

'Listen, quieten down now, or we won't have time for the end which you all seem so keen to see. Sit down, Mark, anywhere will do. Move over a bit, Alex, make room for him.'

'I can't go there, Mr Sorrell. I won't see a thing.'

'Look, just sit down, all right? You'll see perfectly. Or are you so keen to stay on after the end of school? I can be here till midnight, if you like, but I'm not sure the others would see the lab as the ideal place to spend their evening.'

Mark obeyed, but in saying those words Samuel recognised in himself all those qualities he had so resented in his own teachers: uninspired sarcasm, petty bossiness. It was a depressing comparison.

'Lights, someone,' he ordered, and they were duly switched off.

Samuel pressed the video's 'play' button, knowing the plug was not in the wall. •

Nothing happened.

'Oh,' he said, feigning surprise, 'I must've forgotten to put the plug in. Madeleine, could you please?'

Madeleine Good, who had knotted her hair round a pencil, did not move. She just narrowed her eyes.

'Madeleine, did you hear me?'

'Why can't you do it, Mr Sorrell? You're nearest it.'

'Because I asked you to. Now, please will you put it in immediately.' He pointed at the plug which was lying on the floor at the end of its lead. He was shaking inside. Anger and fear.

Madeleine stood up reluctantly. She knelt to pick up the plug. 'Don't you like plugs or something?' she asked menacingly, turning it in her fingers. Suddenly her hand shot out towards him. Samuel took a sharp step back. His heart was punching the inside of his chest.

'Get on with it, Madeleine,' one of the boys shouted. 'I want to see the video.'

Madeleine put the plug into the socket and flicked the switch on.

'Right,' Samuel said, trying to conceal his relief. He hesitated before placing his finger on the 'play' button once more. He was aware that some of his pupils were giving him a quizzical look. Two girls were nudging each other and suppressing giggles.

He felt wretched. Even if Madeleine and they didn't know the exact nature of his weakness, she had managed to make them all too aware that there was something odd about him. If he couldn't win back their respect instantly, his position would become untenable, and he would have failed as a teacher.

'Right,' he said again. The word came out with a resounding tone of authority. Madeline stopped whispering to her neighbour and sat up straight. The rest of the class fell silent. Samuel was able to force himself to press the button.

'Thank God,' he said to himself. Now I mustn't think about this any more.

Fortunately, the cheerful commentary started up, along with the tasteful graphics, and his mind was distracted.

Everybody began to concentrate.

A pretty grim introduction to sex, Samuel thought (though it was questionable for quite how many of them it was an introduction). So clinical, they're hardly even giggling.

There had been, in previous lessons, very sensitive and earnest discussions (part of the syllabus) about the importance of 'meaningful relationships' and 'a loving partner'. He wondered how they were going to manage to equate such abstract sentiment with the clinical proceedings they were now witnessing on screen. It was hard enough for him. A happily married man.

His mind began to meander.

The awfulnes of the phrase 'meaningful relationships'.

Miss Hardcastle wouldn't use such terminology.

She would have passionate affairs, dangerous liaisons, even. Irresistible notion.

There was a movement at the back of the room as if a couple of pupils were shifting in their seats, or the door had gently slipped open of its own accord. Samuel did not look up. Just at that moment a blob of sperm suddenly presented itself on the screen. The video's finale. The pupils laughed loudly.

'He's come,' one of the boys observed triumphantly.

Samuel, shaken from his thoughts, laughed with them. 'That's right, Paul. Now give me the right term.'

'Can't remember.'

'Anyone?' Samuel asked, switching off the film. Looking up, he suddenly spied Miss Hardcastle politely waiting at the back of the room.

Alas, too late.

Only a split second passed. But there was time enough for him to dread what was to come.

Then the inevitable: the general cry went up: 'Ejaculation!'

It was one of those moments in his life he could quite well have managed without.

# CHAPTER

## 4

Friday night. It was hot and dark inside Conrad's car. Nell felt drowsy. Christabel, exhausted by her own chatter, had fallen asleep in the back.

The three of them were heading for a cottage near Welshpool in Wales. The journey from London had already taken three hours, and they had another forty minutes to go. Conversation had frittered out just before Birmingham.

Nell's eyes had grown weary of the pattern on the black dashboard – dots of red, green and yellow lights. She turned to Conrad whose lower jaw was jutting forward: concentrating on the road.

She stared at him. Contemplating.

They had been together for nearly four years.

Met at a party in Hackney and had ended up drinking an interesting amount of Rioja. Awful party, Nell remembered. A couple of people had worn pathetically unwitty wigs in overeager colours.

One man, with a reptilian blink, had pressed her up against the fridge and informed her she was 'an intelligent woman'.

'I don't meet many intelligent women,' he said. 'Are there many?' He was wearing a Hawaiian shirt. Quite unexpectedly his thin tongue sprang out, flick-knife-like, towards her lips. She did not allow it to go so far as to kiss her.

His face was plastered with irritating exuberance. Extricating herself, Nell had spotted Conrad in a grey jersey, and with an expression that was dazzling in comparison: completely depressed.

A kindred spirit.

She introduced herself. Unusual for her – unheard of, in fact. But she was desperate.

Conrad was pleased. He was hating the party as much as she was. They sat in a corner and piled into the Rioja without further ado. Nell had felt like getting drunk.

Some weeks before the party, a boyfriend had dropped in on her to explain that it was over, and to collect his Doc Marten shoes. Totally out of the blue. Just like that.

After the initial shock she developed a considerable hatred for DMs and a resilient sense of pessimism.

Nell was in the mood for gloom. And Conrad Holland was gloomy: overworked and cross to find himself surrounded by people so urgently keen to have fun.

Their affair began a week or two later, on a low.

Nell liked him, but expected it to be a short-lived encounter; straightforward; nice while it lasted.

The pair of them started meeting with increasing frequency. He went to the flat she rented at that time in Primrose Hill, and they watched television. She went with him to the pub near where he lived in Camberwell.

Thus it trickled into a more established arrangement. About a year later they discovered they loved each other. And now, three years after that, they were still happy.

Nell's concept of happiness was not ambitious. She believed, simply, that not to be positively unhappy meant she was happy. To aspire to a sustained state of delirium was naive and pointless. Like someone standing out in a thunderstorm not only hoping to stay dry, but actually expecting to get brown.

But she had not felt depressed once since the day she met Conrad: an achievement in itself. She missed him when he went away on photographic assignments, and never stopped enjoying his company.

She knew, however, that things could change, and any day he might announce his decision to gather up his shoes, just like the last one.

Conrad, on the other hand, turned out to be more of an optimist. He came to recognise an active joy in his association with Nell. And showed it by ready laughter at her conversation, considerate attentiveness, affectionate teasing, interest in her work, very obvious sexual fulfilment.

In the dark, as they drove along, she continued to stare at him, and was aware of a feeling of contentment.

'What?' he asked, putting his hand up to his neck, suddenly conscious of her eyes on him. 'What are you looking at?'

'Nothing. Just thinking.'

'About?'

'The weekend. Looking forward to it.'

'Bit rash, isn't it?' he said, humouring her. 'Goes against the rules. Inviting disappointment, no?'

Nell smiled. 'Not on a weekend with Samuel and Liza. I can't be disappointed when I'm with them. You know that.'

They turned off the narrow lane, and trundled over a cattlegrid on to a mud track which had a lumpy spine of thick grass. As the car heaved itself up the steep incline, its headlights whitened a close-knit gathering of tree-trunks and tried to penetrate the black, black wood.

The small, solitary cottage was set back off the track. The squelching bed of mud on which it stood had been ruffled by tyre tracks and footprints, and looked like a crumpled brown duvet. A single bulb above the green front door shed a thrifty light on a section of the grubby stone façade.

Nell, Conrad and Christabel went inside. Although a fire had been lit in the kitchen, the place was still dank; the brick walls still clammy with cold.

The Sorrells had borrowed the cottage for the weekend, and they and Daniel John were already there. They were drinking wine, and unpacking food from cardboard boxes on the battered wooden table.

The new arrivals shivered, and were given some wine.

'No bathroom, I'm afraid,' Liza told them cheerfully. 'Have to wash in the sink, and go to the loo outside.'

'Won't Max and Nancy die of pneumonia,' Christabel asked, 'if they have to go out in the middle of the night?'

'They've got coats,' was their mother's pragmatic reply.

'Are they in bed? Have we missed them?' Conrad asked.

'Probably still awake,' Samuel told him.

Nell's boyfriend went to say goodnight to the children who were on campbeds in the sitting room. She moved to stand with Christabel by the fire, and could feel its stinging heat through the back of her jeans. Daniel put his arm round her.

Liza and Nell's older brother was thirty. His hair was already going grey. The face was attractive, but only had ten years or so before it would almost certainly give way to the puffiness caused by drink. There was about him an air of irresistible if completely untrustworthy charm. He always carried a fat fountain pen in his pocket, and had never in his life lost a game of Racing Demon. The lenses of his spectacles were rectangular and had shiny black frames. They resembled those worn by sinister characters in films of the early sixties. His trousers were far too big for him. It was as if he was expecting to grow into them, like a schoolboy into his new uniform.

'Liza said you auditioned for the new Braine play the other day. How did it go?' he asked.

'Heard this morning. I didn't get it.'

Daniel squeezed his sister's arm. 'I'm sorry,' he said. 'Bugger Braine.'

'You didn't really want it, anyway, did you?' Liza asked, taking the last thing from the box of shopping, and putting it in the cupboard. Liza's face, Nell noticed, was a healthy brown in the dim light. How did she manage to glow even in such cold?

'No, to be honest. Cillian congratulated me when I told him. Said it was a point of distinction to be turned down for a Braine play.'

Daniel smiled. 'Typical, but quite right of course. How is he? Hard at his new collection of poems?'

'Not very,' Nell answered.

Supper was ready at midnight.

Christabel sat next to Daniel. He could smell the spicy scent she was wearing.

'By the way, what were you up to last Saturday when we were all celebrating the end of Nell's play?' she asked him mischievously.

'I think my excuse was work, wasn't it?'

'And were you working?'

Daniel looked at her over the top of his spectacles. They had slipped a little. He pushed them up with his forefinger before answering.

'Ish,' he admitted. The others were listening to the conversation. 'I really wanted to be there. Something came up though.' He looked at Nell. 'You and Liza wouldn't have approved. Sorting out a couple of things,' he said shiftily.

'By things, you mean women, presumably?' Liza remarked.

'Well, one woman in particular really. Well.' Daniel tapped the table in a gesture indicating that that was his last word on the subject.

But he was in the presence of sisters.

'Who?' the older of the two asked.

'Liza,' Samuel said gently, putting his hand on his wife's knee.

'No, you don't mind, do you, Dan? What's going on in your life that's so important you missed Nell's celebration?'

'I didn't mind,' Nell murmured.

'Come on, tell us,' Christabel urged.

Daniel hesitated.

'I've never known you be so discreet,' Liza said, laughing. 'Kate, was it?'

Her brother shook his head. 'You don't know her.'

'Oh? Another one?' she went on. Her husband and Conrad gave Daniel a sympathetic look, but they said nothing.

'Got in a bit of a muddle, that's all.' Liza's and Christabel's expressions seemed to beckon further explanation. 'All right,' he said, sighing. 'A few months ago I slept with someone. Both rather drunk. All very nice, a casual thing. Happened a few more times over the weeks. Then. Well.'

Nell stood up to get another bottle of wine.

'Well?' she asked, her back to him.

'Cohesion of the flesh, diversion of the minds. She thinks we have an affair on our hands. I don't.'

'And the question of commitment arises?' Liza probed.

'Afraid so. As always, I don't see why it can't continue as it is. We're having a good time. But no. She wants more. I understand that, yet can't give her more. End of story.'

'You're very ruthless,' Christabel said, smiling a little. 'Poor thing. Was she very upset?'

'Wailed a bit, but I cheered her up.'

'How?' Nell wondered out loud, sitting down again and boring into him with her eyes.

Daniel shrugged, and took off his spectacles. He began urgently to rub the lenses with the bottom of his jersey. 'She needed comforting.'

'You bastard.'

'I'm only teasing you, Nellie. Of course I didn't sleep with her again.' Cajoling voice. He hated it when she was cross with him.

'I wouldn't put it past you,' his other sister remarked. 'It amazes me that you're so understanding and devoted to Nell and me, and so kind to all your friends, but the minute you sleep with someone you treat them like dirt.'

'That's the way it works,' her younger sister told her, flatly.

'It isn't. Samuel doesn't treat me like dirt.'

'You two are different,' Nell said.

'I'm not married to these people,' Daniel protested. 'I wasn't married to Penny.'

'You're practically married to Kate,' Liza retorted. 'What about her?'

85

'No longer. She's gone.'

'Left you?'

Daniel shrugged.

'Serve you right. Poor Kate, are you missing her?'

Daniel nodded grimly.

'I'm glad.'

'I think Daniel's probably had enough,' said Samuel, putting his fork down. 'It's a private matter, none of our business.'

'You used her, Dan,' Liza went on, despite her husband's observation. 'I don't think you ever intended to marry her.'

Daniel replied, 'I don't know. Marriage.'

'Frightened. Cowardly. Worried you might have picked the wrong one?'

'I think that's fair enough,' Conrad cut in suddenly. 'Doesn't everyone have that to an extent? I once dreamed I was at my wedding, in the church, everyone there. Turned round to watch the entrance of the bride and, as she walked up the aisle towards me, I realised I'd made a big mistake.'

'I worry more,' Daniel ventured, emboldened by support, 'about being at the party afterwards, feeling really happy, when all of a sudden my wife of two hours comes up to me and says, "Don't you think you've had enough to drink, dear?" '

Nell stood up again, and without a word began to clear the plates.

'I think that's pathetic,' Liza commented. 'Makes me feel slightly sick. Almost as much as what you did to Kate. I'm sure Nell agrees with me.'

Nell shook her head.

'Why not, for God's sake?'

'Because infidelity doesn't surprise me,' came the soft reply. 'I've made a rule for myself: you must never take faithfulness for granted in anyone.'

'Rubbish!' Conrad declared, thumping the table.

'Absurd,' Liza added.

86

'Not remotely. I don't *know* Conrad's faithful to me, for example, do I? One can't know for certain about anyone other than oneself.'

'That completely precludes the whole concept of trust,' Daniel observed.

'Kate trusted you,' Nell pointed out quietly.

There was a split second's silence while her brother opened his mouth but closed it again like a fish.

'But, Nellie, don't you think you're being just a bit jealous, or paranoid?' Christabel suggested.

'No, it's more a defensive thing I've concocted for myself. I don't want to be disillusioned and humiliated. I've been fooled in the past and upset when I discovered the invariable truth. So I've made a conscious decision never to be caught out again.'

'That's just depressing,' Christabel said.

'Makes sense,' Nell murmured.

'I don't think so, I know Samuel's faithful to me,' Liza told her sister.

'Admittedly, you've got a pretty strong case for saying that,' Nell agreed. 'I do have a couple of threads of faith left, and I reckon you two are one of them.' The same, she reflected, could no longer be said of Bill and Rosie Howard, whose shotgun divorce had come like a bolt from the blue. But in Christabel's presence she tactfully didn't mention that theirs had been one of the few marriages in which she really had had total faith. 'Normally, though,' she continued, 'when people claim that X is always faithful to them, alarm bells start ringing in my head because it always turns out that the truth of the matter is that X has been screwing around all along.'

The kettle, which Christabel had put on the stove to boil, started to whistle like a referee.

Conrad sat on the iron bed and took off his socks. The stone floor was so cold it numbed the soles of his feet. He lay back on the pillows, hands behind his head, and looked up at the

87

low ceiling. The spindly beams were peppered with wood-worm holes. The unpainted walls were plaster pink. A flimsy yellow curtain was drawn across the small square window. Patterned with printed roses and redcurrants, and real cobwebs, it reminded him of an old skirt in a dressing-up box.

Supper was over and Nell was cleaning her teeth and washing at the kitchen sink. As Conrad lay waiting for her, his eyelids, like two drunks leaning against a wall, began falteringly to slip downwards. When they closed completely, all he could see was that blank grey of dead television screens. After a minute or two, though, the monochrome flickered into life and he pictured the colourful animation of scenes remembered, small fleeting moments past.

Nell featured in all of them.

Plane to Bombay two years earlier. Crowded and airless. Him gasping with impatience still, after a ten-hour delay, and complaining that the start of their holiday could not have been worse. Her gasping, too, but only with thirst, and actually finding it funny when presented with orange juice in a cup not much bigger than a pen top.

Burglary some months ago at Oxford Gardens. Him shaking and angry at loss of camera equipment, and violation – if only superficial – of the flat. Nell enjoying witnessing for the first time the magical appearance of fingerprints when surfaces were worked on by an officer with a special silver brush.

A couple of years earlier when her mother had called to say her father was dying: Nell had been upset, but had remained calm. He took her to Euston, put her on the train. She had leaned out of the smoggy window and said, 'I'm glad I'm going before it's too late. Papa never spoke to me much, but I've got a strong feeling he will now, now he's got so little time.' Angus died a few days later of emphysema. He was only in his sixties.

Liza told him a long time afterwards that during her father's old-fashioned deathbed scene, it was Nell who had

88

been the bravest of all the family – even more so than Daniel. She had, single-handedly, kept their spirits up.

When he met her off the train, she hadn't mentioned it. She had simply smiled and said, 'The old rascal, you know, in four days he talked so much to us, about everything, he almost managed to make up for a lifetime of reticence.'

She never did say much on such occasions, but her eyes seemed unnaturally bright. And her face did appear to reveal a definite stoicism. It was not that of a pessimist.

'I don't think,' he said to her when she returned from the kitchen, 'you really believe all that stuff you were going on about at supper.'

Nell shivered in her towel and sat down on the bed.

'No?'

'No. I think you've got more faith in human nature than you let on. You know, in your heart of hearts, for instance, that I don't sleep with other women.'

Nell turned to look at him and raised her eyebrows.

'Oh, come *on*. I haven't the time, for a start.'

'The time can be made if the inclination's there.'

'But the inclination's not there,' Conrad asserted, lifting one arm from behind his head and gesticulating to stress the point. 'I wish you'd get it into your mind now that I don't and nor do I want to.'

'You were unfaithful to past girlfriends,' Nell reminded him, taking off her watch and putting it on the upturned packing case beside the bed. 'So why not me?' she asked cheerfully.

'I don't think I can be bothered to answer that,' he replied, turning his back on her. There was a silence as he started to undress, then got into bed. Nell unwrapped the towel from around her and joined him. Conrad turned out the light.

'I might have to go to New York for three days next week,' he said after a couple of minutes in an effort to change the subject, dissipate the tension. As he did so, he stroked her arms.

'Good assignment?' she asked.

89

'Very good. Young architect wants me to photograph a new museum he designed. I've heard it's very beautiful, really impressive.'

'That's very exciting,' Nell said happily. She hugged him in congratulation, and added, 'Don't catch anything.'

Conrad drew himself back from her to take in her expression. 'Like?'

Nell shrugged. His eyes, by now accustomed to the dark, could see she had the very look of stoicism that a few minutes before he had been remembering, visualising.

He told her he thought her remark was misplaced. 'I'm going for three days, if that. I don't want to bloody well sleep with anyone else there, here or anywhere.' Exasperated voice.

'All right, all right. I'm sorry. It was a joke.'

'A poor one. I don't understand why you have so little trust.'

'Pitch your expectations high and you'll always be disappointed. Pitch them rock bottom and they're more likely to be fulfilled,' she told him slowly.

'I call that wilful pessimism.'

'Anybody who has their eyes and ears vaguely open, who observes a little, thinks a bit about their own experiences, other people's, *must* come to the same conclusions as me.'

'But can't you see the danger in that argument?' Conrad asked, concerned. 'You're so determined to defend yourself against disillusion, you deny seeing the good in anything. I'm not saying everything's for the best, but the belief that everything's for the worst is equally extreme. What's more, it allows absolutely no room for happiness.'

He paused, and drew himself closer to her again.

'Anyway,' he went on, 'it's my belief you're not a real pessimist. On an intellectual level, maybe, but not instinctively.'

Then he kissed her so she was unable to protest and thus the conversation came to an end.

'I'd really like to know,' Daniel suddenly declared the following evening, 'what makes a firework red.'

Samuel, in a thick blue coat and scarf, looked at his brother-in-law sceptically, but decided to tell him all the same. 'I think you'll find,' he said, 'if I remember rightly, it's a combination of strontium carbonate, oxylate and nitrate.'

'My God, I wasn't expecting an answer. That's really impressive.' Daniel frowned, amazed. 'I thought you were a biology teacher.'

'That's what I specialise in. But I had to have a general knowledge of science to qualify. I can still remember some of my physics and chemistry. Have to fill in for colleagues occasionally, and I seem to get by.'

'So, what about green then?'

'Are you sure you want to know?'

'Of course.'

So Samuel, laughing, told him.

It was the nearest Saturday to Guy Fawkes Night. The two of them were in the garden, waiting for the others to emerge from the cottage. They had just lit a mountainous bonfire and were standing beside it.

The flames were reaching higher and higher every minute, anxious, it appeared, to challenge and invade the sky which was as black as a deep lake. The heat made the wood pop. Aggressive bullets of sparks shot out at random, their noise like a battle of cap guns.

The intense orange of the fire was reflected, flickeringly, on the men's faces, and transformed their urban pallor. But their gloveless hands, squelched into inadequate pockets, remained cold.

The front door opened, and the Sorrell children ran towards their father, keen to witness the cremation of the guy they had made that afternoon.

Samuel reminded them not to go too close to the fire.

Liza and Conrad appeared, carrying wine, uncooked potatoes and raw sausages. Christabel, practically mummified by layers of thick jerseys, socks and scarves, was

91

hampered in her walk across the stodgy mud. Daniel held out his hand to help her.

'Are you sure you'll be warm enough?' he asked, mocking.

'Where's the box of fireworks, Christabel?' Samuel shouted above the relentless roar and crackle of the bonfire.

'Nell's bringing it,' came the reply. 'But I've got some sparklers. Who wants a sparkler?'

The children leapt, literally, at the offer.

'Careful, you two,' their father warned.

'I'll light them for you,' Christabel said, handing them one each. 'But try not to poke them in anyone's eye.'

They ran off. She lit one for herself, and while they weren't looking, taunted Daniel by making as if to poke him with it in the stomach. 'I hope you freeze,' she joked, 'and when you do, I won't lend you one of my scarves.'

Nell, who was reading the firework instructions inside at the kitchen table, could hear laughter in the garden. She looked up and saw the light of the fire flittering, genie-like, through the window. Setting aside the leaflet, she hastily picked up the box and went to the door.

She stood there for a moment, watching the scene in front of her. Waves of heat and the faint smell of burning sausages invisibly marbled the cold, cold air. Smoke presumptuously knitted itself into her woollen clothes, and stung her eyes.

She could not see Max and Nancy, but the shadowy figures of Daniel and Christabel were chasing and fighting each other with excited childlike gestures, comic strip silhouettes.

Conrad was kicking stray bits of kindling into the bottom of the fire, bolstering its flickering force. Not violent but strangely purposeful. The fire responded well to his attentions. It appeared to groan with pleasure.

Nell's sister and brother-in-law, facing the flames, had their backs to her. Liza was holding a stick and probing at something in the sunset-coloured ashes. In one hand, Samuel was holding a drink. The other rested on his wife's shoulder.

A baked-potato-by-a-bonfire marriage.

Nell, clutching the box of fireworks, smiled to herself, and, mud sucking at her gumboots, she ventured across to join them.

A short while later, the fire was at its height. The darkness immediately surrounding it seemed to have surrendered at last, and become a paler dung brown.

Daniel and Christabel stood a little way off, calmer now. The roar of the fire obscured their voices.

Nell and Samuel were at the bottom of the garden, setting up the fireworks.

'Liza, sweetie,' the latter called, 'grab hold of the kids. We're ready to light the first rocket.'

His wife took hold of the children's hands. He struck a match, meanwhile, and could just be seen running with Nell to safety behind a tree.

There was a white flash in the ground, and a fizzing noise like the sound of effervescent Coca-Cola released from a shaken bottle. A whistling whoosh as the rocket sped into the sky. A split second's silence. Then a clatter of pink and silver polka dots burst out in a flourish, peppering the blackness. But their life was only momentary. Instantly, they began to sink and dim in a death so much more modest than their birth.

Delighted applause.

Nell and Samuel returned to their little launch pad, matchboxes in hand. Their audience was waiting.

'Come on,' Liza cried out, 'hurry up, you two.'

No response.

She crouched down to the children's level. 'Don't think Dad heard me. Go and tell him we want more.'

Max let go of his mother's hand. Liza watched as the child, a keen messenger, ran excitedly towards his father. When he reached him, she could see Samuel lean down to his son and appear to put his palm on his head. Happy, she felt a surge of pride. It warmed her as tangibly as a gulp of brandy.

Then a sharp noise went up. Piercing, like the rocket. Max's cry, followed by an adult shout.

'Liza!'

Samuel was suddenly running towards her, pushing Max in front of him. Face as livid as the bonfire.

'What the hell did you let him go over there for?' he barked, cocking his head towards the spot where Nell could just be seen, still lingering, rather startled. 'Fireworks! For Christ's sake!'

The boy freed himself from his father's grip and, sobbing, bolted towards Liza.

'I'm sorry, Samuel,' she whispered soothingly.

'How could you?' he screeched.

'I said I'm sorry. It was silly.'

'Silly? Unbelievably irresponsible.' Breathless with fury.

Conrad looked down at his feet, embarrassed, and concentrated on shifting from one to the other.

Samuel shook his head, turned dramatically and flung his matchbox to the ground. Then he stormed into the cottage, and slammed the door.

Nell trudged up to her sister. 'What's up?' she asked.

'I shouldn't have let Max go near the fireworks,' Liza explained, stroking her son's head. He had stopped crying. 'Samuel's right.'

'Where's he gone?'

'Indoors.'

'Isn't he over-reacting a little?'

'I should have stopped to think,' Liza reflected, out loud, regretful. The remark was more to herself than to Nell.

'Perhaps,' Nell commented. 'But I think he's being a bit unreasonable, don't you?'

Her sister, troubled, did not reply. Nell assumed this was either because the children were listening, or from loyalty to her husband. She did not press the point but, instead, offered to go and see if Samuel was all right.

'Oh, would you? Please, yes,' Liza responded. Her tone was one of overwhelming appreciation which, though sincere, seemed out of proportion to the offer.

Nell turned to Conrad, and bit her lip, puzzled.

'Here, give me those,' he said helpfully, pointing at the matches in her hand. 'I can go and finish the display with Dan or Christabel. Where are they?'

Nell was grateful for his tact. She passed him the Swan Vestas, and walked off towards the cottage to find Samuel.

The sitting room was cold, unlived-in. Stone floor. One dusty rug. Withering flowers on a sparse bookshelf. The ash in the fireplace was lumpen and grey, like urban wasteland. The corduroy sofa and one armchair had that depressed look of furniture which had been abused early in life: crushed, stained, smelling faintly of damp dog.

Samuel, still in his coat and scarf, was on the sofa, bending forward towards the low chest in front of it. Completely silent, he appeared to be staring at a crumpled, bleached magazine and a parched newspaper. But the room was too dark for him to be reading. The only light was that coming through the window from the bonfire. He was holding a cigarette over a blue grass ashtray, his forefinger tapping at it continuously although there was no surplus ash. Otherwise, he was motionless.

Nell, reluctant to intrude, approached him hesitantly. He did not look up. She sat down beside him.

'Can I turn the light on?' she whispered. He nodded and she stretched across to the small lamp. It was not bright.

For some minutes they did not speak. Eventually Samuel lifted his head, and blinked. Nell was flabbergasted to see he was weeping.

She did not know what to say. She pushed a strand of hair behind her ear, twisted her sock back into position round her heel, and placed a hand on Samuel's knee. The dark trousers had worn a little and she could feel his warm skin through the frayed hole.

'I've been meaning to ask you,' he began, then stopped, putting the cigarette between his lips and wiping one eye with the back of his hand. 'I was hoping you might be able to help me with something.'

'Of course. What?'

'I'm going up for an audition, and I haven't a clue how to set about it. Though I really want a part.'

His sister-in-law stared at him with unconcealed amazement.

'School play,' he explained. 'Only the end-of-term production. *A Midsummer Night's Dream.*'

'That's an odd choice for Christmas, isn't it?' Light note in the voice.

'Old favourite. Think you can help me?'

'I can try, but I'm not much good myself,' she told him. 'My audition technique doesn't seem to have got me very far.' Nell was troubled by Samuel's distress, but was trying to hide the fact. She settled more comfortably on the sofa, tucking her feet beneath herself.

'I could do with a few of your RADA tips. I've only got five days. The audition's on Thursday.' Samuel slipped his hand into his inside pocket, and pulled out a tatty paperback. 'Here. I've learned a speech. Will you hear me?'

'Now?' Nell asked, amused by this sense of urgency. 'You don't want to go and see the rest of the fireworks?'

Samuel shook his head. 'You go, though,' he said, but it was obvious he was hoping she would stay. 'I don't want you to miss them.'

'I don't mind in the least,' she told him.

Samuel sighed with relief, and shrugged his arms out of his coat. 'I doubt the director expects us to learn a speech, but I thought I'd better show willing. Lucy Hardcastle.'

'She the director?'

'English teacher. Yes. Very good at these things. Something about her, everyone wants to do their best.'

'You've been in one of her plays before?'

'She invited me last year to be Caesar. I was very flattered, but I couldn't bring myself. Painted scenery instead. Even so, it was nice to have a break from routine. And there was such a team spirit, I'm determined to be involved again. To act, though, this time. Lucy really makes it fun.'

'Is she a friend?'

'Oh yes, very much so.' Samuel's tone was brighter, enthusiastic even.

Nell was pleased he appeared to be cheering up.

'We share break duty,' Samuel added hastily.

'Has she invited you again?'

'No, but I do know she wants me to audition. That much she did ask. Auditions are a new thing, you see, and everyone has to do them who wants to be in it. Staff as well as pupils. Quite right, really. But it means I can't rely on harmless nepotism as a way in. I have to prove myself.'

'I expect she still wants you to be her leading man,' Nell said encouragingly.

Samuel beamed. 'I hope,' he remarked.

Oh fuck, he thought. If only Lucy wanted me. Lucy Hardcastle. *Miss* Hardcastle.

'Was she upset?' he asked out loud, changing the subject.

Nell knew instantly what he meant and replied that Liza was fine.

'Such is my neurosis. Christ, I don't want to upset her, of all people. But she wouldn't understand. Not really. I can't explain it to Liza. Can't talk to her about it.' Samuel stopped and tried to gauge Nell's reaction. What was she thinking? Suspicious?

Puzzled. Sweetly, generously, naively puzzled. He yearned to explain. He was dying to explain.

Can I tell you? he asked her silently. You would understand, instinctively. Part of your nature. I so want to tell you, I could fucking disintegrate.

Liza's *sister*. Christ. What am I thinking? Can't do that to you, no right to. The burden. So many implications, consequences. It would cut one of your final threads, render that pessimism of yours irrevocable.

Yet it is the truth.

Lump in the throat. Like a sodding lump of coal. Don't say I'm about to cry again. Samuel? Please don't. Samuel.

Shit.

Her comforting hand on my knee again. That means she's spotted that bloody tear. I couldn't keep it in. A science teacher, too. Tears.

And I'm crying over a bit of exploding strontium carbonate.

I *feel* like a bit of exploding strontium carbonate.

I'm crying because I'm so neurotic and frightened.

I'm neurotic and frightened because I love my wife.

I'm crying because I'm madly in love with Lucy.


The next day Nell was quiet, contemplative. But she went through Samuel's speech with him, making suggestions, helping and encouraging him. She thought he was good.

That evening, on the way back to London, Conrad remarked what an enjoyable weekend it had been. 'How long were you up talking to Samuel last night?' he asked Nell. 'What time did you come to bed?'

'I don't know.'

'Must have been late. You look tired.'

'A bit, yes.'

'You seem subdued.'

'Not really.'

'What was that performance with the fireworks? I thought maybe as you and he had sat up most the night, you might have got an explanation out of him. Bit neurotic, wasn't it?'

'No.'

'What then?' Conrad asked.

'It's not fair to go into it.'

'Oh, come on. Did he ask you not to tell?'

Nell shook her head.

'Well then?'

'Disloyal.'

'Come off it. He's not your bloody husband.'

'He has a sort of phobia.'

'What, of fireworks? I've heard of snakes — '

'Not fireworks exactly,' Nell said.

98

'What then?'

'Listen, it's none of our business.'

'I don't see why not.' Conrad paused and added, 'I've always thought Samuel was a bit odd.'

'He's not. Not remotely odd.'

'Okay, not odd. Detached, perhaps. I sometimes get the impression, like that evening after your last night, that his mind's on something else.'

'He's got a lot on his mind. Work.'

'You always stick up for him, don't you? Never hear a word against Samuel, not even the mildest criticism.'

'True.'

'Is he so bloody wonderful?'

Nell hesitated. 'Yes. Yes, he is.'

'I just hope you're as loyal about me as you are about him. Are you?'

'What do you think?'

'I hope.' Conrad pushed a tape into the car's cassette machine.

Nell's reply was drowned by the music. Later, on the motorway, he turned the volume down.

'Still, you had a nice time?' he asked. 'I was worried about you so looking forward to it.' He laughed, but not unpleasantly. 'Has to be said, Samuel and Liza are good hosts. You're right, they don't disappoint, do they?'

This time it was Nell who turned the volume up thereby relieving herself of the need to answer.

# CHAPTER

## 5

Liza made Samuel's coffee on Thursday morning, the day of the audition. He was nervous, and could not have touched the kettle.

Samuel was sitting at the kitchen table trying to concentrate as he went over his preparations for his first lesson. But his mind kept reverting to the lines of the speech he had learned, and he found himself repeating them like a song on the brain.

The children were having their breakfast. He was not. On a normal, less fraught morning, he could usually brace himself and make a slice of toast. But today he was in no fit state to confront or go anywhere near the toaster, perhaps his most ferocious household enemy. This object, in his eyes, was a hotbed of gratuitously violent electricity: orange, burning, explosive. A miniature nuclear power station on his own sideboard.

Damn thing. Damn toast. He wasn't hungry, anyway.

Liza gave him his coffee. He tapped his head twenty-four times, unselfconscious in front of his immediate family. His young son cheerfully copied him. Then, as Samuel picked up his cup, Max picked up his own mug of milk.

Samuel noticed this out of the corner of his eye. 'Don't do that, Max,' he urged anxiously.

'Last time you laughed,' the child replied reasonably.

'So we've had that joke once. Not funny a second time.'

'You do it. Lots. Tapping your head.'

'It's one of my silly habits. I don't want you picking it up,' his father explained, reflecting that even at home he would

100

have to be more careful in future, more surreptitious. He felt uneasy with guilt.

The doorbell rang. A mother to collect Max and Nancy.

When they had gone, Liza returned to the kitchen.

'Audition today,' Samuel told her.

'I know.'

'Oh.'

'What?'

'You're not going to wish me luck?'

'Samuel – '

'Um?'

'Are you sure it's a good idea?'

'The audition? If I want a part in the play I have no choice.'

'I mean the play,' she said. 'I worry.'

'About?'

'Well, just at the moment. It might exacerbate, you know, things.'

Pause. 'Things?'

'Anxieties.'

'Ah.'

'What with nerves. I mean, it'd be quite natural to get nervous. Performing. Understandable. But have you thought – stage lights, and stuff? If you're feeling a bit anxious anyway, then all those big electric lights? The combination. Well.' Liza closed her eyes. She didn't like to imagine.

'You don't think I'm up to it, do you?'

'No, I think you are. I was just wondering if you'd considered what you're letting yourself in for. The possibility.'

'I appreciate your concern.'

'Samuel – ' Hurt voice.

'I think my doctor can advise – ' He stood up. 'It's just a school play, that's all it is.'

'Fine.'

'Good.'

'I merely wonder if it's wise. I'm not saying you shouldn't

101

do it, only you should give it some thought. I feel disinclined to encourage you, I don't know why. If something should go wrong – '

'Blackmail.'

'Rubbish, blackmail!' Liza retorted.

Pause. Samuel looked at his wife. He thought about that incident in class the other day, when he had been incapable of switching on the plug for the video. It was ominous. Up until then, the electricity fear had been limited to the confines of his own house pretty much. The implications of it affecting him elsewhere, particularly in school, were not troubling, but horrific.

Liza was right – it might be risky for him to appear on stage. But he could not bring himself to admit it to her. He put on his coat instead, hating himself for his ridiculous neuroses, and resenting Liza for her lack of them.

He looked at his wife and began silently to shout at her, like never before.

What do you know, for God's sake? What d'you know of the prison in my head where I'm being tortured? My bloody fears are threatening to overwhelm me . . . People like you who don't bloody suffer them can't possibly understand. There're moments when they're intolerable and I feel I can't cope any more. I sometimes just want to give in completely. I look at other people – strangers in the street, pupils, colleagues, friends, family, the children, yourself – and because you're not frightened of electricity, and because you don't have to tap your head, I think that makes you superior, me worthless. You didn't know that, did you? I feel so worthless I don't deserve to be near you. I'm normal. These thoughts are so menacing . . . they frighten me more than you can ever know. Your husband's mind, Liza, is possessed by a whole lot of stuff which you might think you understand. But you've only the tiniest inkling. No real notion of what it's like. When the most ordinary things turn into monsters.

Try living with that.

'Your life is so very comfortable,' he told her out loud suddenly.

Her puzzled expression confirmed to him what he had been thinking, but it also made him guilty. He berated himself for being unkind to her, and felt the urge to apologise, but he could not do so. Later, despite his own secret doubts, he would reassure her, affectionately, that his appearing on stage would be fine. For the time being, though, it was all he could do to muster a hasty goodbye.

In the car on the way to Parsons Green, Samuel was too gloomy to switch on the radio, but he needed distraction. He began reciting his speech aloud to himself, careful to remember Nell's words of advice – speak clearly and loudly, project the voice. His aim was to get his mouth round the words as if each one was a chiselled gem.

Samuel had been aware that his diction might not have been up to scratch. At the weekend session with Nell, he had requested a few voice exercises. She had asked if that was strictly necessary, but had not made him feel at all foolish. Nell was, he noted, not remotely self-important about giving professional help.

At a red traffic light near the school gate, Samuel leaned towards the windscreen mirror. Having said the speech a few times, he decided to practise his diction.

'La, la, la,' he pronounced, with exaggerated movements of the mouth, watching the flip of his tongue.

'Do, do, do,' he added, noting the rounded shape of his lips.

He and Nell had laughed when she told him what her voice coach had urged. Apparently, he had said that with the oooh sound 'the lips should look like a cat's arse'. It was a tip Samuel was unlikely to forget. Very useful too, for the line, 'A crew of patches, rude mechanicals.'

He tried it now.

'Crooo . . . ooode,' he trilled, still staring in the mirror, a little more cheerful.

An admirable imitation of a cat's arse, he thought. But just

103

as he was about to congratulate himself, he noticed the man in the next car giving him a quizzical look.

Samuel, feeling a touch silly, sent him back a nonchalant smile. It seemed to say, I don't care what you think. I don't know you from Adam.

Unfortunately, as he did so, he suddenly realised he *did* know the man. The red beard and the green gingham shirt collar were unmistakably those of his colleague, Ralph Simmonds. Geography teacher.

The traffic light remained steadfastly red. Samuel himself went red and squeezed the steering wheel tight so his knuckles protruded like pebbles, but he managed to smile on at Ralph, wryly. He was curdling with embarrassment.

How the hell would he explain himself when he saw Ralph in the staff room in a few minutes' time? 'I was trying to be a cat's arse'? Ralph would never understand.

The light went green at last. Samuel sped into the school drive and along to the car-park.

Oh, so what? He would say nothing. Why should he? He had never liked him, anyway. Ralph had a vast capacity to irritate, especially when he talked of his relations with the opposite sex. He believed women found him irresistible.

'I can empathise with them,' he would boast, 'in a way other men rarely can. Gets them every time.'

Thus it was, whenever a female colleague was distressed, Ralph Simmonds could be relied upon to be at her side, instantaneously, with his own distressed little forehead. His compassion was collapsible: he could bring it out and fold it away again at a moment's notice, like a deckchair.

Sickening to watch, Samuel reflected as he walked across the tarmac, under the dripping chestnut tree and past the gym. A few of the female staff had fallen for it, though. Cynthia in the stationery store for one. (Literally in the stationery store so the story went.) And Battleaxe Barbara? There had been rumours, when her husband died last year, that Ralph had tried on his uniquely compassionate type of comfort, and succeeded. Had her fat fingers wrestled with

104

the buttons of his gingham shirt? What a pathetic little coupling that must have been.

Ralph is so bloody wet, Samuel said to himself as he pushed open the glass double doors of the main entrance. The sort of man, he fancied, who probably spent his evenings playing with Fuzzy Felt.

He had confided this notion to Lucy once. She had laughed. She didn't much care for Ralph, either.

'Are you coming along to the audition, then, Sam?'

It was Rachel English, and her enthusiasm.

Samuel and she and various others were in the staffroom. The last lesson of the day had just finished. The auditions, to be held in Hall, were about to begin.

'You aren't going to tell me you're not even going to try?'

I'm not in the mood for cheerful chatter, he told Rachel in his head. I'm about to have to stand up in front of Lucy, you realise, and *act*.

Polite, he only shook his head at her, saying grimly, 'I'll try.'

'Lucy told me she wants you to go up for Oberon,' Rachel informed him with a knowing grin. She was wearing another of her unsuitably thin jerseys. Detectable nipples. 'Quite a big part.'

'But I learned one of Puck's speeches,' he burst out, distressed.

Ralph Simmonds, who was working at the table, glanced at him and chuckled smugly. Samuel did not notice as he stood and walked over to the photocopying machine.

Rachel giggled and asked, 'Why did you do that? She wasn't expecting anyone to learn anything at this stage. Puck! Sam, you are funny.'

'I thought it would be better, better to be properly acquainted with a particular speech.'

'I'm sure Lucy will appreciate such dedication, Sam.' Ralph's voice.

Samuel looked up. The geography teacher was at the

105

photocopier, lining up a piece of paper on the glass. Watching him, Samuel suddenly felt gripped with panic. Seeing Ralph close the lid and move his finger towards the 'operate' button, he began to pant. He could not bear to envisage what might happen if Ralph were to press it.

He could not stand it.

The noise; the light; the wanton electricity.

'No, Ralph!' he shouted. He was shaking violently.

Ralph instinctively pulled his hand away, as if from a scorching stove. The room fell silent.

'What?' Ralph asked.

Samuel's colleagues stared at him. He was aware of the quizzical expressions on their faces.

'The photocopier – ' Only a whisper.

'What about it, Sam, for Chrissake? God, you gave me a fright.'

'Just,' he faltered, 'just don't touch it, okay, Ralph.' Heart thumping like a hooligan.

'Why, what's the matter with it?'

'I think it's broken,' Samuel told him quickly, edging towards the door.

Ralph frowned. 'No it's not. Perfectly all right.' He gave a cursory glance at its dashboard of lighted symbols. 'You carry on as if it's going to blow up. I don't know what all the fuss – '

'Ralph,' said Tim Crawford, 'he obviously knows there is something the matter with it, or else he wouldn't have stopped you.'

'Look, it's all right.' Ralph was impatient. His finger headed once more for the button.

'I asked you not to touch it.' Samuel's voice was cool, firm.

The two men stared at each other. Boxers in a ring. Ralph sighed, his finger twitching above the button.

'Please, Ralph.' Samuel, in desperation, was begging now; his voice was imbued with anguish.

'Sam, you've gone as white as a sheet,' Rachel told him. 'You're sweating too. Have you got a temperature? Are you okay?'

'Yes, perhaps you aren't well?' Ralph said, moving away from the machine at last.

Samuel paused to compose himself before answering. 'I'm fine.'

'We're all a bit nervous,' Rachel said, 'but the audition's not going to be as bad as you think.' She took Samuel's arm. 'Let's go, shall we?'

Tim, with a briefcase under his arm, opened the door. 'I'll come down with you,' he said, 'I'm off home. Good luck, Sam. I'm sure you'll make the RSC yet.' His kind smile curled round the cigarette in his mouth.

Samuel shot a look at Ralph who was back at the table. Then he turned and, with Rachel, began to follow Tim down the stairs.

Hall was a vast room. Its windows overlooked the cold, windy football pitch, the turf of which was covered with black mud scabs.

There was a wooden floor, and a smell of polish that was trying to imitate the scent of something pleasing. Roses perhaps. It failed.

The chairs, in long rows or in stacks to one side, were flimsy objects with tinny frames and frayed canvas seats. Fifty or so pupils, ranging in age from eleven to eighteen, were sitting at the end of the room. They and about six members of staff had gathered round the stage upon which a third-former was reading aloud from a copy of the play. Lucy Hardcastle, at a small desk by the window, was writing notes.

Samuel and Rachel sneaked through the swing doors as quietly as possible and softly walked up to the front. Their chairs, as they sat down, scraped noisily on the floor. Loose screws rattled inside the tubular legs.

The sound caused Lucy to look up. Samuel thought he could detect, just beneath the rims of her big blue spectacles, a dash of a frown. He wanted to say he was sorry. There was chalk dust on her old baggy cardigan, a light frost on the copper beech wool.

107

The boy on stage finished and went away. Another went up to read the same speech. Because the director had organised the auditions well, the turnover was rapid and before long there was only a handful of children left to be tried. Samuel was impressed by some of them, and worried that he would be unable to match up to their talent. He did not want to end up as one of Theseus's non-speaking attendants. He would rather paint scenery.

When the last child had read and left to go home, it was the teachers' turn.

Ralph Simmonds, who had slipped in after Samuel and Rachel, went up first.

'I know you want me for Theseus,' he told Lucy. 'Probably on account of my beard,' he added with a chuckle. 'But ducal as my facial carpet may be, I'd rather try for Oberon, if you don't mind.'

Barbara, who was anxious to play Hippolyta, laughed in an almost indecently appreciative way. She had clearly enjoyed such cheekiness in Ralph on other, less public, occasions. She was a riot of polka dots today, Samuel noted, feeling a little giddy. Polka dot shirt, polka dot complexion.

Lucy, graceful, accepted Ralph's presumptuous announcement. 'Read the wild thyme speech then,' she said tolerantly.

Ralph flipped through the pages saying, 'Um, yes,' a lot. He could not find it.

'I know a bank whereon the wild thyme blows,' she said helpfully.

'Of course. Yes,' he assured her, still flipping. 'Silly me. Where am I now? Ah, here we go . . . No . . . Um. Funny, isn't it, I'd know just where to find an actual bank covered in the wretched herb, such is my geographical . . . Yes. But can't seem to place the one in these pages . . .' Flip, flip.

'Act Two, Scene One,' Lucy said.

Samuel was secretly relieved by Ralph's ridiculous performance, for he felt confident his attempt to act would be equally inept. He glanced across to Lucy and was not

108

altogether displeased to see her expression was one of suppressed impatience.

She's thinking, Ralph is a drip, I can tell. Lacks the nobility required for a king. She's thinking, it's getting late, and Ralph's not right for Oberon. She must be. Rachel told me she's got other ideas for Oberon. Ralph's an ass. So he can play Bottom.

Just then Ralph did a self-important little cough and began.

Unfortunately the minute he did so, Samuel realised he had misjudged him. The usurping geography teacher proceeded to read with a strength and elegance of which no one could have imagined him capable.

Lucy put down her pen, and sat up straight. Samuel was not a violent man, but at that precise moment, he found he had an extraordinary urge to rearrange not only Ralph's 'facial carpet', but the rest of what he would doubtless refer to as his 'facial furniture' as well.

When Ralph came to the end, he closed the book very carefully and piously, like a priest closing the Bible after reading the lesson. As he stepped down from his pulpit, Barbara gave him two or three prim claps. Her upright hands came together neatly, like those of a praying child in a kitsch painting on Hyde Park railings.

It was her go next. She walked up on to the stage, and placed her hand on the neck bow of her polyester silk shirt, and recited five of Hippolyta's lines. She sounded more like a Blue Peter presenter than a Queen of the Amazons.

Then the others took it in turns to do their pieces. Samuel was last, and Rachel stayed behind to watch him, keen to lend support.

Standing on stage, he became aware of an irritating tuck in the heel of his sock. He wondered whether to bend down and pull at it.

'Will you try one of Oberon's speeches for me?' Lucy asked.

'I learned one of Puck's.'

109

'Oh?' Lucy said, surprised. 'Well, that's good. You didn't have to learn anything, though.'

'I know. I thought it'd be better.'

'Yes. It's great. Let's hear it.'

Samuel recited the speech, careful not to look in her direction as he did so. As he neared the end of each line, he feared he would not be able to remember the following one. But, despite his nerves, none of them eluded him.

Such was his relief when he reached the end that he forgot his sock was bothering him. He thought he heard Lucy thanking him, though he could not be sure.

'How about reading the speech Ralph read?' she asked politely.

Sorry? You want me to do another? I thought my ordeal was over, and now you're asking me to do it again?

He bent down on one knee and tugged at his sock.

'Would you mind? Is that awful of me?'

Yes, frankly. Awful.

He stood up again.

'I know it's late,' she said, glancing at her watch. It was after six o'clock. 'But it won't take a minute, and I'd really like you to.'

You have a very persuasive manner, Miss Hardcastle.

He turned to the relevant page, and just before he began to read, he looked at her.

She was smiling.


It was after six o'clock.

Something to do with the trousers, Nell decided. Made of moleskin, that thick material, soft as an old sheet, baggy, falling to bits. Only variation — black in winter, cream in summer. He must have had quite a few pairs, all very much alike. Something about them, so constant somehow, you could never believe their wearer could contemplate infidelity.

It was Thursday, the day of Samuel's audition. Nell was thinking of him.

She was alone in the flat on the sofa with Chekhov. Rereading the play. But her mind had wandered.

What was to be made of Samuel's revelation? He was in love with a colleague, Lucy Hardcastle, and he was – what were his words? – 'One of those loonies who's got a thing about electricity and a slightly up and down relationship with the television and the toaster.'

Some revelation. Samuel? For God's sake, was she so unperceptive? How many other people she loved were harbouring secrets, obsessions? Perhaps Conrad, who often voiced a desire not to go out, wasn't 'exhausted' after all, but in fact a screaming agoraphobic? Perhaps Daniel's fondness for women and his tendency to promiscuity actually hinted at a darker truth?

Nell lay back, rested her head on the sofa's arm, pushed her feet under the cushions, and placed the book on her stomach.

She loved Samuel.

Liza had met him first in an off licence. There was some extraordinary statistic about the number of people who meet their future spouse in the supermarket. But it was far more distinguished to meet in Oddbins, wasn't it, amongst the vodka? And typical of Samuel.

She remembered the night well. She and Liza had shared a flat in Primrose Hill. They were about to have a quiet supper together, and Liza had dashed round the corner to buy some drink. She was ages, but came back eventually bearing a small bottle which had a faded label and Polish writing and an illustration of a bison.

'I met this person,' she said, 'who's an authority on vodka. Told me I had to buy this one with the strand of grass in it. It's the best.' Liza was distracted as she laid the table, and could not light the candles. Kept breaking the matches. 'Science teacher at Parsons Green School. A thousand pupils! That's a hell of a lot, isn't it?'

Nell could never forget how twitchy Liza had been, wandering about the room with a spare fork in her hand.

111

'He was buying whisky himself. He said he had a cold and his nose was constipated and whisky was very soothing like a sort of alcoholic milk of magnesia,' she said, smiling. 'He's joining us for supper.'

'How come?'

'I liked him.'

June it was. The first thing Nell noticed about Samuel was his cream-coloured trousers. Liza asked if he played cricket. He said he did, but that wasn't why he was wearing cream-coloured trousers.

'I'm very conventional. My father's influence, most probably,' he explained, wiping his spectacles which were held together with brittle Sellotape. 'Yes, cream for summer.'

He said he was living in a large rented flat in Belsize Park, just up the road, with friends.

'Aspiring actors,' he told Nell and Liza. 'We're quite different, but I like that. They're loud and exuberant, shout a lot. Perhaps that's what big cities do to people, there again, my mother liked to shout and we were in a small village.'

He told them a little about his family, and life in Belsize Park. He had to work hard – preparing lessons and marking – most evenings after school. Even so, a great deal of time seemed to be spent, he added, sitting around on sofas, eating spaghetti Bolognese, drinking cheap wine, and having rather earnest conversations deep into the night. 'You know these acting types, they can get rather earnest at times.'

'Nell's an actress, or at least she's at RADA training to become one, and she's not earnest,' Liza laughed.

Nell could remember Samuel's curling embarrassment, and the profusion of apologies which arose out of it. They were sincere, endearing.

Later on, after supper, he had revealed that his girlfriend, a nurse, had just left him. 'I was fond of her,' he said. 'She told me she didn't really want to go, but she went all the same.' For some reason Nell could recall every word of his description of Kathleen. She was rather small and prim,

112

wore green eye-liner and used to iron her uniform religiously every single day. She had contemplated becoming a Jehovah's Witness. 'She didn't drink alcohol,' Samuel said, 'except that Bailey's Irish Cream. Filthy stuff. I used to tease her about it. Recently I stopped laughing whenever she had a glass of it, and she gave it up. Said it didn't taste the same, not as good.

'She was sweet and calm, but I think it came to an end because she couldn't take my friends. I can understand she might not like them, might have found them too noisy, but her complaint was she thought them "too arty". That kind of narrow-mindedness makes me impatient. It's the small-town mentality. The people in the village where I was brought up suffered from the same thing. I can't admire it. It's sad, because Kathy was lovely, but she'll miss out.'

The thing which Nell instantly recognised and liked about Samuel was that he was completely straightforward, down to earth. For example, when he spoke of the numerous problems his school had to face, the tone was sad, but pragmatic.

He had just transferred from a small school in north London to Parsons Green School, which was a large and tough inner-city comprehensive. A handful of its pupils were the children of white middle-class socialists living in Fulham. But the majority were working-class children and those from ethnic minorities. The staff had to cope with truancy, bullying, and pupils with learning difficulties. Many of the parents were, at best, indifferent to their children, at worst, abusive. All this was quite apart from the endless financial struggles he and his colleagues came up against, struggles which the government seemed to ignore, yet which made their lot virtually impossible.

'Still,' Samuel said, 'we do our best.'

He did manage, though, to convey the funnier sides of school life. He told stories about the people he worked with. The headmaster was obsessive about the telephone, apparently, paranoid about missing a call to the point that whenever the cleaner lifted the handset of the one in his office to clean it, he would insist she held the pips down for the few seconds it took her to do so.

Nell noticed his laugh. It was good. Sheer throaty enjoyment. Not particularly loud, but catching. Funny how the way someone laughed could be so immediately engaging.

Samuel was obviously quite shy. A bit nervous. There was a lot of wiping of the spectacles, especially when Liza addressed him. His eyes were as brown as black coffee. Liza said afterwards, 'Did you notice, Nell, when he took off his glasses, the whites of his eyes were milky-blue, like those special opaque marbles?'

Nell had teased her sister. No, she said, that particular detail had eluded her. They had laughed then.

And now, she wondered, what details eluded Liza, the one who on that first meeting had been so observant in her admiration? The milky whites of his eyes! Today, as his wife, did she notice the guilty furrows in his brows?

Nell looked at her watch. It was later than she thought. She stood up, tucked her thin paisley shirt into her pale jeans and put on her big black coat, an old one of Cillian's. Then she left the flat, made her way to the underground and to the West End.

It was the night of Hilary Black's private view for an exhibition of his sculptures. The small gallery was in a street off Charlotte Street. Nell wandered past a sandwich bar and a photocopying shop, both closed. She stopped a moment and peered into the black window of the latter. The machines within were shadowy, lifeless. She wanted to join them, to go and crawl under one for a while.

But she could hear the hum of the party a few doors farther along, and could see a yellow glow glowering through the gallery's glass façade. Reluctantly she strolled towards it. She had only ever been to one private view before and had not enjoyed it.

The door was open. Nell took a deep breath and stepped inside. Numerous bodies were squashed into the space,

114

talking loudly at each other, but – as she expected – not bothering to look at Hilary's work.

The vicious spotlights, aimed at the exhibits, the walls and the glossy white floor, appeared to pierce the lump of people like skewers.

Nell edged her way to the table with the drink. She was given a small glass of red wine, though it was not really red. More a sort of watery, deep pink. She could have had Tippex solvent from the photocopy shop, she thought, and it would not have been an inferior alternative.

She tried to look at Hilary's work but it was hard to see much. Someone shoved his way past her and in doing so pushed her up against one of the sculptures. It was the shape of an old-fashioned wireless, and made entirely of bones and tin. The man beside her made some pretentious remark about it. His bulging eyelids were like mussels.

In the crowd there were people Nell knew, acquaintances mostly, but nobody she particularly wanted to talk to. At the far end of the room she could just see Hilary. He was surrounded. At his side stood a girl in a big felt cap who had her back to Nell. She watched as she whispered something in his ear, as his face leapt into a grin. He was laughing, but the sound was obscured by the general hum of conversation.

Nell was squashed and hot and her glass was empty. She felt clammy breath in her ear as a puffing man budged into her before moving on.

'Nell! Here, behind you.' It was Christabel's voice. An animated trio stood between the two friends. 'Excuse me,' Christabel said. 'Can I get through, please?'

They managed to reach each other. 'Thank God you're here. Nightmare, isn't it?'

Nell agreed.

'Who are all these people? Have you spoken to Hilary yet? Apparently he's already sold quite a few. He is brilliant.' Christabel's bracelets jangled along with her chatter. 'I've just met his new girlfriend. She's lovely.'

'Is Jodie here? Where?'

115

'In the red cap over there.'

'Oh, I couldn't see who that was. No wonder Hilary looks so happy.' Nell said.

'Go over in a minute. Listen, I've got to talk to you. News.'

Christabel was at her most exuberant, Nell noticed. Full of movement, gestures.

'You're not going to believe this.'

Nell suddenly knew exactly what she was about to be told. 'You're having an affair,' she stated.

'Yes, but who with?'

'Daniel,' Nell replied flatly. There was a curious sensation in her throat, uncomfortable, as if it was being pressed like a tube of toothpaste.

'How did you know? He didn't tell you, did he? I told him I wanted to.'

'I knew anyway,' Nell said. This was not strictly true. She had seen Daniel and Christabel flirting with each other at the weekend, but there was nothing unusual in that. They often did: they had known one another for a long time.

Nell had always liked the fact that they got on so well. Sex, though, was a different matter. Her brother and her best friend. A picture of the two of them plonked itself down intrusively on her mind. It was as unwelcome and persistent as the voice of an obscene caller.

'Started in Wales,' Christabel informed her. 'I thought no one guessed.'

Nell raised her eyebrows. 'He is my brother,' she reminded her friend.

'Aren't you pleased for us? I was for you and Ben.'

'Christabel, I was sixteen. Things were a bit different.'

'Okay, but you can still be pleased for us all the same.'

That 'us' was a touch irritating. Still, the question was clearly rhetorical: Christabel was so pleased for herself. Nell decided an answer would have been superfluous.

'He's here, over in the corner talking to Conrad,' Christabel said, inclining her head in their direction.

'Oh, Conrad's arrived, has he?'

116

'Few minutes ago. You didn't come together?'

'No, he was coming straight from the studio,' Nell told her. She was not enjoying the party.

'Let's try and make our way over to them,' Christabel suggested.

Daniel and Conrad were pressed uncomfortably up against the wall, talking to someone Nell did not know. They greeted her enthusiastically, and introduced her to the girl, who was called Marina. She was a friend of Daniel's, and Conrad knew her vaguely. Her complexion, Nell noticed, was softened by pale face powder and a kind expression. She smelt of lavender.

'Nell, sweetheart, you haven't got a drink,' Conrad noticed, taking a puff of his cigarette. When he exhaled, he had to tilt his head upwards in order to avoid blowing smoke into the faces of those around him.

Christabel offered to fight her way to the table. Nell let her. Her throat was dry with thirst; her tongue seemed to rasp the roof of her mouth.

Nell turned to Daniel and raised an eyebrow. Fingering the belt of his baggy trousers, and hitching them up a bit, he smiled. When he did so, the skin round his eyes had wrinkles like little stitched tucks.

'Why are you giving me that look?' he asked.

'Why do you think? You know damn well.'

Daniel said nothing, so Nell just stared at him.

'What?' he asked at last.

'Our mutual friend.'

'Oh. Yes.'

Conrad, not wanting to intrude on their conversation, carried on talking to Marina. Marina had a large ring on one of her fingers with a very real-looking glass eye set into it. Spooky, Nell thought. She speculated about the sort of person who woke up one morning and thought, 'Why not stick artificial eyeballs on to bands of silver and sell them as unusual pieces of jewellery?' She overheard Conrad ask Marina where she bought it, but did not catch the answer.

117

'Is it a good idea?' she asked her brother, continuing the interrogation.

'Ah. That.'

Nell waited. 'Daniel?' she prompted.

After a moment's thought, he said, 'Why not?' Then the subject of their cryptic conversation returned, bearing some wine. She gave a glass to Nell. Hilary, who had followed Christabel, kissed Nell, then took her hand and squeezed it with glee.

Nell looked into the face of her old friend. It was glistening slightly: a combination of stuffy heat and unchecked joy. She congratulated him.

'I hear you've already sold quite a lot,' she said.

'Nearly all! I can't believe it.'

Behind Hilary's shoulder, there appeared a familiar face – Jodie. The actress stepped past him, and gave Nell a hug.

'I see you're wearing your green tights,' Nell observed, smiling. 'That must mean it's Thursday.'

Jodie laughed loudly.

'What are you talking about?' Hilary asked, a note of protest in his voice.

'Ah, I can see you don't know her quite as well as I do,' Nell teased. 'You can always tell the day of the week by the colour of Jodie's tights.'

Hilary was amazed and amused by this.

'I'm glad you told me that,' he said to Nell as he glanced appreciatively at his new girlfriend. It was as if he regarded this atest piece of information as yet another thing to add to the sum of those he already loved about Jodie.

Jodie laughed and turned to talk to Christabel. Hilary shook his head admiringly, and whispered in Nell's ear, 'I'm so bloody happy.'

'Are you the great artist himself?' a voice interrupted.

It was the man Nell had seen earlier with the rubbery eyelids.

'Might I prevail upon you a moment in order that we might discuss Art?' He put his hand on Hilary's rather

118

surprised shoulder, smiled at Nell as if to say, Excuse me, and took him aside. 'The symbolic use of bones in your work,' she heard him begin, 'strikes me as so unutterably moving as to be almost tangible.' She winked at Hilary and watched him as the man droned on, reflecting that he had the uncomfortable, slightly desperate air of someone at an opera who feels the onset of a coughing fit. All the same, he still looked happy.

A while later, Nell, Conrad, Daniel and Christabel left the party and went to a restaurant in Notting Hill. Nell was disappointed that Hilary and Jodie were unable to join them, for she had found their sense of wellbeing infectious. She had never seen Hilary so spirited.

At supper, she found herself less inspired by her brother's and Christabel's company in their new capacity as lovers. They laughed at each other's jokes as they had done for years, but they had already begun to annoy one another. It was an affair doomed from the start. Before the drinks arrived he had already compared her energy with that of a Morris dancer, which did not go down well; and she had berated him for his habit of holding his earlobe when concentrating.

It would not last. Such was the predictable nature of both his and her romances: short-lived. He would do the leaving; she would be left. As always, Nell thought, fiddling with her fork, and only half listening to the conversation. He, ever discreet about his private life, would never mention it and quite quickly, after a matter of days, find someone else. She would become very low, and talk about it as much as possible but, ever optimistic, fall upon a new diversion within a month or two.

All would seemingly be forgotten and forgiven very swiftly. But, in fact, the nature of Daniel's and Christabel's friendship would shift slightly. The physical knowledge, newly acquired, would impose itself on all platonic meetings in the future. And it would continue to do so, with perplexing inevitability, however civilised they were.

119

Unspoken awkwardness would take the place of un-inhibited friendliness because there would for ever exist a residue of anger on Christabel's part, and the dregs of contempt on Daniel's.

Nell found she drank quite a lot, anxious not to mull over the affair for long. Instead, she turned her thoughts to Samuel, and wondered how he had fared at the audition.

When supper was over, the four of them lingered outside the restaurant a while, finishing off conversations. The November night was cold. They tapped their icy feet on the pavement. None of them could quite summon the initiative to say goodbye. But after a few minutes, as Christabel chatted to Conrad, Daniel turned to his sister and kissed her on both cheeks.

'You don't mind, do you?' he asked.

Nell knew what he meant: his voice was low, presumably in order that Christabel would not hear.

'Not at all. Pleased,' she replied with a note of resignation. 'Think it'll be as short-lived as some of the others?'

Daniel did not reply. He simply shrugged and gave her another kiss.

When Nell and Conrad arrived home, it was late, but she rang Samuel. He was still up, working. He said it had not gone well.

Nell berated him fondly. 'That's typical of you,' she commented. 'Never any self-confidence. I'm sure you did brilliantly.'

'No, that's your prerogative. You're the actor of the family. I think I'd better stick to science.'

'Come on. How do you rate your chances?'

'Daresay I could be in with a small one. About the size of a molecule,' Samuel admitted modestly. He then paused before venturing to add, 'I went to the pub with Lucy afterwards.'

'Oh yes?' Nell hesitated. 'What did she say?'

'Well, she didn't seem to think my performance was an unmitigated disaster.'

'That's good.'

120

'Could be. Nell?'
'Um?'
'Sorry.'
'What?'
'Well.'
'Listen,' she said, 'let me know how it goes, okay?'
'Of course.'
They sent each other love and said goodbye.

# CHAPTER

## 6

'You've still got greasepaint on your neck,' Lucy, smiling, pointed out to Samuel in the pub one Friday night in early December.

It was a month after the auditions. They, and the other members of staff involved in the school play, had gathered for a drink following the first dress rehearsal, which had taken place earlier that evening. It was the pub where the staff went when they had stayed on late at the school. Some more often than others. Stationery Store Cynthia for one. Her not ungenerous bottom was known to keep the stool nearest the door warm most evenings.

The bar was stuffy and crowded. People chatted and laughed loudly, exhaling smoke and beery breath into the stifling atmosphere. The woodchip wallpaper was nicotine-stained. Its browning bobbles glistened like beads of sweat on sunbathing flesh. The carpet was pattered with an exuberance of lurid swirls: Britvic orange, Heineken honey, Bloody Mary red.

'And your eyebrows are still black,' Ralph Simmonds remarked as they all sat down on the red banquette, round a squat table. He was clearly amused by his own remark. He put his fingers to his green gingham throat, and jerked his head sideways in order to loosen his flowery turquoise tie. This Samuel took for a sign that the geography teacher was feeling relaxed.

In his mind's eye, he could see himself wielding a pair of scissors, the size of Struwwelpeter's and, with a swash-buckling flourish, snipping off Ralph's offensive neckwear.

This satisfying image was enough, temporarily at least, to assuage his irritation.

'Well, I think it makes him look very fetching,' Rachel English asserted in Samuel's defence.

She was on her third Virgin Mary, he noticed.

Perhaps she was anxious, in his presence, to keep her head for fear of saying something she might regret. (Playing Oberon opposite her Titania had confirmed Samuel's suspicion that she was in love with him. She had learned his lines as well as hers, by way, he surmised, of a particularly dedicated form of encouragement. He was rather alarmed by it though he knew this reaction was a somewhat uncharitable one. Not a callous man, he was anxious to show appreciation for her kind, if singular attentiveness. Yet he was also concerned not to mislead her. Thus he took great pains to be friendly, but not overly so. It was the least he could do.)

'Thank you, Rachel,' he said, smiling. 'I'll remember that next time I'm going barmy trying to rub the stuff off. What on earth do they make those eyebrow pencils out of?'

'Soot, I imagine,' Ralph suggested imaginatively.

Lucy laughed. Samuel hoped she did so only out of politeness. Ralph had once said that making people laugh gave him 'even more pleasure than polishing the Vauxhall'. Unfortunately, he was not very funny. It was lucky, Samuel pondered, that there were those around like Lucy, who, unlike himself, were prepared to indulge Ralph with the occasional chuckle to keep him happy.

'Anyway, Samuel, we all know you've gone a bit barmy already, quite apart from when you're rubbing off eyebrow pencil,' Ralph said.

'Ralph — ' Rachel said.

'Oh yes?' Samuel asked at the same time.

'Yes.'

'How do you mean?'

The others were listening intently, uneasily.

'Well, all those histrionics with the photocopier that

123

afternoon. Extraordinary performance, wasn't it? Not one of a completely sane man, I should say. What was it all about then, eh?'

'Ralph Simmonds, I really do think . . .' Barbara whispered. 'For goodness sake, mind your own business.'

'No, I'd like to know. I'm concerned about my colleague here. Seems to me he was a bit frightened of the photocopier, forgive me if I'm mistaken.'

Samuel closed his eyes. When he was a child he believed if he closed his eyes and couldn't see people, neither could they see him.

'Eh, Samuel?'

'Ralph, shut up.' Barbara nudged him. 'Now that's enough.'

'Something fishy,' Ralph went on. 'I notice you've been getting Rachel to do your photocopying for you since then.'

'He didn't get me to do it. I happened to offer to do a few of his worksheets while I was doing some for myself, that's all.'

'Well, I think we're entitled to an explanation from our revered professor of science here.' Ralph raised his eyebrows expectantly.

'Well,' Barbara said, 'I think you are entitled to no such thing.'

'Let the man speak for himself.'

Samuel opened his eyes and stared at his feet.

Silence.

'Let the man speak for himself,' Ralph repeated.

The man raised his eyes to pierce the geography teacher's features, and said absolutely nothing.

Ralph cowered in the face of Samuel's voiceless but vituperative contempt. 'Righto, folks,' he began after a pause, 'Ralph's turn to offer you all a bit more lubrication. Liquid reinforcements are in order, I think.' He swigged the dregs of his pint of beer. 'Another Virgin, Rachel, or shall you be graduating to something a bit stronger? Go on, be daring, have a Bloody Mary.' He stood up and tapped his pockets. They jingled with the sound of loose change.

124

Rachel shook her head. 'Nothing, thanks.'

'I can't persuade you?'

She shook it again.

'Same again, Lucy? Samuel? What can I fetch you?'

Fetch, Samuel repeated in his head.

Come to think of it, Ralph is not dissimilar to a dog. Like a slobbery labrador — tries too hard. The way those wide, blinking, watery eyes look at Lucy, all expectant. I never could stand dogs.

'Samuel?' Ralph asked a second time.

'Just half a pint, please. Thanks.'

'And Barbara? What were you on? Gin, was it? Expect you could do with another, eh? After all that scene shifting.'

It was a tactless remark. Everyone knew Battleaxe Barbara had been sad to lose the part of Hippolyta to a fifth-former, however dignified she was being about it. It was hardly fair of him to emphasise the slightly less glamorous role she had been assigned.

'She certainly deserves another,' Samuel asserted, trying to make amends for Ralph's faux pas. 'Most important part in the whole play, the scene shifter. You ran a lot more smoothly than any of us lot. I was so ashamed forgetting my lines like that.'

'Come on,' Barbara assured him. 'Just a couple of seconds. I didn't even notice at the time, only when you pointed it out backstage straight afterwards. I'd thought it was a thoughtful pause.'

'That's a very generous interpretation,' Samuel murmured.

'Barbara's right,' Rachel said. 'Honestly, no one noticed.'

'I did though,' he protested.

'Listen, it was your best performance. You were tremendous.'

Lucy's voice. Samuel looked up. Her Dali-red lips were smiling. Everything else all around blurred. He could see nothing but the lips. The red lips.

How did they stay that way? Always so red. Never faded or

125

smudged. Lucy's lipstick seemed to have a special staying power all of its own. Probably didn't taste of pigs' trotters, either, or whale blubber, or whatever other dodgy ingredient it was that went into it. A superior brand.

The desire to kiss those lips was tangible. He could feel a sharp tingling beneath his tongue (of all places, he thought). It was as if a lemon lozenge had lodged there and was persistently hitting a nerve.

'Do you really mean that?' Although he spoke softly, Samuel was alarmed that his voice seemed to resound like a tennis ball at Wimbledon's Centre Court.

'Of course she does,' Rachel said. 'You were great. And there was me. Pathetic. Tripping over my hem like that. How could I?'

'Well it doesn't matter. It was only a dress rehearsal,' Barbara reminded her.

'I know, but I still felt I let the children and everybody else down. They all did so well.'

'Look, it was fine,' Lucy told her. Her sepia-coloured eyes were kind. The pale rings beneath them seemed to reflect the light grey eyeshadow on the lids above. 'It went well. I was really pleased.'

Ralph returned from the bar bearing a round of drinks, the brims of which jiggled in the glasses as he walked.

'Cynthia's over there, as per usual,' he remarked. 'We had a little chat. She said she was fed up in the stationery store. So what's new? Her line in chat is a bit limited.'

'Unlike her line in almost everything else, from what I gather, Ralph Simmonds,' Barbara commented as he handed her her glass of gin and tonic.

'I am sure I don't know to what you are referring, Barbara,' he told her smugly.

Samuel suppressed a snigger into his beer. Someone nudged his foot. From her conspiratorial expression, he guessed it was Lucy, and he basked in the pleasure of their privately shared amusement. Was this what they called body language? Hearing the phrase had always caused him to squirm. But the reality had a certain appeal.

Barbara, who was sitting next to Ralph, went 'Humph!' Then to further demonstrate her indignation, she shifted her bottom a centimetre or two along the seat, away from him. Samuel, in turn, was forced to move closer to his neighbour on the bench: Lucy. Their proximity meant the warmth of her leg blotted itself into his.

'I'm sorry about this,' he whispered to her.

'It's fine, Samuel,' she said, taking a sip of her vodka and orange. The ice-cubes clanked glamorously in her glass, like semi-precious stones. 'Don't worry.'

Welcome words. Samuel began not to worry with a vengeance.

After their brief private exchange they turned back to the general conversation. The others by now were on to the favourite topic of many teachers – insufficient government funds for schools. They were all complaining bitterly.

Lucy and Samuel appeared to listen, but remained silent. It was a subject they both felt strongly about. This time, though, Samuel found himself disinclined to participate, and Lucy seemed to be equally reluctant. Perhaps she, like him, was tired and could not concentrate enough to join in.

Eventually Barbara, who had been taking Ralph to task on some point, glanced at her watch. The thin silver strap was highly sprung and clung tightly to her pudgy wrist.

'Look at the time,' she exclaimed. 'I'd best be off.' She swigged the dregs of her gin and tonic and plonked her handbag on her lap.

'I'm sorry. You're not leaving just because you and I were having a bit of a ding-dong, are you?' Ralph's tone was apparently one of concern, but arrogance shone through it. His expression was not one of regret. He did not try to dissuade her from going.

'Have one more drink,' Samuel urged Barbara.

'I won't, actually, Oberon, thank you kindly all the same. Perhaps another time when Theseus has reacquainted himself with Mr Manners.' So saying, she threw Ralph a bitter look as if she wanted to peel him like a citrus fruit.

Rachel, embarrassed, pulled the cuffs of her jersey over her hands. 'I'll come out with you Barbara. Are you walking to the tube? I ought to be getting home myself.'

'Party breaking up, is it?' Ralph asked.

'Looks like it, doesn't it?' Rachel replied.

'You off too, Samuel? You could give Lucy a lift home. Earls Court is on your way to Shepherds Bush.'

'Thank you, Ralph. But I don't think we need a mediator. We can sort out our own travel arrangements.'

Ralph shrugged, and put on his bulky brown suede jacket. It had condensed black fake fur on the inside, and when he stood up it only just covered his low-slung bottom. He clumsily did up the big rounded buttons.

Samuel looked at Lucy fleetingly, and wondered about the opportunity which had now presented itself to him. It had leapt on to his lap like a dog. He had a choice: he could push it off, or embrace it.

'Cold as a witch's tit out there,' Ralph observed, 'and what have I got to do this weekend? Correct essays on wildlife in the Sahara. Bit ironic, really.' He glanced at Barbara. She was tying a scarf round her neck. 'Will you want dropping off at the tube?'

Barbara looked at Samuel and Lucy as if anticipating their disapprobation.

'Well,' she said, 'I was rather set on walking but as you say, it is – ' she paused for a second or two, not quite able to bring herself precisely to repeat Ralph's expression – 'very cold out there. So, thank you. Yes.' Her eyes swayed surreptitiously in Cynthia's direction, a touch too triumphantly Samuel thought.

'Rachel, what about you?' Ralph enquired.

Rachel replied, slowly, that she would prefer to walk. Her tone reeked of reluctance. Samuel smelled the hint, but thought he would prefer not to take it.

The five of them walked outside on to the pavement. Their breath was visible in the dark. When Samuel exhaled, he felt a bit like a can of hairspray.

Ralph and Barbara said goodnight and wandered away past some black plane trees to his car. Samuel, watching them, was depressed at the thought of the bleak denouement to their evening. And he wondered about his.

'What was with those two?' Rachel asked.

Lucy raised an eyebrow. 'It'd be doing my imagination a kindness not to have to speculate too much,' Samuel replied, smiling. His fingers were stinging with cold. He wanted to get warm, make a move. He wanted to give Lucy a lift to Earls Court, but did not know how to set about the business of putting the suggestion which Ralph had so brazenly made a few minutes before into practice.

'Right, I'm off,' he announced, with a suddenness that surprised even himself. 'Lift either of you? Rachel?'

Rachel declined. And as she walked off towards the tube station, Samuel did notice that her shoulders stooped slightly. A little lonely regret, perhaps? he conjectured, without satisfaction. On another occasion, he would almost certainly have mustered more sympathy for her.

But not tonight. It was now quite late, and he was, after all, alone with Lucy Hardcastle, and a number of possibilities.

Lucy did not ask Samuel in for coffee. She asked him in for rosehip tea.

Standing on her doorstep, he felt as unsettled as a paper mobile dangling in a draught.

Try to think about something really, really boring, Samuel told himself as Lucy put the key in her front door. Something quite different. What do the children find really boring? Pollination. That's a guaranteed dampener. Okay. So the transfer of pollen from anthers to stigma is called pollination. Now, cross-pollination is the transfer on one flower – come on, Samuel – to the stigma of another flower of the same species.

The door opened. They stepped into a dark hall with a red carpet and a battered umbrella stand.

A good example of a flower that's insect-pollinated would be, say, the buttercup.

Aaah! Bloody buttercups. Bugger bloody buttercups, and their pitiful mockery of a sex life.

What about rosehips?

This method of maintaining control is not working, Samuel.

Lucy flicked on a dim lamp. A few strands of her dark hair had wisped across her pale face and had stuck, irresistibly to her red lips.

Definitely now working. You are a pathetic specimen of homo sapiens, you know that, don't you, Samuel?

'Let's go down to the kitchen. I'll put the kettle on,' Lucy suggested and led the way down a flight of lino stairs to the basement.

The strip lights blinked to life.

'Not very salubrious, I'm afraid.'

Samuel's eyes, accustoming themselves to the scorching brightness, glanced about the room.

There was a filthy window looking on to a black brick wall. It reminded him of one that had been deliberately 'distressed' for use in a stage set.

The paint on the walls had long ago given up its battle against the onslaught of grease and steam over the years. They, like the fridge and the washing machine, had turned that greyish-white of underwear that has seen better days. The thin plywood cupboards were pale yellow and had misty glass sections in their façades. The flowers printed on the plastic tablecloth, though fated perennially to bloom, were fading and clearly longing to die.

'My aunt hasn't changed a thing since she moved here in the fifties,' Lucy told him, taking a small box of teabags from one of the cupboards above the sink. 'Bit grim. But I've grown quite fond of the place, really.'

Samuel said, 'Yes I like it.'

He had tried to imagine the place where Lucy lived, to speculate what it would look like. How odd it now felt to be

130

with her, not at school or in the pub, but in her own environment.

Over the months – since she had joined Parsons Green and he and she had befriended each other in the staff-room – Lucy had not revealed much about herself, her life outside school. Stray details only. This was due to natural reticence as opposed to deliberate secrecy. Samuel had managed to piece together barely more than an impression.

She came from Ireland (and still had a wisp of an accent which lent her soft voice a soothing effect, like a sort of verbal massage). Her parents ran a modest bed and breakfast in Cork. As a teenager she worked there, making the beds and taking tea and toast to the guests every morning, and manning the reception desk in the evenings after school. She left home at eighteen. From what Samuel could gather, she had been engaged to the boy who helped her mother in the kitchen. She had not loved him, and was relieved when he ran off with the girl from the wool shop in the next village. It gave Lucy the perfect excuse to escape, and herself run off to England.

She went to Sussex University and had lived with her aunt since then. Samuel knew little of her private life. Last year there had been mention of a man called Rick. Rick had a small head and thin hair, apparently. He had learned this because Lucy had come to school and said, 'Rick left me last night,' and then had bravely tried to think of reasons why not to mind too much. The fact he had 'a head like a coconut' was one of them; another was his tendency to wear a Walkman in bed, which he claimed improved his performance therein. Lucy obviously thought differently. Samuel remembered her saying that between the sheets Rick particularly liked to listen to punk. 'This seemed to entitle him,' she had ventured with wistful good humour, 'to go in for a kind of horizontal pogo.'

It was the only time she had ever spoken about sex with reference to herself.

A character called Frank had featured soon after Rick, but

131

only briefly as far as Samuel could make out. She told Tim Crawford, whose hobby was ornithology, that her new boyfriend was a keen birdwatcher. Then she rashly let out that Frank's surname was Raven. Tim had laughed.

One Monday morning a few weeks later, Lucy said, 'I told Frank Raven where he could shove his telescope.'

That's curtains for him, Samuel thought, and indeed, since then, Frank Raven had been heard of no more.

'Do sit down.' Her voice was sweet.

'Thank you, yes.'

He pulled out a metal chair from the table. Its plastic seat had split. An excretion of yellowing foam oozed out like pus from a wound. Awkward, he sat down without taking off his coat.

Quick cup of tea then I'll be making my way, Samuel reassured himself.

'Is she about?'

'My aunt? No. Gone to Ireland.'

'Holiday?'

'Visiting my family for a few days.'

'Ah, yes.'

The kettle on the gas stove began to squeal. Lucy poured the water into two mugs and sat down.

Thank God for her rosehip tea. Couldn't have come in for coffee. How would I have explained away the headtapping? Rosehip tea I could get to love.

'Does anyone else live here?'

'No. Just the two of us.'

'Nice and peaceful, I expect,' Samuel remarked, nodding.

The inanity of that observation does not become you, you ass. But she doesn't seem to have noticed. Or maybe she's just too polite to comment.

'Sometimes too nice and peaceful. Can get lonely every so often if I've got a lot of work on. But I suppose it means I get it done, no distractions.'

Samuel attempted a light-hearted chuckle but it went a bit wrong, and he choked instead. He sipped at his tea to soothe his throat.

132

Don't drink so fast. When it runs out, so does the excuse to be here. Don't want to go just yet. I've got this curious sensation. Compelling. Like milk and honey running through my veins. Come off it, that's alcohol, you fool. You're drunk.

Resume conversation now!

'Ah, distractions. I know all about them. That's what comes of having a family. Not necessarily an antidote to loneliness though, not necessarily,' he remarked, and paused before adding, 'funnily enough.'

'No, of course.'

'Terrible business, loneliness.'

'Oh, don't get me wrong. I'm not really lonely. Just occasionally. I have a nice time. I go out, have people round.'

'That not a problem? With the aunt, I mean.'

'No, she's very good. Likes my friends.'

'That's good.'

Pause.

'More tea, or – ?' Lucy asked, standing up.

'It's very nice, your rosehip,' he told her, peering into his mug. He needed some more.

Top up the tea, top up the excuse to stay a while longer. Must be off soon. Liza will be wondering where . . .

'Lovely,' he said, handing her the mug. 'Thank you.'

'Perhaps I'm keeping you?'

'Not at all. No. No.'

'It's funny, it's the end of a heavy week and I don't feel at all tired. Must be the adrenalin, still, from the dress rehearsal,' Lucy said.

That must be what that flip was, too, inside my stomach just now: adrenalin. Of course. Like that feeling you get in a lift.

'Me too,' he agreed. 'I think I've still got stage fright, though the performance ended, what, over two hours ago?'

'More like over three.'

'God, is it eleven already?'

Samuel made a show of looking at his watch.

133

'I feel so awake,' he said. 'During term, I'm usually dead by this time on a Friday. Powerful stuff, this adrenalin.'

'The body's natural amphetamines.'

'Absolutely. It's a brilliant system,' he told her enthusiastically.

'How does it work exactly?' Lucy asked, smiling.

'Well, inside the adrenal glands, which are round about here – ' he began, pointing at his kidneys, 'there is an area called the medulla – the inner zone, if you like. It's that part which is stimulated by the nervous system to produce adrenalin. When it's released into the blood it quickens the heartbeat and diverts blood from the alimentary canal and skin to the muscles.' He was gesticulating energetically. 'Then the pupils start dilating away; and the rate of breathing and the oxidation of carbohydrates speeds up, you see – ' Samuel stopped abruptly. He hastily thrust his hands into his coat pocket to keep them in check.

What do you think you're doing? You're getting carried away here. This is rosehip tea at Lucy Hardcastle's flat, it is not a biology lecture. Shut your stupid mouth.

'I'm sorry, you don't want to hear all this. Goodness, you probably know it anyway – '

'Not really. I'm interested.'

'Seriously?' Samuel's pupils dilated. 'Are you sure? That's more than can be said for most of the children I teach.'

'Rubbish. Go on.'

'Yes. Well.' He started again more gently. 'So. Anyway, it produces a sensation of fear. You know – thumping heart, hollow feeling in the stomach, pale face, etcetera.' He paused. 'That kind of thing. But it's secreted not only when people are in a position of danger. Also in situations which promote anxiety, for example. And yes, excitement, too . . .' His soft voice tailed off.

He released one hand from his pocket and took the last sip of his tea.

The sleeves of Lucy's copper beech cardigan were pulled down over her knuckles, Samuel noticed appreciatively. Her long fingers clutched each other around her mug as if trying to warm themselves. She looked so cold. He thought he could discern small goose pimples on her white neck.

'Well,' he said inconsequentially. Just to fill the silence. Pause. 'I think perhaps – ' Another pause.

Yes, what do you think? I don't know. I don't know what I think.

My heart is beating so vigorously I can feel it in my ears. What I think is: someone's doing drum practice in my semicircular canals.

Still sitting, he inched his chair back from the table so as to be able to stand up. But he did not stand up.

'Maybe it's time – '

For what?

Confused, he stood up.

Lucy hesitated before doing so herself – possibly wanting to prolong the moment? But it was only a split second's hesitation. Samuel wondered if, too hopeful, he had imagined it.

She switched off the lights and they went upstairs.

Bugger it, he would kiss her goodnight. In the near darkness of the hall it would not be taking that much of a liberty.

As he did so, he held her elbow with one hand. Lucy closed her eyes in a prolonged blink. Suddenly he felt her woollen sleeve and the tips of her fingers in his free hand.

As they fell, kissing each other, on to Lucy's lumpy single bed, Samuel hit his head on the mahogany bedpost. The table beside it shook a little, causing the parchment lampshade slowly to sway like a ballerina's skirt.

Lucy giggled, and apologised for the candlewick bedspread.

The room was small and dark and cold. An antique lace curtain wafted breezily in front of the little window above a wooden chair with a straw seat. On the chest of drawers a vase of dried flowers stood by a pile of books. A towel or a dressing gown hung on a hook nailed to the back of the door. There was a faint smell of damp.

Samuel and Lucy manoeuvred themselves under the thick blankets. The mattress springs groaned with quiet tolerance. Once between the soft sheets, Samuel pushed Lucy's loose cardigan up over her shoulders, and then slowly ran his hand along her legs. He peeled away her tights and dropped them, silken husks, still as warm as flesh, on to the black floorboards.

When the last pieces of clothing had been discarded, Samuel held Lucy in his arms for a moment, and closed his eyes.

My head is still pulsating. Farther down, there's a sort of tango taking place. Joy and guilt make for rather ill-matched dancing partners. Joy is currently leading.

Is Lucy aware that all this commotion is going on within me? Can she guess that my seeming apathy isn't reluctance, but deliberate procrastination?

I'll open my eyes in one minute. Let her have patience just a little while longer.


Less than an hour later, Samuel stepped out of bed to dress. A touch dazed, he groped about on the floor for his clothes.

Lucy, naked, walked across to the door. Her hair, untied and unbrushed, fell almost to the small of her back. Samuel watched as she lifted her dressing-gown from the hook. In the darkness her skin had a milky-blue quality. Neither of them said much.

He shivered and concentrated on hoisting up his socks. He did not notice as Lucy knotted the towelling belt around her waist and bent down to flick a switch in the skirting board.

As the old-fashioned heater began to warm up, it turned steadily brighter, and illuminated a section of the floor. The snake markings on the silk flex that slithered from its side, and a stray shoe belonging to Samuel, became visible.

By now he was grappling with the buttons of his shirt. Such is the frenetic nature of the adulterous husband, he reflected, a touch ruefully.

136

'Here's one of your shoes,' Lucy said. She managed, he registered, to enrich even this prosaic remark with that inimitably sweet tone of hers.

He looked up sharply.

Until that moment he had not been aware of the heater.

And suddenly he spotted the bright orange bars. Like two rigid glow-worms being tortured on a rack. Their protestations took the form of sinister noises: sizzling and spluttering.

Samuel's eyes widened, and as he kept them open, aghast, the heat began to sting them.

That thing is ten times worse than any goddamn toaster, he thought.

And then, without further ado, he keeled over and fainted.

Letting herself in to Cillian's flat, Nell could hear the noise of laughter coming from the sitting room. She peered round the large vase of flowers on the hall table and into the old mirror. Her nose was red, and she sniffed. The place smelled of dust, smoke and winter jasmine.

'Nell, my darling, is that you?' Cillian's shout sounded excited. Before she could answer, he had appeared from a door at the end of the book-lined corridor. He leaned against the wall, and took a sip of his drink. Nell glanced at the thin wrists, and long white fingers sticking out from the sleeves of his dark grey jacket. She was intrigued that they were strong enough to hold the thick-set glass, and instinctively felt the urge to relieve him of it, as if it were a heavy suitcase. She wanted to carry it for him, but when she approached him to kiss him hello, she managed to refrain from offering.

'You seem surprised,' she remarked. 'You weren't expecting me?' she asked as they walked into the sitting room.

'Of course I was,' Cillian insisted, a little offended that she could imagine he might have forgotten. 'Lunch. I've been looking forward to it. We've run out of fags. I was just about to ask Jake to go and get some.'

137

'Don't worry, I've got lots,' Nell assured him, smiling at the man who had politely stood up when she and Cillian had entered.

'My God, I haven't introduced you,' the old poet said, apologetically, putting his fingers to his mouth. 'Jakey, where are you?' he added, spinning round with agitation, listening for his grandson's whereabouts.

Jake stepped towards Cillian and gently touched his elbow. He was taller than his grandfather, but was of the same thin frame. Nell, who had seen photographs of Cillian in his youth, could detect a distinct resemblance. Jake had bad teeth – crooked, yellow, neglected – but his deep brown hair was shiny. He smelt strongly of mothballs.

'Nell John – Jake O'Neill,' Cillian declared triumphantly. 'At last you meet. It seems so odd you never have before now. Jakey, you've been living away for too long. This is my little bee. Now tell me, is she in her black and yellow today?'

Jake, shaking Nell's hand, looked at her old jeans, faded with age, and her dark blue bomber jacket, the suede of which was worn. There was a black ink stain on its breast.

'Yes,' he replied with a wink at Nell.

'That's my black coat she wears, you know,' the old man told him. 'And I gave her the yellow scarf, too. Very appropriate today for meeting the bee expert,' he said chuckling, 'though she insists bees are brown. But her nature isn't wasp-like. A bumble-bee, she is. Here, my darling, give us a fag, and for God's sake get yourself a drink. How are your preparations for the Chekhov audition?'

Ten minutes later, the three of them went through to the kitchen to have lunch.

'Well, I think before we know it you're going to be on stage at the National,' Cillian declared, sitting down at the table and opening a bottle of red wine.

'That's hardly very likely,' Nell murmured. 'I really don't think I – '

'Don't be an ass,' the poet interrupted. 'If Belinsky has any

138

sense he'll see you'd make a wonderful Varia. What do you reckon, Jakey? He'd be foolish not to, wouldn't he?'

'Foolish,' the younger man reiterated.

'And Jake should know. He's mad about Chekhov.'

Nell looked at Jake as he knelt down to pull the plates out of the oven. As he did so, the bottom of his white shirt, which was sticking out from his baggy black jersey, brushed the lino tiles on the floor.

'You saw *Wild Honey* at the National, didn't you, Michael Frayn's production?' Cillian asked.

'I loved it,' Jake said, standing up again, and putting the plates on the table. The shirt tail now hung over his dark flannel trousers and covered his bottom.

'Not pure Chekhov, of course, but how could you resist a title like that? You know, Nell, before you came, he was telling me how he'd spent his morning − examining the remains of a honey bee found in a can of peaches sent to him by some environmental health inspector.'

Nell screwed up her nose. 'Really?'

'He wanted to know my theory as to how or why it had got there,' Jake explained.

'What did you say?'

'Well, my answer wasn't very technical. Common sense, really. I wrote back saying it had probably got into the crate of fresh peaches long before reaching the canning factory.'

'I could have told them that,' Cillian announced. 'Doesn't take much expertise to work that one out.'

'Yes, but could you have worked out what sort of bee it was and where it had come from?' Nell enquired, teasing.

'Well, no, but I don't see why a health inspector should be so hung up on detail.'

Nell and Jake laughed.

'You should be busy identifying all the new bees you collected in Indonesia,' Cillian went on, 'not wasting your time corresponding with pernickety environmental health officers.'

'I've just come back from a month in the Indonesian rain forests,' Jake explained to Nell.

139

'It was an expedition organised by the Royal Entomological Society,' Cillian informed her, buttering a roll. 'Please could you pass the houmous, my darling?'

'Taramasalata,' she corrected him as she handed over the pot.

'Damn, why must they always alter the layout in Marks & Spencer? I was used to houmous on the left. He was one of about forty or fifty scientists out there and they had a military support staff with them.'

'Three Landrovers,' Jake added.

'Yes, but you did lots of walking. That was a big joke. Farthest he'd ever walked was the corner shop for cigarettes,' Cillian said, biting into his roll. Crumbs scampered down his shirt front.

Nell looked at Jake's long thin limbs, still brown from the Indonesian sun.

'I got quite fit. The forest was on a mountain, very steep, and enclosed. And being on the Equator, it was unbelievably humid and hot.'

'They couldn't wear shorts because of all the thorns, mosquitoes and leeches,' Cillian said.

'We were staying in this wooden base camp built by construction workers who had made a nearby dam. It was crawling with a virulent form of harvest mite, so we were bitten to pieces anyway.'

'He came back with spots all over him. Not only that, they had to contend with the threat of rabies, and the horror of tinned army food. But that's a bee boffin for you.'

'What was the aim of the expedition?' Nell asked Jake as she poured more wine into their three glasses.

'To make a revision of the species in the region. There are two or three hundred on that particular island, but many more in Borneo.'

'He netted three or four scarce specimens that can only be found in Indonesia.'

'The *Xylocopa Smithii*,' Jake said, nodding. 'I'm not sure Nell's really interested in all this,' he murmured to his grandfather, looking at Nell and biting his lip apologetically.

'Well, I'm interested,' Cillian said.

Nell nodded in agreement.

'See, she's nodding,' the old man remarked. It was a characteristically canny guess.

Jake said, 'Typical,' and smiled.

'He described the *Smithii* family to me. Bloody enormous. We're not talking about the type of bee you find making eyes at a bit of honeysuckle in the Cotswolds, you know. No, these lot are over an inch long and all black.'

'White heads,' Jake reminded him.

'Sinister little buggers all the same. Bet they give the monkeys there a run for their money. Salad, my darling?' Cillian asked, pushing the wooden bowl in Nell's direction. 'Don't worry if you find a caterpillar in it – Jakey'll be able to tell you if it's a boy or a girl.'

'I used to be in moths.'

'Yes, and two years later you still haven't managed to get rid of the stink of their balls,' Cillian observed affectionately.

'Cillian, you're insufferable,' Nell told him, grinning.

'No, he's right,' Jake agreed. 'It's the naphthalene crystals we use to preserve the specimens. The whole place reeks, and so do we.'

'He's all right, though, he can't smell them any more,' Cillian pointed out. 'Used to it, like dustmen get used to the smell of rubbish. It's everyone else around him who suffers. Times I've visited him at work, I've been practically knocked out by it.'

'It doesn't put him off coming, though,' Jake told Nell reaching for the salad bowl. As he did so, a woollen thread sticking out from the sleeve of his old jersey, dipped itself into the pot of taramasalata. When he licked it off, Nell noticed the large hole in his elbow.

There was something endearing, she thought, about a moth expert with holes in his clothes.

'He visits me quite a lot,' Jake went on. 'Likes me to open all the cabinets for him, and describe my special bees to him in great detail, what they look like, their habits, and so on.'

'I bet you're a real bore, Cillian,' Nell commented.

141

'Nonsense. I keep him on his toes.'

'Yes,' Jake affirmed. 'Asking all sorts of difficult questions.'

'I've caught the bugger out more than once,' the old man said. 'Asked the same question on separate occasions, and got different answers.'

'Accused me of being a fraud,' his grandson recalled, shaking his head.

Cillian laughed, and asked if either of them wanted coffee.

Nell stood up. 'I'll do it,' she said, moving to put the kettle on.

Jake looked at his watch. 'In fact, I ought to be getting back to the museum.'

'What do you mean? It's Saturday, for Christ's sake,' Cillian protested. 'Don't go.'

'I must. Yesterday was hectic, and I've got to finish some stuff.'

'What's on the agenda this afternoon then?' The old man lit one of Nell's cigarettes. 'Examining a jar of marmalade with a bumble-bee in it?'

'No. I've been sent a few specimens from an amateur entomologist in Canada. I've got to identify and label them, then log them into our collection. I better go, but I'm worried about leaving this mess.' Jake stood up and put the plates on the sideboard.

'Leave it,' Cillian instructed nonchalantly waving his arm. 'Bugger off back to your bees, you bloody boffin, you.'

'Sure?'

'Sure,' the poet repeated.

The younger man kissed his grandfather and said he would call him later. 'Meanwhile, get on with your poems. The deadline's approaching. Encourage him, Nell, won't you?' Jake asked, putting on his coat.

'Of course,' she assured him.

'No, I think a bit of Tolstoy with my bee here, then a little sleep. That's what's on my agenda this afternoon,' Cillian claimed defiantly. 'Unlike you, I think I'll give work a miss this weekend. Just this once,' he laughed.

'You're hopeless,' Jake said, and looked to Nell. 'Goodbye. Nice meeting you.' He hesitated momentarily.

Nell wondered if, like her, he was considering the small social dilemma which confronted them: was it to be a casually friendly kiss on the cheek or, the more formal option, a handshake?

A second passed, then simultaneously they held out their hands to one another, and said goodbye before Jake smiled, turned, and made his way out of the flat.

You can binge on anticipation, Samuel told himself, so much so that reality can give you a headache.

It was early on Monday morning. He was in Out Patients. There were fewer people than usual. His elbow rested on the wooden arm of the blue plastic chair on which he had sat down. A rolled-up copy of the *Independent* stuck out of his jacket pocket. On his lap was a pile of exercise books. The top one was open. He was chewing a red biro and staring into space.

Why, bearing in mind it had augured so well, had it been no good, sex with Lucy?

The inevitable disillusion brought about by hope, would doubtless be what Nell would say. And there may be something in that. But there are other reasons too.

Let's face it, Samuel, on a very basic level, things didn't, well, work, quite, exactly, did they? I'm not talking about the obvious things that can go wrong, like impotence and so forth. It was more subtle than that. Call it physical incompatibility. There's no particular reason I can see for it. Of course, sex with someone new always has its awkward sides – inhibitions, and the over-polite eagerness to please giving rise to clumsiness. (There was a difficult moment when my arm was in the wrong place, squashed beneath her; pins and needles, should I say anything? And it was embarrassing when, rolling over in an embrace, I tugged her hair by mistake, caught it under my shoulder blades.) These things can be overcome in time. But there was something more than that, something which I felt could not be remedied.

I'd almost forgotten that ghastly syndrome of it all being over – just – and suddenly not only not wanting to be touched, but not wanting to be there at all any more. Awful, but I'm afraid I had that with Lucy. It's a chemical thing. Hormonal, must be.

There again, I don't get it with Liza.

I've been spoiled by Liza.

Samuel shifted in his chair uneasily as he admitted this to himself. One of the exercise books on his lap slid to the floor. He leaned down to pick it up. A girl whom he recognised to be the lime-green girl, asked him if the next seat was taken. He shook his head, and she sat down. Today she was in that orange which railwaymen and bicyclists wear so as to show up in the dark.

I'll have to tell Dr Oak about all this.

I wonder what he'll have to say about the bar heater incident?

Actually, I know what he'll say, don't I? That I'm not making things easy for myself. And he'll be right. I set myself up for it. I mean, I put myself in a situation that was bound to have consequences.

Yes, a fucking fainting fit.

Only last time Dr Oak said to me, 'Samuel, I don't think you'd be very good at infidelity. Even just thinking about it sends you into a frenzy with a plug socket.' I remember that, because we laughed when he said it.

He advised me against seducing Lucy but for my own sake. He's interested in getting me better, getting me over this dottiness of mine.

We're both agreed it's partly to do with guilt. And we've discussed the familiar formula: guilt equals anxiety equals crisis.

No wonder there was that ridiculous performance with the bar heater. It was inevitable and I've only myself to blame.

Only myself to blame. Oh, yes, not my poor, darling

Liza. It's me who's risking all, while she remains unaware, blissful as ever. Darling Liza. Do I honestly want the fabric of my marriage to crack? Christ, do I? Because that's what I'm doing. How can I be doing this?

Fool, so much, no – everything – to lose. And for what?

I'm really no better than Ralph Simmonds who speaks of 'the thrill of the chase, and the catch'. In fact, I'm probably worse. At least he's open about trying to fulfil some sort of dubious macho ideal. Me? This is just infatuation . . . yet . . . so compelling an infatuation.

Oh, honestly, it's pathetic. I'm not proud of myself. And it can hardly be described as macho, can it, to sleep with someone and afterwards promptly faint at the sight of her bar heater?

Samuel's thoughts were interrupted by the appearance of Dr Oak. They walked along the corridor which had worn felt tiles, manure green, and into a plain little room.

The window had small metal frames. It overlooked the hospital garden. The flowers, reminiscent of those on a municipal roundabout, were purpose-grown. Their reds, oranges and yellows were artificially bright, like the colours of the décor in a Happy Eater restaurant on a motorway.

Samuel, as usual, ignored the high narrow bed which was covered with a giant strip of loo paper, and sat on one of the chairs beside Dr Oak's bare desk.

Dr Oak opened his file, and smiled as if genuinely, as opposed just to professionally, pleased to see him.

'I've got a confession to make,' Samuel began. 'I slept with Lucy Hardcastle.'

The older man nodded with a sympathetic expression which encouraged his patient to admit everything, including the experience with the bar heater.

'Oh dear,' Dr Oak commented. 'Well, at least it wasn't a sunray bed,' he joked, his tone not remotely mocking.

Maybe that's why he doesn't get exasperated, Samuel reflected, laughing: he's a shrink with a sense of humour.

'I felt such a bloody fool when I came round,' Samuel told

him. 'I saw her concerned face, bending over me, as I lay on the floorboards. And I thought, this is a nightmare, I've got to go, I can't face her. Lucy! When have I ever not been able to face Lucy before? Bugger sex, you know.' He stopped and sighed. 'So, anyway,' he began again, 'she asked me what was wrong.'

'Did you tell her?'

'Oh no!' Samuel replied, appalled at the idea. 'I couldn't possibly. She doesn't know, and I couldn't bear it if she did.'

'She wouldn't understand?'

'No, I think she would. She's very understanding. I can tell her all sorts of things, it's just I could never tell her that. The humiliation! It's hard to talk to anyone about private madness. You; and Nell to an extent. Otherwise, I keep it to myself.'

Dr Oak nodded. 'So what did you tell Lucy?'

'I managed to cobble together some sort of excuse – fatigue, drink.' He paused and added with a chuckle, 'I've been doing a bit of acting recently, as you know, which helped. So I don't think she guessed.'

The session was helpful. Dr Oak did not regard what had happened as a major disaster. He called it a minor setback.

'Unfortunately, you weren't making things easy for yourself. But I suppose if you sleep with Lucy again, you'll know to ask her not to turn the heater on. However, that only eradicates the direct precipitator. It doesn't take away the underlying cause: the guilt. For that reason, you must think carefully before going to bed with her a second time.'

Samuel nodded, pensive.

'Do you think you will?'

'I can't tell. Every atom of my common sense implores me not to – my God, I'd pay to die rather than lose Liza – but there are other impulses which urge me to try again. Pride, perhaps. And that self-destructive impulse too, the one which convinces the alcoholic who's trying not to drink that an off licence is as good a place as any to go and buy a bottle of Perrier. It's not rational. There again, rationality isn't one of my strong points.' Samuel smiled stoically. 'To be honest, I'm terrified of even seeing her, I'm terrified of having to go into school this morning. I might go mad with the lab lights. Who knows? Anything could happen. See – ' Samuel stopped, and held up one of his hands. 'I'm trembling. Can you see? I'm shaking. Yes.'

'How do you feel about a practical, Samuel?'

'Now?' The trembling had worked its way into his vocal chords.

'Yes. Just a short one.'

'Goodness.'

'We don't have to.'

A high-pitched 'Oh' of relief from Samuel.

'But it might be helpful.'

'Do you think so?'

'We could give it a try, and stop if you hated it. Remember, it's like with an injection. The anticipation is always worse than the real thing.'

'Funny,' Samuel remarked, 'the same can't be said, at least in my limited experience, for adulterous sex.' He managed to raise a chuckle. 'Just the opposite, in fact.'

Dr Oak smiled, and lifted a large briefcase from the floor beside his desk.

'Ah, your box of tricks,' Samuel said gloomily. 'For a wonderful moment, I thought you'd forgotten it.'

'I'm sorry.'

'Ah, well. If it's going to do me good.'

The doctor put the briefcase on the desk and undid the locks. The two metal clips sprang back against the leather with a small but violent thudding sound. Samuel shuddered.

'Perhaps you'd prefer it if we did the coffee exercise first?' Dr Oak enquired softly.

'I think so. Yes, please.'

Dr Oak picked up the cream-coloured handset of his flat telephone and prodded a couple of digits. 'Mary? Yes, please would you be very kind and ask one of the nurses to bring a couple of cups of coffee to my office? Both milk no sugar.

147

Thank you.' He replaced the receiver. 'Someone'll be along with them in a minute. How did you do this week, by the way? Last week you did so well. Down to twenty taps every time, and no lapses, wasn't it?'

'That's right.'

'Brilliant.'

'And that was the case again up until Friday, when I had that little disaster – '

'Hiccup,' Dr Oak corrected.

'All right, hiccup. Anyway, since then, it's gone straight back up to twenty-four.'

'Never mind,' the grey-haired man said cheerfully, standing up to answer the knock on the door. 'Let's see if we can reverse the trend together, eh?'

The nurse who was normally to be found behind the reception desk in Out Patients, stepped in, put two steaming cups of coffee on the desk, and went out again.

The steam reminded Samuel of the sight of his and Lucy's breath, visible as it had been on the cold air outside the pub, the night he took her home.

'It helps, doesn't it, if I drink some too?' Dr Oak said cajolingly.

Samuel, staring anxiously at the frothy liquid, bit his lip. 'Okay,' he said heavily.

'Right. Think you can touch it?'

'Oh yes.' He put his hand forward and gently lowered his fingertips on to the polystyrene side of the cup. It felt warm and smooth. 'You see, that bit's okay. I can do that.'

'Good, very good. Now, how about seeing if you can tap your head just eighteen times before you take your first sip? It doesn't matter in the least if you can't.'

'I can try.'

'Great. Let's see what happens. No hurry.'

Dr Oak's voice was so utterly patient and understanding, Samuel prayed he would not disappoint him.

'You know,' he said, trying to sound light-hearted, 'any idea that right now I don't feel like a complete crackpot – '

148

'You're not even half a crackpot,' Dr Oak interrupted, reassuring.

'I'm an ordinary happily married man with two kids and a respectable job,' Samuel observed with an incredulous smile and shaking his head. 'This minute that might be quite hard to believe. All right, here we go.'

He lifted his left hand and pushed the sleeve of his black Shetland jersey up a little by way of preparation. Then he bent his head forward, tentatively began tapping his crown with two straight fingers, neatly joined, and started, very steadily, to count out loud. As he neared tap number sixteen, the control in his voice wavered a little. But, glancing at Dr Oak, whose expression was willing him to succeed, he forced himself to blank out any nightmarish images in his mind, of road accidents and his children.

'. . . fifteen, sixteen . . .' he said, sighing with effort. Another two taps, '. . . seventeen, eighteen . . .' He slowly drew his hand away from his head and with the other one forced it down to between his knees, away from temptation. He looked at the cup of coffee, knowing he should now try and attempt to drink it. But there was this unreasonable force inside, propelling him to give his head two more taps . . . possibly four.

Suddenly, he could bear it no longer, and the left hand shot out from his knees, like a lone bat from a cave, and gave his forehead two more taps. 'Twenty!'

But before he would allow it to do twenty-two, even twenty-four he hastily picked up the cup and took a big gulp of the coffee.

'Oh, blast!' he cried, crestfallen, when he put it down again. 'You see, I didn't quite manage it, did I? I didn't think I would. I'm in a guilty, guilty mood, a funny mood today.'

He watched Dr Oak for his reaction.

'I don't know what you mean,' the older man said, beaming. 'I think that was wonderful. Given the circumstances, twenty this week is better than twenty last week when you hadn't had a crisis. And you jolly nearly made only eighteen this time. Marvellous progress Samuel. I'm impressed.'

'Seriously?'

'Seriously,' the doctor reiterated, pulling the briefcase nearer to him and lifting open the lid. 'And last week, too, you did so well with the electric razor, I thought we could graduate today to something perhaps a little more troubling, and see how you fare.'

Samuel gulped as Dr Oak put his large hand into the case and began pulling out a household plug which was fixed to a yard-long piece of plastic flex. Finally the object to which it was attached, and to which the doctor had referred, emerged.

'I don't expect you'll have any problems handling a hairdrier, will you?' he asked, and threw Samuel a supremely confident smile.

When the session was over and Samuel was passing through Out Patients, he bumped into Eddie McLean, the man afflicted with Delusory parasitosis. Since their first encounter some weeks before, they had met on a number of occasions while awaiting their appointments with their doctors, and they had got to know each other quite well.

Chance friendships pleased Samuel. He had met Liza in an off-licence. It was a good story, which she often told: complete strangers who, over the vodka bottles, exchange a few glances, mutter a word or two, and end up getting married.

It was unusual for Liza to meet people in that way. Her friends were mainly those she had met through her family, ones she had made at school and university, or people in publishing.

Of course, like her, he had friends from university and work. But he had also met people more arbitrarily. Colin, for example, was the man who worked in his local newsagent and who sold him his paper each morning. Colin had revealed one day that he couldn't read or write. Samuel had teased him, and asked if he was not possibly in the wrong job. They had both laughed. Then Samuel had offered to teach him, and they became friends when he started giving him lessons.

It was the same with Joy. Samuel had been out shopping for Liza and was on the number 12 heading home. A woman was having a row with the bus-conductor. While everyone else remained silently indignant on her behalf, Samuel stuck up for her. Her gratitude was open, sincere. She had a Liverpool accent, a T-shirt with the name of a theatre on it, and a sharp, bright wit. He had taken her for a performer of some sort – an actress or a dancer. Joy was in fact a prostitute.

Liza liked most of his friends, old and new. She admired his ability to make good friends, such as Colin and Joy, through chance. But she was puzzled by it too: he was more shy than she was.

'Different attitude I expect,' he had told her when they had talked about it.

'What do you mean?'

'I don't know, maybe I'm not as constrained as you by social convention.'

Grossly put out. 'By that you mean I'm more narrow-minded, don't you?'

'I never said that, not at all.' He had been surprised by the offence he had unwittingly caused her. 'Perhaps just a little less open to suggestion, a bit less receptive to circumstance?' In the end she had reluctantly agreed.

Eddie, who was scratching his neck, stepped forward and said hello. Samuel shook him warmly by the hand.

'You look very happy,' the Scotsman said.

'I am.' Samuel's eyes were coruscating. 'Dr Oak's been amazing. He's just achieved the impossible.'

'What's that then?'

'Well, don't laugh – he got me actually to lick the handle of a hairdrier.'

'Blimey, it'll be no time before you're giving the nozzle a blowjob,' Eddie declared.

151

The two men laughed.

'Well, you're not the only one, Sammy. I've got a bit of a cause for celebration too, as it happens.'

'Oh, yes?'

Eddie nudged his friend in the ribs. 'Oh, yes. Reckon my infestation is down by fifty per cent, which is another way of saying the itching's down by half. It won't be long now before I get rid of those dirty, jumping little buggers altogether.'

'That's great news!'

'My opinion precisely. Here, listen, what're you up to?' Eddie enquired in a whispering, conspiratorial tone.

'What, now?'

Eddie slapped his jaw, examined his palm, and nodded.

'Well, I'm on my way to school.'

'Oh,' came the disappointed response.

'Why?' Samuel asked.

'Do you want to?'

'Funny you should ask me that,' he replied. 'Every so often I wake up and think I really can't face going in, but I always do. And when I'm there, of course, it's not so bad, you know. In all my years of teaching, I've never missed a single day of work. Still, just today, I feel I'd choose to get into bed with a whirring Magimix, rather than go to school.'

Eddie's eyes were brightening. 'What you're saying here, you realise, is music to my ears. Samuel, just for once, I want you to throw responsibility to the wind.'

Monday night. Oxford Gardens.

The telephone rang.

Conrad, who had been out to supper and had just come in, answered it.

'Hello. Very well, and you? Samuel? Oh, where is he? Oh. Do you want to speak to Nell? Yes, she's right here. She's been in all evening, boning up on her Chekhov. That's right, tomorrow. We've got our fingers crossed. I know she'll make it. I hope so, too, very soon. You must come here. All right,

I'll pass you over.' He cupped his hand over the mouthpiece. 'It's Liza. She sounds a bit distraught.'

Nell was lying on the sofa, embedded in the cushions. She was wearing a huge jersey, pyjama bottoms, and thick baggy socks.

'What's up?' she whispered as she took the receiver from him. Conrad shrugged.

'Liza?'

'I tried ringing you earlier. You were engaged for ages,' Liza said.

'I was talking to Cillian about my audition tomorrow. Listen, are you all right?'

'Not really. Samuel's disappeared.'

'What do you mean?'

'Well, he left at the normal time this morning, but the school rang to say he hadn't turned up. And now it's past midnight and there's still no sign.'

'He didn't mention anything?' Nell asked.

'No, not a word. He got back late on Friday night after his dress rehearsal. They'd all been to the pub, then on somewhere I think. He spent most of the weekend working. And today there's no sign of him.'

'You didn't have a row?'

'No, nothing like that. It's so unlike him not to let me know. Normally he goes into such detail about his movements. You've heard me tease him about it.' Liza attempted to sound lighthearted, but failed. 'What if he's had an accident? Do you suppose he's had an accident?'

'I very much doubt it,' came Nell's reply. She told her sister to remember Cillian's observation that women always expect the worst.

'He's probably right, but all the same – '

'Do you want me to come over?'

'Don't worry. It's past one, and you've got your audition tomorrow.'

'Are you sure? I can be there in five minutes. It's no problem.'

153

'It's not necessary, honestly,' Liza said. 'Just, if you hear anything – '

'Of course. And promise to call me, whatever time, if you need or hear anything.'

Liza promised, and they said goodbye. Nell replaced the receiver. It made a loud clack. Conrad passed her a cup of coffee he had brought from the kitchen. He sat down on the sofa, rested her feet on his knees, and raised his eyebrow.

'Poor Liza,' Nell whispered gloomily.

'What?' Conrad enquired, taking a sip of his coffee.

'Samuel's having an affair.'

# CHAPTER

## 7

The sea and the sky were the gloomy grey of pale tarmac. Through the drizzle, they seemed to smudge into one another so the indistinct horizon was barely discernible. Far away, one skirt of light had broken through the clouds, and fallen on to a small area of water near the tiny dot of a distant boat.

As Samuel and Eddie walked down one of the steep streets towards the front and turned the corner, the famous pier came into view. It was paddling in the feebly flopping waves.

They crossed the road and made their way over to the wide entrance. Below the clock tower was a sign saying Brighton Palace Pier. They wandered past it and through the gates.

Between the gaps in the wooden boards on which they walked, they could see the water. Samuel wondered, briefly, what would happen if the floor gave way, and he joined his companion who had leaned against the railings. The white ironwork was rusty. It looked like antique lace which had been scorched by a candle flame.

'Bit of sea air, Samuel. Do you good,' Eddie remarked, smiling. 'You're looking a bit pasty. Deep breaths.' He inhaled and exhaled loudly by way of example.

Samuel followed suit.

'Oi, got a light?' Eddie asked, taking a packet of cigarettes from the pocket of his thick jacket. He nudged Sam, and winked. 'Don't want to overdose on the fresh air, now, do we?'

Samuel produced some matches. Eddie, striking one, cupped his hand over it to protect it against the wind.

'Bloody hell, it's a bit breezy out here, isn't it?' he said. 'Never mind, maybe it'll blow some of my bugs away. They deserve to drown. Come on, let's go and have a look.'

The two men wandered away from the railings and began to stroll towards the other end.

They passed the little kiosks which ran down the centre of the pier. In their windows were soft toys, sticks of Brighton rock, and an abundance of fluorescence. In one booth, there was an assortment of different popcorns – bubblegum, cinnamon, fruit cocktail. In another, which had crude pictures of pizzas, crêpes and hot dogs painted on its door, a dusty boater with a red, white and blue band was perilously perched on a bottle of ketchup. None of the stalls was open.

They passed a little hut which stood on its own to one side. There was a board in front of it which read: 'World famous clairvoyant palmist Eva Petulengro, whose knowledge does not come from books but is a gift from nature.'

'Perhaps I should ask her if the wind will blow these buggers away,' Eddie commented, as he leaned over to scratch his knee.

'Doesn't look like she's there,' Samuel observed, laughing. 'Must be her day off.'

They moved on. A lone figure with a stick nodded at them.

'This place isn't exactly crowded at the moment,' Eddie whispered when the lame old man had gone by. 'Relief.'

'I remember coming here as a child. Holidays,' Samuel told him. 'It was then.'

'What?'

'Crowded.'

'Oh, yes. Sorry.' Eddie was scratching his cheek. 'July, August, you came?'

'That sort of thing.'

'Would have been. Crowded, I mean. We used to spend our holidays in Fort William. Fucking odd, that, seeing as we used to live only about eleven miles outside it. My parents could never have been accused of being over-adventurous, I'll say that for them. You from here, originally, then?'

156

'The North,' Samuel said. 'Staffordshire. My father was a vicar. I think he met my mother here. Both on holiday with their parents. He loved Brighton, loved to come back.'

'I like it,' Eddie said. 'Does he still come here?' he asked as the pair of them approached the amusement arcade.

Samuel shook his head, and stopped. Standing before the wide entrance the machines could be clearly seen and heard. Their lights flashed ruthlessly, and their sound effects deafeningly pinged, trilled and fizzed.

'You hesitate, Samuel? Not a gambling man?'

Samuel stared a moment into the huge room full of video games and fruit machines.

'It's because you're a fucking vicar's son,' Eddie went on.

'No, I do bet sometimes.'

'On the horses?'

'Yes.'

'That's good. Remind me. I want to place a tenner on one I quite fancy at Newmarket this afternoon. Right, are you on for a quick game of something?'

'Electricity,' Samuel murmured, embarrassed.

'Oh! Fucking hell, mate, I forgot,' Eddie cried. 'God,' he added, slapping his arm. Samuel wondered if the gesture was one of self-reproach or whether the Scotsman was zapping another of his 'bugs'.

'It's okay. It's usually fine outside my own house. Only recently it's also been getting at me a bit elsewhere, but not badly.'

'Come on, you sodding great wimp, we can walk round the outside.'

'We don't have to,' Samuel said anxiously. 'I'll be fine, really.'

'Are you sure?' Eddie enquired, laughing. 'That place must be like the gates of hell for someone like you.'

'Not a bad analogy,' Samuel agreed.

'My idea of hell is to spend any time in the company of hedgehogs. I have nightmares about it. You know, one of them fucking animals has got more bugs crawling over it

157

than all this country's Delusory whatsit patients put together.'

Samuel raised a smile.

'Okay, wimp, shall we give it a try?' Eddie continued. 'We can always come straight back out again. Tell you what, if you get through to the other side, I'll treat you to one of those donut fuckers they have here! How about it? You on?'

'I'm on.'

'Here, hold on to my sleeve. I'm with you.'

Eddie proceeded to guide his friend through the arcade.

'Nearly there,' he repeated a couple of times, full of encouragement.

When they reached the exit and emerged at the other end, Samuel sighed with relief.

Eddie, more extrovert, clapped and whooed. 'That was great, that was fucking great, you know?' He dashed up to a stall beneath the huge orange and yellow awning. It advertised 'hot 'n' fresh doughnuts', and it was open.

'How many do you want, Sam, eh? You deserve a bagful.'

Samuel said, 'Just one please.'

His companion leaned his head through the little glass hatch to place the order. 'Three big doughnuts with holes, please,' he said to the fresh-faced teenager in a white coat and boater who was making them. 'That's one for my brilliant friend, and two for me!' Huge smile. 'And while you're at it, can you get them to switch that bloody muzak off?' he asked, pointing to one of the speakers above the kiosks. 'Sounds like the singer's about to croak. How about a bit of jazz or something?'

'Sorry, sir,' the boy replied, giving him the doughnuts. 'It's always music hall.'

'Ah, well,' Eddie said, shrugging and handing a doughnut to Samuel.

They turned away and carried on walking to the end of the pier, stopping at the railings to finish their doughnuts, and look at the view.

The buildings along the sea front were tall, narrow and

pale. Many were white or cream-coloured. Their mainly Georgian façades rose up behind the turquoise-green iron fence above the beach — an impressive sight even through the steam of drizzle.

Near the Grand Hotel another pier, West Pier, jutted out of the water. A large section near the shore had fallen away completely. The rest had been left to rot. From where he stood, half-closing his eyes, Samuel thought the disfigured structure looked like an old, old skull: its white bones and teeth were blackening with neglect and decay.

They stayed there a while, not saying much, just staring out to sea. After a few minutes, Eddie drew himself back from the railings.

'Fancy a walk along the beach, followed by a few beers in the pub?' he asked, hunching his shoulders against the wind.

They turned and began strolling back. This time, though, they went round the amusement arcade rather than through it.

'I don't expect you to visit hell twice in one day,' Eddie said.

Stepping on to the beach, they headed for the edge of the water. The small waves curled lazily on to the shore, as if weary of their eternal motion.

Eddie and Samuel wandered along in silence, happy to listen to the sound of the pebbles crunching under their feet, and to the screeching seagulls which swooped above them.

After a while, they came across of pile of deckchairs. They unfolded a couple and sat down.

'I haven't done this for a long time,' Samuel admitted. 'Luxury. All I'm missing is a bucket and spade.'

'Not been here since you were a kid, then? Eddie asked, handing Samuel a cigarette.

'Not since I was about fifteen, no.'

'I bet you were playing with more than a bucket and spade when you were fifteen, weren't you?' Eddie wondered out loud, teasing. 'There again, your dad was a vicar. Vicars.

159

Poncy sods most of 'em. Wouldn't know what sex was if a girl sat on their face.'

Samuel laughed.

'Did you get on with him?'

'Oh yes, very well. I had one of those country childhoods. Lots of walks with him and my brother and coming home to the fireplace, and books, and my mother's cooking.'

'Spoilt bastard. So what went wrong?' Eddie asked, 'Where along the line did you get your electricity thing? I thought that was for the likes of me. You know, the sort whose parents collect divorce papers like others collect postage stamps. We're the loonies who end up as out patients in psychiatric hospitals, and working for the BBC! Not the children of vicars with books and mothers who make Yorkshire effing pudding or whatever it is you make up there.'

Samuel laughed again. 'You make it sound idyllic and it was far from that. My mother was an alcoholic. But that's not necessarily the reason why I'm the way I am. I think anyone can be afflicted,' he said. 'In fact, I think everyone is, to a greater or lesser degree. Some of our private madnesses are madder than others, that's all. In my case, I can only imagine it all stems from guilt.'

'Yes, maybe we all have private madnesses which we never tell anybody about. Until, I suppose they get out of hand and we can't control them any more. My doctor says my problem arises from stress and depression. He tends to say things like that. Bit of a prick, see.'

'What do you reckon the reason is?'

'Well, his theory's a bit like saying the reason a kid's got head lice is because he's being bullied at school, but I dare say the man's got a point. I admit I've been feeling pretty fucking depressed for the past two or three months.'

'How long have you had the infestation?' Samuel asked, pushing his hands into the pockets of his big black coat. The drizzle was turning into rain, and his fingers had become damp and cold.

'Since about the time my wife left me. Eight weeks or so, now, must be.'

'I'm sorry.'

'Och, well, who gives a shit?' Eddie said, shrugging and pushing up the the collar of his jacket to protect his exposed neck. 'I'm liking the rain, Samuel, but maybe it's getting a wee bit too much now.' He threw back his head, opened his mouth wide and let the drops splash on to his tongue. 'Time for the pub, eh?'

They both lifted themselves up from the sunken canvas seats, and began walking towards a bar they had spotted which was on the beach itself, under the seafront.

Before entering, the two dripping figures shook themselves like dogs, and rubbed their hair vigorously.

The interior of the pub was, predictably, modelled on a ship theme – wooden floors and walls, a huge fishing net draped from the ceiling, prints of seascapes and sailing vessels.

Samuel ordered two pints of lager and took them to where Eddie had found a couple of seats, by a small window. He sat down on the hard chair and placed his drink on the table: an old beer barrel.

For an hour they talked about sport: racing, football, cricket. As they became drunker, they began to speak of other things – politics, their work. Samuel was fascinated to hear Eddie on the subject of his job. The Scotsman was a cameraman for the BBC. He was currently making a series of documentaries.

'I'm fed up, to tell you the truth,' he admitted. 'Been working my arse off these last few months, every weekend, never a break.' He picked up his glass and took a swig of his fifth, maybe sixth, pint of lager. 'It's hardly surprising – ' he added, before stopping abruptly.

'What?'

Eddie sighed deeply, before replying. 'Well, that my wife left me. Yes, she ran off with a fucking dentist.' Eddie scratched his scalp with his fingers. 'Funny, I've never trusted dentists, never liked them.'

161

'Nor me,' Samuel agreed.

'Cuthbert!' Eddie spat, aggressively striking a match and lighting a cigarette. 'That was his name. What more need I say? Poxy name, poxy guy.' He paused. 'I loved the lass,' he added, his voice quiet, pensive. 'She was called Faith. What a bleeding irony that turned out to be. Fancy a game of pool?'

Play pool? Samuel's puritanical side suddenly reminded him it was a Monday. He was playing truant as it was, but then to play pool too. It was a bit like a Calvinist gambling on Sunday.

He hesitated. Then he thought, aw, fuck it. 'Yeah,' he said smiling and nodding, 'let's go to the pub next door and see if they've got a table.'

The pub next door was rougher than the first; featureless and seedy. But Samuel and Eddie were happy. They bought more drinks, and began playing pool.

Over an hour later they cheerfully reeled outside, determined to go and find a betting shop. As they staggered up to the town, Eddie slapped his forehead, but this time it was not another bug.

'I've had a brainwave,' he declared. 'Let's place our bets and then why don't we go and book a room for what's left of the afternoon, and evening? I really fancy settling down to watch the race on telly, and calling up room service for some very late lunch and more booze. What do you say?'

Samuel liked the idea, and was thrilled that, for the course of his wholly irresponsible day, someone else was taking the initiative.

They found a bookmaker, and soon afterwards a grim little bed and breakfast with a cracked façade, and a fat landlady with a lilac apron, a figure like a cottage loaf, and a motherly expression. She seemed perfectly willing to take them in, even if it was only for a few hours, and even though the two visitors were bedraggled and drunk.

'It's the winter season,' she explained, taking them up the steep, narrow stairs. They were covered with a grey and red patterned carpet. 'And trade's very slow,' she said bleakly.

162

'I've given you a room overlooking the sea,' she declared proudly, opening the door.

Eddie thanked her politely, although Samuel suspected he was not in the ideal state really to appreciate the view.

The room was simple: bobbly wallpaper painted magnolia, two single beds pressed up against two padded plastic head boards with buttons, two chairs, one teak dressing table. Some silver swirls decorated the edges of the white formica wardrobe. His daughter, Samuel remembered, had a similar piece of furniture, only smaller, in the miniature bedroom she had set up for her Cindy doll.

'Should you wish to watch telly,' the landlady said, 'the remote control is on the bedside table. The kettle, the tea tray and some chocolate wafers are on the side there. If you want anything else – '

Eddie interrupted her with a gentle cough. 'Any chance of a drink, love?'

'Of course,' she replied, and touched her stiff bath hat of white hair.

The two men ordered some beer, and ventured to ask for something to eat. 'A couple of rounds of fish and chips?' Eddie suggested tentatively. The woman blinked but did not seem unduly put out.

'Will that be all?' she enquired. When her guests nodded, she smiled and went out of the room.

Samuel and Eddie, wasting no time, lay back on their beds against the pale blue pillows to watch the race. They became extremely excited and shouted encouragement at the horses on which they had placed bets. In vain. A matter of minutes later, they had lost £20 between them. But it soon did not bother them for there was a knock on the door and they were quickly consoled by the arrival of room service.

Eddie did not lower the television's volume with the remote control panel when the landlady came in and placed a tray on the dressing table. 'Thanks, love,' he shouted above the noise. After she had gone, he handed one of the plates to his friend.

163

'Fucking brilliant,' he said, shaking his head and picking up his fork.

'Best fish and chips I've had for ages,' Samuel remarked, taking a mouthful and grinning with pleasure. 'Here, pass the ketchup.'

'You don't mind the telly then?' Eddie asked, sprinkling some salt and vinegar over his food.

'Sometimes. When I'm at home. But it's not troubling me now in the least. Though I admit I wouldn't actually relish using the remote control.'

'That's good. It'd be a bugger if we couldn't watch it. You know, I came to a place like this with some lass once, I think it was in Weston-super-Mare, or some place. Bleeding bloody disaster. Rows and that. She wasn't into what we're doing now. Oh no. She wanted to spend all the time in goddamn wine bars, chucking Tia Marias down her neck.'

Samuel, grinning, choked on a bit of batter.

'About as raunchy as an effing clothes peg, she turned out to be too,' Eddie added. 'When I asked her for a blowjob she said, "I'd rather not, I hate the taste." I told her to get on with it and when the time came just to spit it out or duck. But she still wouldn't, the stupid bitch. That was before I got married.'

'To Faith?'

'No, before my first marriage. Faith's my second wife. And the best.'

'What happened to the first?' Samuel set aside his plate.

'I buggered off, didn't I?' Eddie sighed. 'And now the same's happened to me. Not worth it, marriage. How many times have you been married?'

'Just once. Eight years.'

'Bloody miracle.'

'Well – ' Samuel shrugged.

'Not the type of lass who wouldn't give you blowjobs, then?'

Samuel shook his head, embarrassed.

'You're all right then,' Eddie said. 'Oh, look, here's the results.'

164

Their eyes were fixed on the screen.

'Let's get room-service back again. I want to get bladdered.' Eddie laid the tray on the floor and stood up. He opened the door and shouted down the stairs to the landlady. 'Can you bring us up a bottle of whisky, please, lass?'

Then he settled down on the bed again. 'Shit, I missed that. Who won at Kempton?'

Samuel named the horse.

'Amazing.'

The landlady appeared with the whisky and two glasses, picked up the tray and went away again.

The two men carried on watching the television and began to drink in earnest. An hour or so later Eddie turned the volume down.

'What's her name, the wife?'

'Liza. Partly Scottish.'

'That's good.'

'She was brought up in Argyllshire,' Samuel told him, leaning over to reach his coat which was squatting in a heap on a chair beside the bed. He took out a battered leather wallet from one of the pockets, opened it and handed his friend a photograph.

'She looks a great lass.'

'She is.' Samuel's tone was sincere, but he was unable to conceal from his canny companion a note of regret. 'I don't ever want to lose her.'

'I bet she swallows it. So what's the problem then? You're screwing someone else.'

'How did you know?'

Eddie laughed wickedly. 'Christ, I'm so fucking pissed.' He swigged back his whisky and poured himself some more. 'Here, Sam, give me your glass. Right, that's better. Get it down you, fast. Very soon I'll have you so rat-arsed, you'll be trying to fuck that plug-socket down there.' He pointed at the skirting-board. 'One of them mistresses at that school of yours, eh?'

'How – ?'

165

'Well, you'd be fucking stupid not to, wouldn't you? Sitting ducks, I'd have thought, these lot. I remember doing it with my maths teacher when I was fourteen. She was a walk-over.' He kicked off his shoes so hard they hit a chair on the other side of the room. 'A doddle.'

'Miss Hardcastle – '

'Miss Hardcastle, oh, Mr Sorrell.' Eddie shrieked with laughter.

'Lucy,' Samuel whispered quickly. 'Lucy's not like that. She's not – '

'Not what?'

'Well, easy. You were implying she was easy.' He stopped, thinking he sounded pompous and feeble. Then with more vehemence he added, 'You're a sexist bastard, Eddie, you know that?'

'Och, balls, Samuel, I love women. Maybe I used to be a bit, aye, I agree.' The whisky made his accent stronger. 'But Faith, I'd do anything for her, you know, I love her.' Pause. 'Fucking pissed I am, I can tell you.' Another pause. He scratched the back of his hand so hard with his nails that the flesh turned the colour of raw steak. 'Blimey,' he said glancing at the television, 'that horse could do with some of these bugs. Might make him move a bit. Come on, jump, you lazy sod.'

Samuel thought he could detect a spot of blood on his knuckle where he had rubbed the 'bite'.

'You in love with the lass at the school then, this teacher?'

Samuel shrugged,

'Probably persuaded yourself you were.'

'Why would I have to persuade myself?'

'Guilt, and all that shit.'

'Is that true?'

A shout went up on the screen. Another race over. Samuel and Eddie cheered.

'Another drink, Sam?'

'Thanks.' The whisky made a satisfying glug as it poured.

'Should leave off adultery if I were you,' the Scotsman suggested unexpectedly.

'But a few minutes ago you were saying I'd be daft not to be sleeping with one of my colleagues.'

'I wasn't being entirely serious, Sam, you know. Fucking around, well, fucks everyone up, doesn't it? It fucked my poor wife up, the first one. She had a face like a boiled haggis and about as much humour as a pot plant, but she wasn't so bad. Now Faith's fucked me up: you're fucking yourself up.' Gulp of whisky. 'You love your wife.'

'Very true,' Sam agreed. 'Fuck things up and my whole world'll fall apart.'

'Too right it will, mate, so don't you go fucking it up then, eh?'

At that moment the programme ended.

'Eh, is it that late? Brilliant. Let's leave here and hit a few more pubs, and maybe a club before we go back to London? Dance. You never know, I might get to flirt with some Brighton birds.'

'You might get lucky,' Samuel said lifting himself into a standing position.

'What? You joking? I couldn't get it up now if you hoisted it with a bleeding crane.' Eddie rolled off the bed and fell on to the floor.

They laughed and staggered to the door.

'Anyway,' Eddie told Samuel, 'even if I could, I wouldn't. I'm in love with my wife, even if she does have such sodding rotten taste she can screw dentists with wanky names like Cuthbert. Come on, hurry up, Sam, put your coat on. We're going to pay and say goodbye to the landlady, then we're going to have some fun.'

'Right,' Samuel grinned.

'Yes, for a start, we're going to go back to that amusement arcade on the pier, and I'm going to play all those big machines.'

Samuel did up a button on his coat. 'Right,' he repeated.

His voice was slightly slurred but he was still grinning.

The two men stepped on to the landing and began to make their unsteady way down the stairs.

Nell was going up for the part of Varia in *The Cherry Orchard*. On Tuesday morning, the day of the audition, she awoke early, feeling anxious. It was not nerves. Auditions could not frighten her in the way they frightened the majority of aspiring actors and actresses. Unlike them, she held out little hope of success, and therefore did not mind if she was turned down.

The reason for her anxiety was that she had not heard from Liza.

Presumably, she thought, as she climbed out of bed, Samuel arrived back late last night, some time after she rang me. Otherwise, she would have called again, wouldn't she?

Conrad was still asleep. In the light which came through the antique curtains, she watched his shoulders slowly moving up and down as he breathed deeply beneath the thick blankets.

Nell put on a big cardigan and a pair of socks, and went into the sitting room to telephone her sister.

'Have I woken you?' she asked, whispering.

'Absolutely not,' came the reply. 'I'm giving Max and Nancy their breakfast.'

'I was worried about Samuel.'

'He got back not long after I spoke to you. He's fine, except for a crippling hangover this morning,' Liza told her. 'He's upstairs, shaving.'

'Oh. Where was he?'

'Brighton. Went there with a friend. He was so funny. Completely pissed.' Liza giggled. 'Could barely walk.'

'What was he doing in Brighton, for God's sake? Wasn't he meant to be at work?'

'He took the day off.'

'Why?'

'I don't know. He said he suddenly just felt like it.'

'Aren't you a bit cross?' Nell enquired, a touch impatient.

'Not really. Should I be?'

'Well, it's quite irresponsible and selfish to miss a day at school, isn't it? And not to let you know.'

168

'It was a spur of the moment thing,' Liza explained brightly.

'I see,' Nell rejoined. She paused momentarily, then quizzed her sister about the friend who had accompanied Samuel. She tried not to sound suspicious.

'I forgot to ask. Must have been someone I don't know, otherwise he'd have mentioned it. Perhaps one of his colleagues.'

Nell gulped. Precisely, sweetie, don't you see? she said to herself. I can't tell you. I couldn't, but how can you be so naive? How long can you go on not seeing the truth for yourself?

'He brought the kids back some rock,' Liza went on. 'And when we went to bed, he went on and on about how much he loved me – he's so funny when he's drunk.'

Samuel's really pushing it, Nell thought. She didn't much want to hear more details, and swiftly changed the subject. 'Listen I suppose I ought to be getting ready to go. My audition.'

'Oh, of course. The best of luck. Ring me when you get back, I'll be longing to know how it went.'

Nell replaced the receiver, and went back into the bedroom.

Conrad rolled over and opened his eyes. 'What's the time?' he asked sleepily.

'Eightish,' she replied, picking up her jeans from the floor. 'I have to go quite soon.'

'Not for a little while though. Come here a minute.' Conrad tapped the bed and grinned. 'I want to wish you good luck.'

Nell smiled, and let her jeans slip out of her hands and back on to the carpet.

An hour or two later, Nell was sitting in a small room at the National Theatre with the friendly figure who was to direct *The Cherry Orchard*.

Belinsky was a short man with a gentle voice, a soft

169

Russian accent, and splayed, white eyebrows, like the bristles on used toothbrushes. He was wearing a dark jersey, and old-fashioned shoes. Nell noticed that he blinked a great deal. His unpretentious and sympathetic air reminded her of a country doctor.

'I hope you'll forgive me for having kept you waiting,' he began. 'There seem to be an awful lot of people to see. I fear it's dreadful of me to be so slow, keeping everyone in suspense out there.'

Nell smiled.

'I'm glad you came,' he man went on. 'Did Annie tell you I wanted you to try for Varia?'

'Yes.'

'Oh, good. You see, she rang me the other day, and we were talking about you. I said I'd seen you in one of the D. H. Lawrence stories they adapted for television.'

'That's right. "Daughters of the Vicar".'

'I seem to remember I enjoyed that very much. It was the Bib?'

'The Beeb? Yes, BBC-2.'

'My pronunciation,' he said apologetically. 'It leaves a lot to be desired.'

They talked a while about what Nell had done. It did not amount to much, but Belinsky appeared unconcerned.

'Perhaps I could ask if you would read for me a little now, my dear?' he asked after a few minutes. 'Varia is a big and important part, as you probably know – ?'

Nell nodded.

' – but she doesn't really have any long speeches, so I'll read with you. That's best, the bit at the end of Act One, when she's talking to Gayev and Anya.'

Nell opened her copy of the play and found the relevant conversation.

'I'll start here,' Belinsky told her, 'where Gayev asks you "What did he say?" Found it? Okay, here we go.' The director paused, and smiled at her encouragingly before they began.

170

When they had finished, he took the biro from behind his ear and gently tapped his nose with it.

'Did you enjoy that? I did, you know, although I think I'm going to have to do a little work on my Anya. I'm not sure I've got her quite right,' he remarked, laughing. 'Perhaps we should have another go? I'd like the practice. Would you mind? I liked the way you said, "Well, why aren't you asleep, Anya?".'

The two of them began again. Nell felt she benefited from doing it a second time.

'We did better then, don't you think?' Belinsky enthused when they had come to an end. 'If we did it a third time, I'm convinced we'd be even better still.' He looked at his watch. 'Alas, my dear, I don't think I have the time. I must relieve the other people waiting.' He stood up and shook Nell's hand. 'I promise to let you know something as soon as I can. I hope we might be meeting again. It was a pleasure. Thank you.'

Belinsky walked with Nell to the door and opened it for her. Such courtesy was uncommon in directors when casting a production. Nell thought back to the smooth pseud she had encountered at the Braine play audition, and winced at the comparison between him and his Russian counterpart.

'Goodbye, my dear. And thank you again,' he said with warm civility. '*Dosvidanya.*'

'Thank you,' Nell said. As she began walking away, along the corridor and down the stairs, she heard Belinsky call the next girl into the room. She wondered how she had fared.

It was cold outside. Making her way to Waterloo underground station, her feet felt damp and hard with cold. Nonetheless, Nell found herself walking with a surprising lightness of step. This was because she had allowed herself, for a treat, momentarily to hope she might be in with a chance.

# CHAPTER

## 8

Samuel was woken by a poke in the cheek. He retrieved his hand from beneath his pillow, and with a finger propped open one of his eyes. His son, who was standing beside the bed, was trying to show him a book.

'Ow, the corner's very sharp, Max,' Samuel groaned. 'Will you take it out of my face?'

'It's *Shark-Infested Custard*, Dad.'

My brain feels like shark-infested custard, Samuel said to himself, clutching his head.

'I got it out of the library. Will you read it to me?'

'Not now, you're meant to be having breakfast,' he told him, endeavouring to sound normal.

'Boring,' Max declared. 'You've got a take-over. What comes of too much whisky, right?

Samuel nodded painfully.

'Mum said to tell you you've got to get up, Dad, or you'll be late for school.' There was that very childlike sense of urgency in the boy's voice.

'I'm getting up,' his father assured him, not moving.

'You better, or maybe the police'll get you,' Max shouted and ran out of the room.

Samuel inched himself out of bed and shuffled to the bathroom. Shaving was always a slow process – he used a brush and cream because an electric razor was not an option – but today it was slower than usual. Moving his head was a painful business. As he stared in the mirror above the basin, he was riveted by how bad he looked: puffy eyes, dulled complexion. Then he thought back to the day before and reasoned that it had been worth it.

I wonder if Eddie's feeling half as terrible, he asked himself, and wandered back to the bedroom rubbing his temples. He managed, with considerable effort, to smile all the same.

Having dressed, he went down to the kitchen. Liza was busy helping the children into their coats and strapping on their sophisticated satchels – like mini rucksacks.

'Coffee,' Samuel muttered, heading for the kettle. 'Have I got time for a piece of toast?' he wondered out loud.

'Just, if you're quick,' came Liza's reply.

Samuel glanced at her. She had her back to him and was bending down in front of their young daughter, doing up the toggles of her duffle coat. Samuel's eyes moved from his preoccupied wife to the toaster, and back.

I can't ask her to make it for me, he thought, when she's busy dealing with the children. Ridiculous. Make it yourself.

He went to the sideboard and cut a slice of brown bread. Then he neared the toaster and, at arm's length, dropped the bread into the slot. He tentatively put out his finger to the plastic lever on the side and, closing his eyes, pushed it down at an exaggerated speed before quickly retreating from it with a loud sigh of relief.

The doorbell rang. Max and Nancy said goodbye to their father and raced out to join the school run. When they had gone, Liza joined him at the table. As she sat down, the toast popped up with an energetic spring that Samuel, in his present state, envied more than feared. Liza automatically moved to fetch it for him.

'Don't worry, I'll get it,' he told her, standing up, and kissing her on the forehead. She smelt, comfortingly, of baby lotion. 'Got to take the bull by the horns,' he explained, grabbing the toast. 'It's not easy, but it can be done,' he added, his fingers jiggling beneath its heat as he took it back to the table.

There was a note of triumph in his voice: he had managed to broach the mini-nuclear power station, and, what's more, he was still alive to tell the tale.

'Lucy said you weren't feeling very well after the pub on Friday,' Ralph Simmonds commented when Samuel arrived in the staff room.

'That's right, Ralph,' Samuel said casually as he peered into his pigeonhole for any post or messages.

'Yes, we were worried about you yesterday, when you didn't come in.'

'Thanks. I'm better now,'

'I am glad. Come over all queer, did you?' Ralph's tone was soaked with insinuation.

Samuel nodded, and turned to smile at Ralph. Wryly.

'I expect she took care of you, though, didn't she? A kind-hearted soul is Lucy.'

Samuel thought what a pleasure it would give him, now, if he were to smother Ralph with that short padded jacket of his, and suffocate him in its fake fur lining.

A few minutes later, the bell rang. Samuel and Tim Crawford, 'the History Man', left together to take their lessons. Groups of boisterous pupils chatted, argued and laughed loudly as they strode along the corridors.

'Keep the noise down,' Tim told them, glancing at Samuel. 'Mr Sorrell's still not feeling particularly well. He's got a headache, so voices quiet, please.'

'What's that, Mr Crawford?' a teenage girl, chewing gum and reeking of smoke, shouted. 'I didn't hear you.'

'Shut up, Madeleine,' Tim said authoritatively,

Madeleine did so and went into the classroom. The other pupils followed her while the two teachers remained outside a moment for a brief word.

'How did you know I've got a headache?' Samuel asked Tim, impressed.

'That exchange just now with Ralph. He's enough to give anyone a headache, eh?'

174

'A pain in the arse, more, I think. The headache's just a hangover. I wasn't ill, exactly, yesterday, you see.'

'No?'

'No. I went on the piss I'm afraid.'

Tim laughed. 'Not like you, Sam. Was it stress of the job, or troubles of a domestic nature?'

'Combination of the two.'

Tim opened the door of his classroom and, before entering, gave Samuel a knowing wink.

Samuel smiled and made his way to the labs in time for the first lesson.

During the lunch break, Samuel went to the small office which he shared with two other science teachers in his department. Neither of them was there. Samuel was relieved. It meant he had an hour to himself. He could work undisturbed.

It was a poky room on the fourth floor of the main school block. The metal-framed window, similar to those at the hospital (both buildings went up in the early 1960s and were equally grim) overlooked the playground. On its sill were piles of exercise books. An ailing plant was trying to flourish in an old yoghurt pot on a sulky-green saucer. The edges of its leaves had turned yellow and crinkly, like the page of a book which had been dropped in the bath. Letters and old memos vied for attention on the hessian noticeboard which hung against the chipped walls.

Samuel looked at the communal desk. In fact, calling it a desk elevated its status. It was actually just a plain table. It took up most of the room, and was cluttered with papers, textbooks and files. The telephone was hiding behind a wooden stand holding five dirty test-tubes.

He sat down and pushed some things aside to make way for the latest heap of work he had to deal with. There were a number of letters to parents he needed to write, and revisions to the various science modules to fit in with the national curriculum, as well as endless marking, and tedious admin.

Samuel's head was thumping and he began to despair of ever finding the time to do all the tasks. Four weeks ago he had promised a pupil who had bad eyesight that he would enlarge the worksheets to enable her to read them. The poor girl, through no fault of her own, was getting behind. Yet it was nothing to do with his fear of the photocopier, which Dr Oak was helping him to overcome – he simply hadn't managed to reach the machine, let alone use it. Every time he had joined the queue, either the bell had gone, or someone diverted him with an even more urgent problem that had to be seen to immediately.

There was a knock on the door.

'Yes?'

It was a couple of boys in his tutor group who had had a fight and who he had asked to come and see him for a pep talk. He had forgotten he was expecting them.

'Oh God, it's you two,' he said. 'Right, what was all that trouble about on Friday, then?'

A rush of explanations followed.

Samuel put up his hand to quieten them. 'Okay, okay, I don't want excuses,' he said, tired. 'You're fourth years, for goodness sake, fighting like first years. It's pathetic. Boring.'

'Yes, Mr Sorrell.'

He proceeded to admonish them for a minute or two. 'It's not me you'll be reporting to next time, but you know who in school HQ. Got it?' he said towards the end.

The boys nodded.

'Right, be off with you. Now, leave me to get on with my work, and here's a novel notion, why don't you go and do some of yours? Have you mastered the difference between a cervix and a urethra yet, Mark? I seem to remember you were rather confused by them in the last lesson. And I feel you'd probably do well to learn the difference sooner rather than later, bearing in mind your well-voiced sexual desires, if not your desires to pass your GCSE exam.'

Mark, who, at fifteen, had enough sexual bravado to keep a football team going, but not enough sexual knowledge to label a basic diagram, bit his lip, embarrassed. He and his companion slouched out of the room.

Samuel breathed deeply and picked up his pen. Under a minute later there was another knock on the door.

'Oh, what?' he called impatiently. 'Who is it now? Come in.'

When the door opened he did not look up from his papers. 'You'll have to wait a second,' he murmured as he continued to write. When he had finished his sentence, he put down his pen.

'How can I – ?' he began, turning to see the intruder.

It was Lucy.

He leapt out of his chair.

'Oh, my God, I'm sorry. It's you. I assumed it was one of the kids. I've been plagued by – well, anyway. Er, goodness here, sit down. Yes.'

Samuel went round to his colleague Nigel's side of the desk and pulled out his chair for her.

Lucy thanked him and sat down. Her long dark hair was shiny and well brushed. The fringe appeared to dip into her eyes. Samuel felt the urge to brush the strands away for her, just as he had removed a hair from her lip the other night. But he restrained himself.

'I know you're very busy,' Lucy began.

'Well – ' Samuel shrugged, 'no more than usual. It's good it's you. You're a much nicer distraction than the two loutish fourth years I've just had to see, Mark Beck and Pete Stevens.'

'Oh, them,' Lucy said knowingly. 'Pains in the neck, those two. Poor you. What was it?'

'Had a fight. It's the third time in a fortnight and, you know, I could do without – ' he stopped abruptly. 'Sorry, this is very boring, it makes me so cross.'

Lucy nodded.

Awkward silence, momentarily.

'Listen, goodness, I mustn't keep you,' she began again. 'I only really wanted to make sure you were happy with everything for tomorrow night?'

177

'Well, as long as you think I performed all right on Friday night?'

Pause.

There was an almost tangible ripple of embarrassment in the air.

'You know,' Samuel went on quickly. 'I mean, acted, yes, as long as you think I acted all right on Friday night?'

'Yes . . . yes,' Lucy assured him, nodding.

'Despite the line fluffing?'

'As Barbara said in the pub, no one but you noticed.'

'No? No. Of course. That's right, isn't it? She said. I remember. Yes.'

Samuel picked up his pen and chewed the lid.

'Costume all right, and everything?'

'Absolutely. Fine, thanks,' he replied.

Lucy stood up. Samuel stood up too.

'I must let you get back – ' Lucy glanced at his pile of work, but she did not finish her sentence. She picked up a buff-coloured folder she had brought in with her, and clutched it to her breast. Looking over it and down at her feet, she quietly said that she hoped he was feeling better, 'after yesterday, being off sick'.

'Oh, yes, thank you. Much better today,' he lied. 'Last week – a hard week. Over-tired, I think, mainly, what with work, and the play. Anyway, I'll be even better tomorrow. I won't be letting the side down, I can promise you – Lucy.'

'No, I didn't think – '

'Raring to go, I am, for the first night,' Samuel declared, holding the pen between his teeth and forcefully pushing up the sleeves of his charcoal Shetland jersey.

'I think it'll be good, if the dress rehearsal was anything to go by,' Lucy remarked, edging towards the door. Still facing Samuel, she put her hand behind her back and held on to the handle. 'I'm glad you're better anyway,' she added brightly.

He smiled and thanked her. 'Thanks.'

'Yes . . . well . . .'

Lucy rubbed her fingertips up and down the edges of the

178

buff-coloured folder. Samuel, still standing pointlessly, shifted papers about on the desk.

'I meant to thank you,' she ventured quietly, nodding, 'for giving me a lift the other evening. Friday.'

'Ah yes. No problem,' Samuel stated emphatically. 'No, it was a pleasure. It was on my way home.'

'Of course,' Lucy muttered, turning the handle and stepping aside to open the door. 'Well, if I don't see you later, tomorrow then.'

'Let me know if there are any last-minute panics, and I'll help you out.'

'I will, but I hope there won't be,' she said girlishly, holding her hand up with her fingers crossed. 'See you, then.'

'Bye,' Samuel said softly as she closed the door behind her.

Left alone, he slumped himself down on to his hard chair, plonked his elbows on the table, and put his throbbing head into his hands.

Samuel pulled on a pair of dance tights. He stood up and walked about to get used to them. The thick nylon clung to his legs like the rubbery skin round a frankfurter.

It was the opening night of *A Midsummer Night's Dream*. The curtain was due to rise in half an hour. Samuel was in one of the tiny music practice rooms behind the stage, changing into his costume. He put his hands in the air and dropped a long kaftan-like robe from the school's wardrobe over his head. It was rather too short for him, reaching to just above his ankles.

'Samuel, are you in there?'

It was Ralph's voice. Ralph was sharing Samuel's dressing room. Typically, he had been ready at least three-quarters of an hour earlier, and had gone off to see if he could give a last-minute helping hand on stage.

Doubtless, Samuel thought, he's been making a nuisance of himself, being bossy with scenery and Barbara has sent him back to wait here.

'Come in,' he said limply.

'Oh my,' Ralph proclaimed with a theatrical flourish. 'You look quite the part.'

'Shut up,' Samuel ordered him, with a fierceness that surprised himself.

'Oooh, do I detect just a little bit of a sense of humour failure there, Sam? Or is it the first-night nerves?'

Samuel looked at Ralph's long white beard which Rachel had stuck on for him with special glue, and was tempted to tug at it like a bell-rope and so scorch his silly face, challenge his smug smile. He ignored Ralph's question.

'Is Rachel coming along with the make-up box?' he asked him instead, slipping on a pair of purple velvet Chinese slippers.

'Very King of the Fairies, very appropiate,' Ralph remarked, looking at the Henry VIII-style footwear.

Samuel scowled.

'Yes,' the geograpy teacher went on. 'She's just finishing off the children, and will be along the corridor in a minute. The hall's getting packed out there, you know. I think we're going to have ourselves a full house. Listen,' he said, opening the door ajar. 'The noise.' He closed it again.

'That's encouraging, anyway.'

'Is your wife coming tonight, tomorrow or Friday?'

'Tonight. With the two children and my sister-in-law, who's a professional actress.'

'Oh yes? What's she called then? Is she famous?'

'Not yet. But she will be. She's been in a few things. She's very good,' Samuel enthused, doing up the few unfastened gold bobbles at the top of his robe. 'Nell John.'

'I'll look out for her. Blimey,' Ralph said, 'the collar of this canvas jacket doesn't half scratch my neck.'

Inwardly Samuel rather wished that the collar, while it was at it, might sever Ralph's neck altogether.

There was a knock on the door. It was Rachel English. She smiled at Samuel but forgot to smile at Ralph.

Her costume was a chiffon dress which flowed like a

180

ballroom dancer's, but, in soft green and greys, was far more understated, nowhere near as vulgar. The only conspicuous clue that perhaps a slightly starrier nature might lurk beneath her quiet and modest exterior, was in the hair accessory – wound into a Greek plait was a twist of gold tinsel.

Samuel noticed Rachel was also wearing Dali-red lipstick. Like Lucy's. Playing Titania had given her the excuse, obviously. He allowed himself, silently, to be touched, before berating himself for making self-important assumptions.

He felt he should tell her how nice she looked, but it didn't come out quite as he had planned. He told her she looked 'right', which was a bit different, and not as good, but she seemed pleased all the same.

Then, spotting her opaque white tights, he rapidly changed the subject.

'How can you bear to wear these things every day?' he asked, bemused. 'They're so uncomfortable.'

Rachel put the blue metal make-up box on top of the stand-up piano, sat him down in front of the keyboard, closed the lid, and placed a small round mirror on the narrow ridge meant for sheet music.

As she did so, Samuel fancied she shimmered, slightly, with delight.

'You get used to them,' she replied with cloying sweetness.

Ralph watched keenly as she sponged foundation over Samuel's face and blackened his eyebrows.

'We had real giggles when I was doing this next door,' Rachel said. 'The girls were all teasing Jeff because he looks so pretty with make-up on. He makes a very striking Demetrius, I think. Kathy said she could almost fancy him in real life, not just as Helena, and got so embarrassed it was really funny.'

'Poor Jeff,' Ralph remarked. 'He's in my tutor group. Cripplingly shy. I have to hand it to Lucy, she's really boosted his confidence by giving him such an important part in this, and it's paid off. I think he's good, don't you?'

Samuel and Rachel agreed.

'Lucy's in with them all now, encouraging them along, wishing them luck,' the latter said. 'Did you two contribute towards her surprise bouquet?'

Samuel nodded.

'Yes, Kathy was organising it. She came round earlier today,' Ralph said. 'Some of us were more generous than others,' he added, eyeing Samuel. 'I didn't have much loose change on me. But this one here came up trumps. A positive walking bureau de change you turned out to be, didn't you, Sam?'

'I gave two pounds,' Samuel told Rachel, his voice frigid with irritation.

'A grand gesture, nonetheless. As befits your kingly status,' Ralph pointed out. 'It was more than most of us managed.'

Loud voices were heard outside the door. Ralph opened it. A gaggle of children and young teenagers in colourful makeshift costumes were waiting to take their positions on stage.

'Oi, you lot, keep quiet. You don't want them to hear out front. Silence please.'

'Where's your ducal crown, Mr Simmonds?' a gawky girl asked. She was wearing a muslin dress of pale blue with maroon felt diamonds sewn on to its bodice. On her feet were leather ballet shoes, baby-lotion pink, with grubby elastic straps.

'Oh my God, good point. I clean forgot,' he exclaimed, clutching his head and looking about him with the frantic air of Lear's Fool. 'Help! We start in three minutes, I can't go on without it. Where is it?' Stepping back into the dressing room, he searched everywhere. 'You're not sitting on it, are you, Samuel?'

'So likely I'd be lounging on a chair, calmly allowing my face to be covered with Max Factor liquid skin, if I had a ruddy great crown up my arse,' he whispered in reply, as Rachel dabbed one or two extra spots of foundation on to his forehead. She then applied to his chin a stiff and matted beard which looked like a spaniel's ear, and smelt like one too.

'I can't find it,' Ralph moaned desperately. 'I shall have to ask Barbara.'

'Barbara's far too busy,' Rachel informed him, putting her brushes, creams and pencils back in the make-up box. 'Okay, Samuel. Stand up, let's have a look at you.'

Samuel, restricted by his tights (he had never felt so packaged) rose slowly.

'Wow! You look brilliant,' she declared with a nervous giggle. 'I love the way the heavy arched eyebrows complement the dark brown beard.'

'Never mind his bloody eyebrows, what about my crown?'

'For goodness sake, Ralph, stop fussing. I'll come and help you look for it in the other music rooms. It's bound just to have got muddled up with everyone else's stuff. What is it like?'

'Cardboard, sprayed gold, with coloured fruitgum jewels.'

'Is this it?' she enquired, on her way out, spotting one on the floor in the corner and bending down to pick it up.

'No,' came the reply. 'That's silver. That's Samuel's,' he added, following her into the corridor. 'Mine's rather grander than that.'

A minute later, Samuel heard a small commotion in the corridor swiftly followed by a fanfare – in truth, that was a somewhat generous description – of toy trumpets, and a hush in the hall. Then the crank of the curtain mechanism, brief silence, and Ralph's lofty acting voice:

Now, fair, Hippolyta, our nuptial hour
Draws on apace . . .

183

Pity poor Hippolyta, Samuel said in his head. Fate worse than death.

He picked up his crown, left his modest room and tiptoed to join the other pupils and members of staff who were in their costumes and watching from the wings.

Lucy was sitting on a tall stool with a copy of the play open on her lap, poised to prompt if necessary. She wore dark colours, as usual – a brown wool skirt, black jersey and tights. Although she had her back to him, he was impressed by the way she looked, taken by her stillness.

At the end of Scene One, she turned round. Spotting him, she smiled and mouthed, 'Good luck'.

During Scene Two he went back to his room to go over his lines.

'Ill met by moonlight, proud Titania,' he whispered. 'Met . . . moonlight . . . Titania . . . t . . . t . . . t . . . t. Diction, remember, Samuel. Nell'll be wanting to see the fruits of her labours.' He carried on practising.

Ten minutes later, there was a knock on the door. Barbara burst in, a sartorial fanfare of pink and yellow. She had dressed up for the occasion: shiny shirt with neck bow attached and a woollen skirt covering the extravagant bottom.

Samuel refrained from telling her she reminded him of a Battenberg cake.

'You're on, Samuel, come on. Best of luck.'

Moments later, he stepped out on the stage and into Barbara's bower.

The scenery was made of cardboard stapled to wooden frames, and painted with powder paint – brown treetrunks, green leaves. This scanty 'wood' was dimly lit with blue 'moonlight'.

Samuel surreptitiously glanced out at the audience and was aware of hundreds of dark, invisible eyes upon him – among them, somewhere, Max's, Nancy's, Liza's, Nell's.

What would they make of his purple slippers?

There was a moment of panic, just before he had to say his

first line, when his stomach seemed to curdle and turn to pigswill.

Alliteration, he reminded himself before beginning –

'Ill met by moonight, proud Titania,' he said out loud.

He just had time to wonder if Nell had appreciated the formation of his lips for 'moonlight'. He felt – since her lesson in Wales – he had improved on the cat's arse no end.

'Tarry, rash wanton! am not I thy lord?' he asked, his voice spurred on by a little more self-confidence.

During Titania's long speech, shortly afterwards, Samuel's nerves slowly started to abate so that he was actually able to listen to her words and become more aware of the other characters on stage. Following her exit he found he could pronounce

Well, go thy way: thou shalt not from this grove
Till I torment thee for this injury

with all the appropriate forcefulness the words required.

Left alone with Puck (played by a talented third former who had a naturally comic sense, and who looked mischievous in a green leotard and green tights) Samuel began to enjoy himself to the extent that he even laughed spontaneously at one of Puck's jokes.

Before he knew it, it was the end of the performance and the cast was taking its bow to loud claps. There were cheers from the audience as Lucy was presented with her bouquet.

When the curtain fell, the children exuberantly whooped and laughed, and spilled into the hall to find their parents. Some of the girls hugged each other, while the boys slapped their friends on the back with shouts of 'Congratulations, mate, you were brilliant'.

Rachel was the first to tell Samuel he was brilliant. He thanked her warmly, and returned the compliment.

'Is Liza here?' she enquired, studiedly bright. 'Coming to the backstage party?'

'I hope so. I better go and look for her, if you'll excuse me.'

185

Another smile. He trotted down the steps and found his family in a middle row. Nell fluffed her hand through his hair with affectionate enthusiasm for his performance.

'Moooonlight,' he mouthed, making her laugh. He lifted Nancy to carry her up on to the stage. The others followed.

Barbara, who was walking round with a tray, came up to them, effervescing with cheer, and offering them plastic cups filled with orange squash.

Then Ralph joined them with a boot-faced expression (he never did find his crown). But he smiled as he said hello to Liza, and lit up when he was introduced to Nell.

'Ralph Simmonds,' Samuel uttered grimly. Max had knelt down amongst the grown-up calves, and was examining his father's slippers, tickling his ankles.

'Geography,' Ralph informed Nell, holding out his hand. 'Head of the department, in fact. Will you be coming to the pub afterwards with the other members of the staff involved in this our modest little production? You're a professional actress, I hear.'

'Er, I don't know, are we invited?' She turned to her brother-in-law. She noticed the lady who had been given the flowers was standing just behind him: Lucy Hardcastle.

Nancy, who was now in Liza's arms, and whose upper lip was the alarmingly artificial colour of orange squash, began to cry.

Samuel hesitated before replying to Nell's question. 'Of course, you all are.'

'I think I should be getting home,' Liza remarked, wiping her daughter's face and trying to soothe her. 'Bed, I think, for these two. They're both exhausted.'

'I ought to come home with you,' he told her.

'Don't be daft. You must to go to the pub with the others.'

'I suppose they might think me a bit unfriendly if I didn't go for at least a short while,' he explained.

'Yes, you must,' Liza urged cheerfully.

'I'm going to see to it I get Rachel English a little bit tipsy tonight,' Ralph boasted. 'You can't miss that, Samuel. I failed

186

after the dress rehearsal. Couldn't wean her off the Virgin Marys for love nor money,' he added, winking lasciviously at Nell.

Samuel experienced a bolt of resentment, but before he could say anything, someone bumped into the back of him in the crush, and knocked off his crown.

'Steady now, you lot.' It was Lucy's voice behind him.

Nell, Ralph, Liza and Lucy all within a square foot of each other. Did this constitute a crisis?

The spotlights at the foot of the stage were beginning to bother Samuel. Such heated, gratuitous electricity.

Don't even think about it, he told himself, quickly averting his eyes. Max, who was still on the floor, passed him his fallen crown.

'I'm so sorry, Samuel,' Lucy apologised. She was pressed up against him and he caught a nostalgic whiff of her rosehip breath. 'You were wonderful.'

As he thanked her, he felt Nell's eyes fall heavily upon him.

Liza shook Lucy's hand. Samuel simply shook.

'I loved it,' he heard her saying. He glanced at his wife, whose words were touchingly sincere. Her brown hair was tied back in a pony tail. Loose strands fell about her pale face which was innocent of make-up. She looked little older than a teenage schoolgirl.

'You must be Liza,' Lucy said, sweetly, shyly. Then she cast her eyes towards Nell, and guessed she and Liza were sisters. There was an awkward silence when she imagined Samuel might be going to introduce them. He did not.

'I think I'd better squeeze through this lot,' Lucy said hastily, 'and go and check everything's in order backstage.' She made to move away, but Ralph stopped her.

'You haven't met Samuel's sister-in-law, Lucy, I don't think,' he said. 'Nell John . . . Lucy Hardcastle.'

Samuel stared at Ralph, incredulous.

I've a good mind to take a bunsen burner, ram it up your arse, and switch it on full blast, he yelled at him, in his head.

187

'Oh yes, sorry, I forgot,' he muttered. 'Nell . . . Lucy . . . yes.'

'This young lady's a professional actress, Lucy,' Ralph said, nudging her elbow and winking at the same time. 'And she's coming to the pub for a drink with us tonight, so perhaps you can discuss the performance.'

'Actually,' Nell chipped in very politely, 'I think I'm going to go back with Liza.'

'Why?' her sister and Ralph said simultaneously.

'I ought to be getting home,' Nell replied softly, her long fingers fiddling with the zip of her suede bomber jacket.

'Conrad's not expecting you till much later,' Liza stated. 'Go on, you must go. It'll be fun.'

Nell glanced at Samuel. He had pushed his hair away from his face to reveal his widow's peak and an anxious frown. She was not angry with him, but she was adamant.

'No,' she told her sister firmly. 'I'm coming with you.'

Liza did one of those semi shrugs. It seemed to say, Oh all right then but I don't see why.

Barbara came round again with another tray. She thrust it in front of Liza and Nancy.

'Would you like a biscuit?' she asked the latter in that sugary voice middle-aged spinsters often reserve for children.

Nancy declined, but Ralph stretched his hand out and said, 'Barbara, if I may?'

'My pleasure,' said Barbara and seemed to shimmer with it. Her smile suggested to Samuel she might have preferred to give Ralph more than a chocolate digestive. Perhaps dizzily, certainly a little unsteadily, she leaned over to Lucy.

'I'm afraid,' she whispered loudly, 'there's been a bit of a whoopsie in Music Room Two. Our Little Peaseblossom's had one too many of these.' Barbara pointed at the biscuits. 'And been sick all over Mustardseed's costume. I've cleaned it up, but she's rather upset. Might you go and have a word?'

Lucy nodded, excused herself, and disappeared through the throng towards the wings.

188

'Time to get changed out of these fancy togs and into gear a bit more suitable for the pub,' Ralph said. 'Chop, chop, Samuel. Everyone's beginning to go home, so we can be off in a minute.'

Liza jogged Nancy more securely on to her hip. 'We must go. Come on, Max, up you get.'

Nell took her nephew's sticky hand.

'Will you be at home when I get back?' Samuel asked her.

'I'm going to help Liza put the children to bed, but then I'll be taking the tube home. Depends how long you're intending to be?' Light tone. Loaded question.

Barbara was complimenting Liza on her children.

'I'll get away as soon as I can,' Samuel told his sister-in-law quietly, desperately.

'Huh!' barked Ralph, nudging Nell, winking and tapping the side of his nose with his forefinger like the unsubtle quizmaster of a cheap game show. 'We've heard that one before, now, haven't we?'

Samuel looked at Ralph. He stared at his nose, which resembled a snail, and his horse-manure eyes.

The geography teacher had one of those inane smiles which caused the science teacher's hands automatically to form into fists. Samuel hastily pushed them deeply into the pockets of his robe. It was a necessary precaution: he feared at that moment that the violent dislike he felt for his odious colleague might well have manifested itself in a manner rather too animated to be acceptable.

Samuel had one drink in the pub, but was agitated. Rachel talked to him energetically – Ralph had managed to persuade her to have a Bloody Mary – but he could not wholly concentrate on what she was saying.

Lucy, who should have been triumphant, seemed subdued. His eyes strayed in her direction. She was sitting on a low stool talking to Barbara. A clipboard and a box of rosehip tea stuck out of the straw basket by her feet. She was looking down at her busy fingers which were playing with the strap of the handbag on her lap. He wondered at the fact that his

189

hand had meandered over the creamy skin visible through the ghostly weave of her thin tights. He still felt the urge to caress it once more.

'I can't believe it's the end of term in two days' time,' Rachel was saying to him excitedly. Her loose hair, released now from the tinsel's spidery binding, was unusually corrugated. 'And Christmas upon us any minute. Less than a week.' She sipped at her bright red drink, her gaze lingering on his face appreciatively.

Samuel could not think of Christmas. He was busy begging himself not to offer Lucy a lift home.

Ralph was at the bar chatting to Stationery Store Cynthia.

Samuel stood up. 'I'm going to be making my way,' he announced softly, weakly, and paused before adding, 'if anyone wants a lift?' He rubbed his eyebrows with the side of his finger.

Barbara, Rachel and Lucy all looked up.

'Already?' the pink and yellow spinster asked. 'That's a shame.'

Rachel said nothing.

Lucy bit her red lip and said simply, 'Please.' She picked up her basket from the swirling carpet, and said goodbye to her colleagues. Then she and Samuel made for the door without another word, both careful to avoid Ralph on the way out. He was still at the bar, talking to Cynthia, but neither of them felt it was necessary to interrupt his conversation to let him know of their departure.

They walked the short distance to Samuel's car in silence. On the way to Lucy's flat, they might have exchanged a comment or two, but nothing of consequence.

Outside her building, Samuel parked, yet did not switch off the engine.

Lucy stared ahead, her eyes rigidly fixed on the black raindrops which measled the windscreen.

A couple, arm in arm, tottered past Samuel's side window. The girl's heels clicked hard on the pavement, like nails hammering into a coffin.

'The play,' he began awkwardly.

'Yes?'

'I think it was a success.'

'Yes.'

'One performance down. Two to go.'

Lucy nodded.

'I'm exhausted,' Samuel remarked. His tone managed to imply something more than mere fatigue.

Silence.

'What are you thinking?' Lucy enquired, barely audible.

'I don't know.'

'No.' Her eyes had graduated to the windowscreen mirror. 'Everything all right with your costume, and everything?' she said to spike the silence. 'I mean – '

'Lucy?' Samuel turned to her and gazed at her dark, upturned profile. 'Everything's fine.'

'That's good.' She nodded to emphasise her point.

'I'm expected back at – '

'Yes. Of course.' Pause. 'My aunt's still in Ireland, so I was thinking we wouldn't be disturbing . . . well . . . I was thinking, just a cup of tea. Rosehip? There again . . .' Her voice petered out.

'Perhaps better . . .'

'Not?' Tremulous, that one syllable.

Samuel nodded and reiterated, 'Not.' He could hear his companion swallow loudly. 'I don't know what – ' he said.

'What?' she asked too quickly.

'I don't know what the time is?'

'Eight thirty-five,' came the disappointed response. She added, 'I don't know what to think.'

'To think?'

'Yes.'

'Ah,' Samuel whispered.

'Well.'

Pause.

Nor me, Samuel thought. I don't know what to think about what. I can think of nothing.

191

'Rosehip tea?' she prompted reasonably.

'Miss – Lucy, you see, Lucy, I love, oh, I don't know, I love . . .'

Lucy anticipated the end of the sentence. It didn't come.

'I love it too. But rosehip isn't everyone's cup of tea,' she commented, managing to raise a feeble smile.

'I can see its charms entirely,' Samuel assured her. 'It's just that, I'm sorry, but I expect, supper, it's probably nearly ready.'

'Absolutely. I mustn't keep you. You must be hungry as well as tired.'

'Oh yes.'

Lucy reached for the door handle and cocked her finger round the black plastic lobe. Then she turned her face towards him.

'Thank you for the lifts,' she said rather formally. 'I've appreciated the lifts.'

Samuel, who fancied that her eyes glistened – maybe it was the reflections from the street lamps? – said, 'Any time.'

Conrad was not expecting Nell back until late.

Nell arrived back home earlier than expected.

Conrad was not in the sitting room.

Nell went along to the bedroom.

The door was ajar. Through it could be seen the faint glow of the bedside lamp, barely stronger than that of two candle flames, shedding its feeble light on the walls which were painted with rough brush strokes of deep burnt sienna. Strewn across the floor's rush matting were shadowy droppings of clothes, shoes, books. The looming antique wardrobe of shiny wood, conker brown, was open. The yellowing long mirror fixed into its door was as bespeckled as a free-range egg. In it was reflected the thick dark material of the old curtains which were drawn across the casement window.

The place smelt unfamiliar, but lovely all the same. Lavender.

A damp towel had been flung over the black wrought-iron bed-end. The bed itself, as usual, was unmade – sheets and blankets twisted, falling over the edges of the mattress.

Conrad was lying on his back, eyes closed. There was about his face, resting in profile on one of the squashed pillows, a look of considerable joy. He might have been dreaming.

Nell stood silently in the doorway. For some moments she remained there, undetected, watching her boyfriend, identifying and recognising from some distance that particular expression.

She wondered if the naked girl who was currently sitting astride his naked body, and therefore able to focus upon his face close up, appreciated it in the same way she had done on similar occasions.

Perhaps she was not looking. Nell could not tell: the girl had her back to her. Maybe her eyes weren't open as she groaned breathily, and slowly rocked back and forth, her compact little bottom prettily rubbing the tops of his thighs

Nell saw her boyfriend reach his hand to his guest's breasts. As the girl in turn put her hand out and stroked his uplifted bicep, Nell, a sharp observer, did not fail to notice the ring on her third finger.

She had seen it before, that silver band with the one large glass eye.

It seemed, unblinking in the smoky dimness, to stare at her. Like Cyclops.

'I thought I'd open a bottle of wine.'

All of a sudden the gentle movement on the bed froze.

'I'll be next door,' Nell, who was leaning against the doorframe with her arms folded, said breezily. 'So, when you're ready.'

She turned away into the dark passage and walked along to the kitchen.

'Red or white?' she called, taking three glasses from the cupboard. Then she laughed to herself, but could not have explained why.

In fact, she decided, she would like red; and because Conrad and his friend did not appear to have heard her, or anyway weren't answering, she took it they had no preference, so went ahead and opened some cheap claret.

Conrad came running in, as white as the damp towel wrapped around his waist.

'What are you doing?' he asked desperately.

'I told you, opening some wine. I hope Miranda – '

'Marina,' he corrected automatically.

'Sorry, Marina – I met her at Hilary's private view, didn't I? – likes red?'

'Nell, don't do this,' he pleaded. The bedroom expression had disappeared completely. 'Please, sweetheart. For God's sake, this calm.'

'I feel very calm,' she assured him sweetly. 'I promise I won't suddenly go mad like a psychopath, and attack you with a kitchen knife. You caught me – or rather I caught you – in a good mood. The school play was great. Samuel was wonderful.'

'I'm glad,' Conrad said in a voice too heavy to muster anything but a whisper.

'You should've come,' Nell told him, stopping abruptly, realising what she had just said. 'Is Marina getting dressed?'

Conrad nodded.

Nell picked up the bottle and the glasses and, without another word, left the kitchen. She came across Marina who, fully clothed now, was sneaking out of the bedroom.

Nell said hello.

The visitor looked alarmed.

'Hi, I'm Nell, Conrad's girlfriend. We've met. Drink?' she asked, striding past her and into the sitting room.

Marina did not know how to respond, so remained silent.

'Come in,' Nell encouraged her, lowering herself on to the sofa.

'Where's Conrad?' the girl enquired meekly, following her.

'Probably still freaking out in the kitchen,' came the honest reply.

'Oh.'

'I'm so glad you didn't clutch the sheet to your breast like people do in films,' Nell remarked. 'Needlessly melo-dramatic.' She gave Marina a glass of wine.

'Are you sure?' the girl said, before taking it.

'Why not? You're here.'

'Yes,' agreed Marina, embarrassed.

Conrad appeared at the door. 'Marina, I think you better go,' he said firmly.

'It's all right – ' Nell began, taking a paper handkerchief out of a pocket. She noticed its colour for some unknown reason. Yellow. Like Cillian's socks, she thought, as she blew her nose. She was not crying, she just had a cold.

'No,' Conrad shouted at Nell unexpectedly, 'it's fucking not all right.' He then yelled at Marina. 'I said go.' He literally pointed at the door.

Marina clutched a rather nice kelim bag to her middle. It was a pretty pattern of pale muted colours – pink, cream, brown – a good combination, Nell reflected. And it had a sturdy leather strap. She wanted to ask her where she got it, but inwardly acknowledged that it was not perhaps the most appropriate moment to do so. And she resisted.

Marina made a swift exit.

When Conrad and Nell were left alone together, silence fell, and she saw that he was shaking. He looked like a man with a severe case of flu – shivering and sweating at the same time. He parted his lips, but no words came out. She feared he might have been going to be sick.

'Here, have some wine,' Nell said, holding a glass out to him. 'Marina didn't have time to finish this. I don't expect you'd mind drinking hers, would you? Pity to waste it.' She leaned back against the sofa cushions, stretched her legs forward and rested her feet on the low table in front of her.

Conrad approached her slowly.

'You must be cold,' Nell pointed out, sipping her wine.

He did not reply, but moved closer to her. She looked him up and down. In the half light he appeared to be especially pale, the colour of goat's milk; and she could see he had goose pimples. She wondered if she were to touch his bare flesh whether it would feel like the rind of a mild goat's cheese. But she found herself disinclined to try.

As he sat down beside her, he still did not say anything. So Nell spoke again, instead.

'The sheets needed a change,' she told him pragmatically. The thought had suddenly entered her head. Pensive, she rotated her tongue round the inside of her glass. 'Yes, I've been meaning to do it for a couple of days. But I might leave that to you, now, if you don't mind. You know. Well . . . other people's . . .'

'A bit below the belt, Nell,' Conrad spat, incredulous, endeavouring to control himself.

'Domestic detail, merely, I'm sorry if it upsets you in some way. I didn't mean to – '

'Fucking hell,' he blasted, taking her shoulders in his hands and shaking her. 'Scream at me, be angry. Christ, Nell, do something. Hit me.'

'I've no intention of hitting you. Why should I?'

'Because,' he gasped, 'you have just found me fucking someone else in our bed. You might react. I just want you to react. You don't give a shit, do you?'

'Listen, of course I give a shit,' she informed him beadily, 'but I'm not prepared to go in for melodrama when it comes as no surprise.'

'That's precisely why I did it.'

'Why?'

'Because you were so bloody untrusting. You drove me to it, with all your pessimistic predictions. I thought what the hell? Why not? I might as well if Nell thinks I'm doing it anyway. Comes to the same thing.'

'I admire your sense of logic,' Nell laughed. 'You should be grateful to it. It's served you rather well, hasn't it? You looked as though you were having a very agreeable time with Marina. She's sweet, and pretty. Nice bum, too.' As she spoke, Nell noticed there was about his hair that familiar

196

post-coital dishevelment. It seemed to her, now, rather less appealing than it had on those occasions when she was responsible for it.

'Nell, don't,' Conrad ordered aggressively.

'Don't what?'

'Just don't. You know damn well what I mean.'

'You don't want me to refer to your erotic little interlude. Is that it? All right, I won't.'

Nell, who was leaning back with her folded arms resting on her ribs, was watching her foot. It was fiddling with a book on the low table, nudging it about a bit. She pushed it nearer and nearer to the edge. Then it fell off on to the floor. Neither Conrad nor she bent forward to pick it up. Nell just poured herself some more wine.

'You look almost happy,' Conrad commented bitterly, tightening the towel around his waist.

'Do I?' she asked, genuinely surprised.

'Your expectations fulfilled.'

'Oh yes,' Nell agreed gently. 'I never doubted they would be, sooner or later.'

'So, now you've witnessed this fulfilment of your singularly pessimistic expectations, and got off on the perverse pleasure you clearly derive from it – '

'Not, alas,' she interrupted, 'half as much pleasure as you were clearly deriving from fulfilling Marina's – '

'Shut up!' he snapped. 'Christ!' he added more calmly, but no less resentfully, 'you're really relishing this, aren't you?'

'What, walking in on my boyfriend as he's fucking somebody else in my bed, seeing the smile on his face as he's about to come? Relish? No, that's not the word that springs to mind, I must say.'

'You've been proved right, though, haven't you? Admit you're feeling a bit pleased.'

'I'm not remotely pleased, I'm resigned,' Nell sighed. 'I'd have been pleased to have been proved wrong.'

'I see,' Conrad said, sceptical. 'I'd have liked to have proved you wrong, too, because I think the doom-laden philosophy by which you live is wrong. But it was an uphill struggle to convince you. I gave up because I wasn't getting anywhere.'

'And you rather fancied Marina, so of course, why not?'

'Nell, sweetheart, please.'

There was a pause. Nell, who could not be bothered to fill the silence, just shrugged. Then she thought of something.

'I take it Cyclops wasn't the first?'

Conrad was so obviously flabbergasted and appalled that, when he cried, 'You take it wrong, of *course* she was!' even Nell knew he was telling the truth. Then the nickname she had used sunk in, and he managed to smile.

'I never want to lose you,' he muttered, and lovingly started rubbing his hand up and down Nell's thigh, over the soft denim of her old jeans.

Her eyes followed his hand. They were as emotionally aloof from what they saw as those of a bored spectator at a tennis match who watches the ball for the sake of it, but who could not care less about the outcome of the game.

She did not respond immediately. However, after some moments, while Conrad continued to caress her leg, she eventually said, 'Ah.'

'Ah, what?' he whispered. His brow was as furrowed as the pleats round the toes of Desmond Sprout's loafers.

Nell gazed at his anxious face. She loved him, but nonetheless felt curiously detached from his misery.

'It's boring, the predictable, you know,' she said flatly.

'I know.'

'Still,' she began, then stopped tantalisingly.

'Yes?' he enquired hopefully, inching closer to her.

'Things are going to have to change,' she went on.

'Of course,' Conrad agreed. 'We've had our experiment now. I'm not going to sleep with Cyclops again, nor anyone else for that matter. I promise. And you're going to have to start trusting me.'

Conrad was eager about his new arrangement. He rubbed

her thigh more feverishly and slipped his hand up inside her jersey and around her warm flesh.

Nell did not object, and he carried on.

But nor did she reciprocate his affectionate attentions. She allowed him to open her lips with his tongue. A moment or two passed.

'Incidentally, tomorrow,' she remarked casually, drawing herself back a little so she could look him straight in the eye as she informed him of her plans.

'Yes?' His tone, so full of optimism.

She paused before delivering her devastating blow. 'Tomorrow I'm going out,' she said with more than a note of finality, 'and I'm not coming back.'

# CHAPTER

## 9

'Oh, Nell, my angel, thank God you're here, my head's throbbing as if someone's inside it playing with a punchball,' Cillian moaned, sitting down at his kitchen table. 'Mystery how I managed to drink so much last night.'

'Mystery how you manage to remain mystified by it,' Nell said. Standing at the sideboard, she lifted the kettle, filled the battered coffee pot with boiling water and poured some coffee into a large cup. She put it on the table in front of Cillian, and steered his hand towards it.

'Is it very strong?' he enquired hopefully, lifting it to his lips.

'Need you ask?' Nell was well acquainted with his needs and tastes.

'Smells good,' he said appreciatively. 'You know, I got completely hammered last night. My nocturnal companion – '

'New girlfriend?'

'No, my friend I told you about once, the fellow with the pigeon phobia, he came round.'

'The one who can't ever go out during the day in case he comes across a pigeon in the street?'

Cillian nodded. 'Makes his life awkward. Means he stays up all night, getting pissed mostly. Completely round the twist when it comes to pigeons, but otherwise he's great. I'm very fond of him. You know his definition of hell?'

'What?'

'Trafalgar bleeding Square,' Cillian answered, laughing. 'I know that because years ago I suggested he came along with me on one of my visits to the National Gallery and he bloody nearly passed out just at the thought of it.'

Nell chuckled quietly, took a cigarette out of her packet, and lit it.

'Oooh, give us one, would you, my darling,' Cillian said, hearing her strike the match and patting his trouser pockets. 'I must have left mine next door. Actually, shall we go next door? Now we've finished *Anna Karenina*, I think I'm in the mood for a little Turgenev. What do you say to *Fathers and Sons*? Or maybe you'd like something quite different? Something modern for a change?'

'I'm very happy with Turgenev,' Nell told him.

They went through into the sitting room. 'I know,' he cried out, suddenly inspired as he ran his fingers along his shelves, feeling the books' spines. 'Perhaps a few Chekhov short stories would be appropriate? Would you like that?'

'Very much.'

'Speaking of which. . . ?' the old man said, urging her for some news.

'Oh, I got a letter this morning,' she responded, flatly.

Cillian was disappointed. 'You didn't get a part?'

'Well, as a matter of fact, I did. A small one, though, not Varia.'

'That doesn't matter in the least. You're completely brilliant to get any part in a Belinsky production. Who'll you play?'

'The parlour maid.'

'Dooniasha. My Nell, that's wonderful,' he enthused. He held out his hand to find her and embraced her by way of joyful congratulation. 'When do you start rehearsing?' he asked, with his arms still round her, and his cigarette secured in the corner of his lips.

'January, I suppose.'

'You don't sound very pleased,' he told her, leading her to the sofa.

'I'm very, very pleased,' she assured him. They sat down together, side by side. 'You know me, I find it hard to risk

201

hope, so it was an amazing surprise. I never supposed for a minute I'd be lucky.'

'So, what's up then? You're not your normal spirited self.'

'I'm fine.'

'No, you're not. Your eyes, they're pink, like a rabbit's.'

'How do you know?' Nell quizzed him. His canniness never ceased to surprise her.

'I can tell.'

'Balls.'

'Not balls. I've an extra sense, you know. I can see you in my own sort of way. In fact, I know you so well, I reckon I can see you a lot better than most of those who've got sight.'

'I've got a cold. You heard me sniffing, and just guessed my eyes are streaming,' Nell rejoined, mustering a smile. 'You lying old bugger.'

Cillian did not reply, but folded his arms and pressed his lips together, waiting. With his white hair sticking out of his head at eccentric angles, he looked like a wise, aged, schoolmaster.

Nell opened his leatherbound copy of *The Kiss and Other Stories* which she had found and picked out from one of the shelves.

'No, no,' he whispered gently as he heard her turn over the pages to find the beginning of the text. 'Before you start, I have to know you're all right, that's more important.'

'I promise I'm fine.'

'You sound as convincing as a Tory politician promising help for the homeless. The Irish don't believe in all this stiff-upper-lip stuff, load of English fucking humbug, eh? Hung over, like me?'

'Possibly, a bit,' she replied. 'I went to Samuel's school play last night, and had rather a lot of red wine when I got home. Didn't sleep much.'

'That photographer friend of yours keeping you awake, being his usual amorous self?'

Pause. Nell rubbed her knee with the tips of her fingers, as if trying to soothe a bruise. 'You could say that.' Ironic chuckle.

Another pause.

'I was going to ask you later,' she went on.

'What?'

'Fancy a guest for a while? I need somewhere to live.'

There was a silence while Cillian thought about what she had said. He placed his palm on his forehead like someone suffering from a headache. His face twitched as two conflicting expressions – huge pleasure and deep concern – battled it out to win over his features.

'My God,' he exclaimed at last. 'You know how much I would love that. Of course you can. I've always said you could stay here as long and as often as you like.'

'Thank you,' Nell said.

On hearing her glum tone, Cillian's glee gave way to anxiety.

'Never could trust a photographer,' he remarked knowingly. 'Been shitting on his own doorstep?'

'Mmm.'

'Steaming little – ' the poet spat.

'Not really,' Nell interrupted. 'No worse than anyone else. Considerably better, in some ways. Only, unfortunately just as predictable. That's the thing which most upsets me, really. Not him screwing someone else.'

'I'm angrier than you are,' Cillian observed. 'You're not angry, and you should be.'

'But you said infidelity didn't matter terribly,' she reminded him.

'That's perhaps true,' he came back quickly, 'in theory, though. When it actually happens to oneself or somebody one cares about, one's entitled to feel fucking furious, I've a mind to garrotte the bugger with his own camera strap, sling him one with his sodding tripod.'

Nell laughed. 'He accused me of being quite pleased about it. He said it confirmed my pessimistic outlook on life.'

'That's exactly what a photographer would say,' Cillian complained.

'He had a point. There is something rather satisfying about being proved right. He always said he had no intention of sleeping with anyone else but yesterday I happen upon him in bed with a girl who smells of lavender and wears a glass eye on her finger. I think now I really have got an excuse to embrace pessimism wholeheartedly.'

'What do you mean?' he asked.

'Well, there was Hilary, who seemed for once to be genuinely in love – with the girl I understudied, Jodie Wells. But that didn't stop him, did it, from making a pass at Christabel, when she went round to see him after Daniel had left her.'

'Oh, God, really?'

'And,' Nell continued, 'the so-called blissful couple, so perfect even I believed in them – Liza and Samuel. The usual miserable sub-text lies beneath that ideal marriage in exactly the same way it does with every other marriage you care to mention. Samuel, the most straightforward, down to earth and loving man you could hope to meet, turns out to be so obsessed by the English teacher at his school and the conviction that poisonous electricity seeps out of wall sockets, he's visiting a psychiatric hospital once a week. Is everyone completely mad?'

'Of course,' Cillian replied nonchalantly. 'Take my friend – seems normal enough, but discovers after twenty years his wife's been knocking off one of his best mates who he plays snooker with every week in Balham. And what does he do? He doesn't even divorce her. No, he goes and develops a morbid fear of ruddy pigeons.'

'So depressing,' Nell remarked.

'Keen lessons that love deceives,' the old poet muttered, leaning forward to pull up his yellow socks. Sitting upright again, he lit another cigarette. When he exhaled, a pale grey tongue of smoke curled over his upper lip and licked the end of his nose before disintegrating. 'And wrings with wrong,'

204

he went on. 'Have you read any of Hardy's poems? I think they'd be right up your street. Terribly gloomy.'

A mahogany grandfather clock chimed in the hall.

'Ahah!' Cillian exclaimed. 'The hour has come for a pre-lunch drink.'

'Post-breakfast,' Nell corrected.

'What shall it be? Champagne to celebrate?' he enthused. 'So many things to celebrate.'

'Oh yes?'

'Dooniasha; you moving in. When will that be, by the way?'

'Today?'

'Excellent. Another reason for champagne − Christmas. You were spending it with the photographer's family, weren't you?'

'Yes, Samuel and Liza did ask us to go with them to the cottage they rent in Wales, but we had to turn them down.'

'So now you can go after all.'

'Too late. They asked a friend of Samuel's and there's no room.'

'Who?' Cillian enquired gruffly.

'A Scotsman. Liza said she doesn't know him.'

'Maybe he could be persuaded to sleep on the sofa.'

'That's already taken. One of the children.'

'So, sleep with the Scotsman,' he suggested helpfully.

'I've never met him,' Nell protested. 'Apparently he's very nice, but he thinks he's got bugs.'

'My angel, your last boyfriend was a photographer. I shouldn't dismiss a man because he's got nits.'

Nell slapped him playfully on the knee.

'I'll get the champagne,' she announced, standing up. 'We don't seem to be getting much reading done,' she added, walking through to the kitchen.

'Anyway,' he shouted to her, 'Jake could sort him out, he knows about bugs.'

'Forget it, Cillian,' she called back. 'I'm not sharing a bed with a stranger.'

'I detect a distinct lack of adventure verging on the prudish. You never know, this man may turn out to be charming.'

Nell went back to the sitting room with a frosty-looking bottle and a couple of antique glasses as delicate as spiderwebs.

'So, my bee,' he said in a quieter voice when she returned, 'will you spend Christmas, here, then, with me? I would love that.'

'Are you sure? Me imposing on your family Christmas?'

'You live here, and you are family. So that's settled,' he said, rubbing his veined hands together with satisfaction. 'Anyway, it's only me and Jake this year. The rest of them are away, thank God. We neither of us much care for his father. Pompous ass. We'll be far happier on our own and even more so with you here. I cannot imagine two people I would prefer to spend Christmas with. So there.'

Nell, holding the bottle of champagne, peeled away the goosepimpled gold foil and unlocked the silver cage clasped to the cork. Then she forced it open. A surge of spume flopped into one of the glasses. At the same time, the doorbell rang.

'Who's that?'

'Jake, most probably,' Cillian answered. 'He mentioned he might drop by for a few minutes to see me.'

'I'll let him in,' Nell said, handing the old man a glass. She went along the booklined passage to the front door. Striding past the hall table, her eyes skated over the mirror which hung above it. Cillian was right: they did look rather pink. She regretted the fact she had not put on any eyeliner that morning. But it was now too late: Jake was waiting. As a less effective but last-minute alternative, she shook her long fringe forward so it nearly covered her eyes; and then opened the door.

Jake was surprised to see her.

'How nice,' he said, kissing her hello. Nell smelt the comforting whiff of mothballs, and glanced at his green tweed suit.

'You're looking very smart,' she observed, smiling.

'Old one of Grandfather's,' he explained, holding the side of the jacket and opening it out to look at the label. 'Very old, in fact,' he said, reading the ink-written date.

'Go on through, I'll just get you a glass. We're drinking champagne.'

Nell joined Cillian and his grandson in the sitting room a moment later. The old man was telling Jake that she was moving in with him.

'I am delighted,' he exclaimed, clutching the younger man's sleeve to stress his point. 'But this one needs cheering up,' he added, tilting his head towards where he had heard Nell sit down.

'Cillian,' Nell said, smiling weakly. 'I'm really all right.'

'Photographer friend of hers has been a shit. What can you expect?'

'Perhaps Nell doesn't want to discuss it.' Jake gave Nell an apologetic look.

She shook her head and assured him she did not mind.

'She's got a part in *The Cherry Orchard*,' Cillian went on. 'But that boyfriend of hers, so considerate in his timing, has managed to put paid to any pleasure she might otherwise have derived from hearing the news.'

'You know that's not true. I am very pleased.'

Jake congratulated her. A while later he asked when she was moving into the flat.

'Today,' she replied. 'I'm going to go and collect a few things from Oxford Gardens this afternoon.'

Jake looked at his watch. 'Have you got time to come and see my bees? I ought to be getting back to work. You could come with me now. That's if you're not in a hurry.'

Cillian swigged back his champagne and drained his glass.

'I'd love to, if it's really not inconvenient.'

'Not at all,' Jake assured her, standing up quickly.

Cillian saw them to the door.

'I'll be back later, with my suitcase,' Nell told him, giving him a kiss goodbye on the cheek.

207

'I'll expect you when I see you,' the old man said. He wandered on to the landing outside the door to his flat, and opened the gates of the lift opposite. Jake and Nell walked inside, then snapped the gates shut again, Cillian waved at them and pressed the button, before turning away and going back into his flat. As the ancient elevator began slowly to descend, Nell thought she could hear him laughing.

The December rain splattered on to the streets with exaggerated force like in a film when the director has been overzealous with his special effects. The imposing sky was the same grey as the damp pavements. Yet Knightsbridge glittered with the headlights of the cars and buses and the bulbs adorning the opulent Christmas windows.

Despite the weather Nell and Jake decided to walk quickly to the museum. It was not very far. They jostled with the shoppers. Passing a chestnut seller outside the tube station, Nell momentarily felt the warmth from the glowing coals. She shivered.

Across the road, outside the entrance to Harrods, the crowds appeared to multiply. 'Like a swarm of bees,' Jake observed with good humour, taking her arm so as not to lose her. Together they pressed their way in the direction of South Kensington. Normally she would have resented having to contend with so many people and would, unreasonably, have cursed them for hampering her progress. But a Christmas spirit seemed to abound. She was reminded of childhood Christmases.

A few minutes later they arrived, drenched, at a side door of the National History Museum. Once inside they walked up some worn stone stairs and down a long corridor lined wih dark wooden cases.

'What's in all those drawers?' Nell asked.

'Hundreds and thousands of specimens,' Jake replied as they approached a grand doorway. Above it, in old-fashioned gold lettering, was written 'Entomology Department.' The bee expert pushed himself against the solid door and swung it open. An overwhelming smell of naphthalene crystals assaulted and tickled Nell's nostrils. She sniffed.

'Now you can understand why I stink like I do,' Jake said apologetically.

'I like the smell,' she insisted.

'This is the room where I work,' he explained.

It was a huge space with a very high ceiling. More blocks of elegant mahogany cases, each with a series of beautifully crafted shallow drawers, rose up above Nell's head and formed a pattern of aisles.

'Follow me,' Jake encouraged her, walking through the maze. 'It's very confusing in here.'

They turned a few corners until they came upon the small square niche which acted as his study. A window towered above an old-fashioned buxom radiator. The walls were made from the backs of three of the wooden cases. Pressed up against them were his desk and rows of bookshelves brimming with jacketless volumes. Nell liked the dowdy colours of their spines. Jake's little private sanctuary reminded her of a hidden corner in a dusty second-hand bookshop.

He pulled a chair forward for Nell to sit on and offered to put her coat over the radiator.

'Are all those drawers full of bees?' she asked him, amazed.

He nodded. 'There are thirty-five thousand species of bee worldwide. We've got about twenty-five million insects in the department. My first priority is the maintenance and curation of the national collections.'

'Of all of them?'

'No, just the bees.'

'But that's enough to be going on with?'

'Certainly. And then there's all the research, and dealing with thousands of enquiries I get on the telephone and through the post.' Jake pointed to a pile of letters. 'That's just what arrived this morning.' He laughed.

'My God,' Nell exclaimed.

'Are you very cold after that drenching?'

'Not at all. This radiator's scorching.'

'Warm enough to come and have a quick look at some of the specimens?'

'Absolutely,' she said, nodding.

'I promise I won't show you many.'

They stood up and he led her out of his study and back into the maze. Halfway along one of the aisles, Jake stopped and slid open one of the numerous drawers. Inside were perhaps three dozen large insects. Each was an inch or so above the bottom of the drawer, held up by a small pin in the underside of its abdomen. Attached to every one of them was a tiny label with miniature brown ink hand writing.

Nell gasped. 'Are they all bees?'

Jake, obviously appreciating her amazement, smiled and nodded.

'But I didn't know you could get metallic green ones. And look at these blue ones. They're as shiny as dupion silk. They're beautiful.'

Jake opened another drawer. He pointed to a row of black and white bees.

'That's the *Xylocopa Smithii*, the one I was telling you about the other day at lunch.'

'Which you found in Indonesia?'

'Exactly.'

'Bet he has a mean sting.'

'It's the females that really do the stinging,' Jake explained, gazing at them respectfully. 'These are Cillian's favourites. He calls them wicked nuns.'

Nell laughed and watched as Jake put his hand into the drawer to straighten one of the specimens which was falling off its miniature plinth. It was a fiddly business, but he nonetheless readjusted it with a deftness which seemed to belie the size of his fingers.

'That was very impressive,' she commented.

'Oh?' Genuine surprise.

'Yes. I'm sure I'd have knocked all the others over.'

Jake glanced at her as he gently closed the drawer with his hip. His eyes, she noticed, were very hollow and the skin beneath them had that faint purplish-blue tone that comes of too little sleep. Nell imagined he had been sitting up late at night, perhaps in his flat in Bloomsbury studying his bees under a magnifying glass beside a single dim lamp. He had the air of someone who relished solitude, and was gregarious only when with the small winged objects of his affection. In their company he seemed less shy.

'Practice, I suppose,' he ventured, 'I spend most of my life with bees, you see. Far better at handling them than I am with people. Few can understand my passion for them,' he said, starting to walk to his study. The voice sounded sad. 'Come. This way. Let's go back to what Grandfather calls my hive.'

'That's absurd,' Nell remarked, almost crossly, as she followed him. 'I can see people might not necessarily share the passion, but they must at least be able to understand it.'

'You'd be surprised. Grandfather's one of the few exceptions.'

She sat down on the chair, he leaned against the window.

'Your parents?'

'I read law at Cambridge. They were rooting for me to be a barrister. A little disappointed, I think, that I became a bee boffin.'

Jake took off his jacket and pushed up the sleeves of his big white shirt, revealing skin that was still honey-brown from the Indonesian sun. By the large veins on the inside of his forearms were a number of old mosquito bites.

'Grandfather thinks my father's a pompous ass and has encouraged me all the way.'

'Cillian's very good like that. He stuck up for me when I told Dad what I wanted to be. It's lucky I didn't want to be a photographer. He's got a thing about them.'

'Only because your boyfriend's one,' Jake told her. 'Had you gone out with a painter, I suspect he'd have affected not to have liked them.'

211

'Ex-boyfriend,' Nell corrected.

'Yes. Sorry,' he said, quickly, embarrassed.

'I wonder what he'd have done if Conrad had been a poet?' She smiled at the thought.

'Then he would doubtless have accused him of being a bad poet,' Jake laughed. 'Grandfather's so fond of you, he'd be jealous of anyone you went out with.'

Nell looked at Jake and wondered. He hastily turned his eyes away from hers and began rearranging a pile of papers and books on his desk. Perhaps he regretted having made a remark that was too flattering, too personal.

Nell uncrossed her legs and stood up quickly. 'I must let you get back to work,' she muttered. 'I've disturbed you long enough.'

He immediately stopped tidying his desk and assured her to the contrary. 'Not at all,' he insisted and offered her a cigarette. 'The Thursday before Christmas – ' he said, breaking off to strike a match.

'Hard to get down to it,' Nell went on.

'Everyone revving up for the office party,' he whispered so his colleagues would not hear him over the partition walls. 'God forbid. Everyone hates it, but it's the annual ordeal.'

Jake helped Nell into her coat.

'It's still damp, I'm afraid.'

'Not to worry,' she said cheerfully. 'Thank you for letting me see your bees.'

'A pleasure.'

'I can see why you're so passionate about them,' she told him emphatically. 'More fool those who don't. They're beautiful.'

Jake grinned. He had been about to shake her hand, but her remark prompted him instead to kiss her goodbye on both cheeks.

They smiled and he showed her to the door. 'Can you find your way out?' he asked anxiously.

'Of course,' said Nell, and made her way downstairs. Outside it was almost dark and still pouring with rain. The cold drops stung her face, and trickled down her bare neck. But as she walked towards the tube station it seemed she did not really mind that she was getting wet. Maybe she had not even noticed.

It was Monday morning. There was little indication in Out Patients that it was Christmas Eve. A straggly strand of red tinsel had been pinned to the reception desk.

By the swing door leading to the Pathology Department (or the path lab, as it was otherwise known) stood a small Christmas tree. Piled at its foot were a number of old shoeboxes and empty cornflake packets all covered, somewhat haphazardly, in wrapping paper. A man was crouching beside them. His legs were so thin that the contours of his knee joints appeared to have been as crudely fashioned as those of a wooden puppet's.

Samuel sat down on one of the free chairs a couple of feet away from him. He had seen the man before, on an earlier visit to the hospital. Then, he had been rather alarmed because the man had repeatedly yelled that he wanted a 'sanwitch'. Now, though, as he squatted by the colourful parcels, he was quiet. He just gazed at them unblinking, longingly.

Samuel crossed his legs and cast his eyes down at his own knees.

Black trousers, as usual, he said to himself, but no exercise books. What a relief, for once, not to be frantically marking a great pile of them. No chalk dust, either, come to that.

School holidays. Absence of any tell-tale signs. Other than the regulars who've often watched me working while I wait, no one would guess I was a teacher. The new patients couldn't know.

Everybody eyes everybody up and down. Natural, I suppose. I'm used to it, now. Blimey, I do it myself enough. I don't mind if they mistake me for a local politician, even a plain clothes policeman, as long as they don't say to themselves, Him over there, he's probably the type who's unfaithful to his wife. Do I look like an adulterer?

213

I don't think I do. But you can never tell, can you? I hope I look more like a picture restorer, and I would go so far as to say a person couldn't be both: a fornicating picture restorer. Somehow it doesn't ring true. As I see it, the one precludes the other. Rather like Stationery Store Cynthia and virginity.

Anyway, I'm no longer an adulterer. For the few minutes that I was one, I wasn't very good. I'd be far better at picture restoration.

Samuel leaned forward to pick up his copy of the *Independent*, which had slipped to his feet. The shoelace of one of his brown brogues was undone, so he retied it. It was wet from the rain outside, and felt flaccid and slimy like a dead earthworm. Sitting upright again, he wiped his fingers on his moleskin trousers, and started reading the paper.

Some moments later the man by the tree began to make muffled groaning sounds. It was hard at first to make out what he was trying to say. 'I wan tapress sent.'

A newcomer, an anorexic girl, stared at the man's pained face. She cowered like an emaciated alley cat, at once frightened and moved. Everyone else, including Samuel, either vaguely glanced in his direction for a second or two, or ignored him completely.

'I wan tapress sent,' the man repeated softly, rocking backwards and forwards. 'I wan tapress sent.'

'Wait for Father Christmas, love,' a smiling woman suggested after a while. 'He's coming tonight.'

Samuel looked up and a few people laughed.

As they did so, the man's face became contorted with anguish. He cupped his hands over his ears and began violently to shake his head. The laughter seemed to pain him. A couple of tears stood in his eyes. He was crying softly. For some moments nobody did anything. Then the man unsteadily rose to his feet, his eyes darting about the room. He sniffed, and turned to Samuel.

'All laff-ing at me,' he muttered desolately, clinging to the arm of Samuel's chair. His knee jiggled like that of a nervous child performing in a school concert or play.

214

'Not at you,' Samuel assured him gently. He had rarely seen another man cry. He felt in his pocket, pulled out a clean paper handkerchief and gave it to him.

The man bit his lip, touched by the modest act of kindness. Calmer now, he thanked Samuel and started, rather clumsily, but with huge dignity, to wipe his tears. Then a nurse came over to them. She had mean, slitty nostrils, and smelt of chlorine.

'Is Mr Roberts bothering you?' she asked. She spat the words 'Mr Roberts' ironically, as if he did not merit such respectful nomenclature.

'Not at all,' Samuel insisted.

The nurse's pinched expression relaxed a little. 'Come on, Mr Roberts. Your doctor's waiting,' she said, detaching his hand from the chair's arm and leading the man away.

Samuel watched their slow progress. He hoped that the following day Mr Roberts would get a Christmas present from someone, but wondered.

A minute or two later, Dr Oak appeared and the two of them went along the corridor. The consulting room was extremely hot as usual. Samuel was prompted to speculate whether those responsible for the hospital's heating had taken the greenhouse effect into account when they had turned the dial on the thermostat. He looked at the radiator beneath the window and fancied he could see the heat emanating from it.

The doctor sat at his desk and opened his blue folder. A modest frown had formed just above the bridge of his nose.

'Samuel, is my radiator bothering you?' he asked, noticing his patient's troubled stare and turning over the pages of his notes. 'I thought it was bar heaters. Forgive me, I didn't realise that radiators were also one of your – '

'Oh, no,' Samuel interrupted, 'I'm just rather hot.'

The two men laughed. Dr Oak immediately leapt up and opened the window overlooking the municipal flowerbed. Samuel hastily removed his jersey and felt the same relief as

215

a sweaty sportsman who strips off his shirt after an energetic game.

'How's this week been?' the doctor enquired, settling down in his chair again.

'You're not going to believe this,' Samuel began, 'but last night, guess what? I didn't get out of bed to check the telly's plug socket downstairs.'

'That's the first time in a long while.'

'For ages. Years, literally,' Samuel enthused. 'Of course, I'm exhausted today: I didn't sleep much. But at least I slept a bit. In the past, if I'd prevented myself from checking I'd have lain awake the whole night worrying, listening out for an explosion or something.'

'How did you feel?'

'A bit twitchy, I must admit. I got up to go to the loo a couple of times, and was tempted to check on the children, to see they hadn't been . . .'

'Go on.'

'Well, you know, sounds so silly, doesn't it? Poisoned by invisible electricity fumes.'

'And did you?' the doctor asked, as if he did not think Samuel remotely silly.

'I managed not to. And, of course, there they were at breakfast this morning as perky as ever. I was so chuffed. I then coped with our new number of head taps quite well.'

'Oh, good. This is good. Fourteen we're on, aren't we?'

Samuel nodded. 'Unfortunately, it was asking a bit too much of myself to deal with the toaster on top of everything else. I had to get Liza to do that today, I'm ashamed to say.'

'No need for shame. We're progressing apace. How do you think you can do with just twelve?'

'Might as well try while the going's good.'

'Fancy a cup of coffee?' Dr Oak asked, reaching for his telephone in order to call the nurse. Some minutes later she appeared with two mugs and the doctor and his patient went through their weekly ritual together.

216

Samuel sighed when it was over, and took a sip of the steaming liquid.

'That wasn't too bad,' he said.

'It was excellent,' the doctor corrected, noting down the figure twelve in his file. 'Do you suppose you can keep that up the rest of this week?'

'Touch wood.'

'Speaking of which, how about touching a few of my things in here?' Dr Oak enquired, lifting his huge box of tricks from the floor beside him and putting it on the desk.

Samuel smiled a little weakly, and went through with the next exercise. They started with an electric toothbrush – who'd ever actually use one one of these pointless contraptions? Samuel wondered, opening his mouth and fingering the button. They'd have to be barking. Then he and the doctor proceeded with a range of other small electrical devices. And eventually they graduated on to an antediluvian Kenwood mixer which Dr Oak produced from a cupboard behind him. Samuel had to plug every object in, turn them all on, and fiddle with their individual switches as well as those on the wall sockets. He fared a little better than he had the week before, although the Kenwood's aggressive steel blades caused him some grief. They sat at the bottom of the tall glass container spinning round noisily.

'The electricity propelling them at such a force has to be strong,' he told Dr Oak, panic starting to bud inside him.

'Okay, think logically, Samuel,' the doctor said calmly. 'You're a science teacher, do what we've done before. Picture the school textbook, turn to the chapter on electricity. Can you see the simple diagrams explaining it?'

'Yes.'

'Remind yourself of the text. Any mention of poison – ?'

'No, but – '

'All right, watch me,' Dr Oak suggested, putting the lid on the container and turning the dial to 'High'. 'I'm removing this little lid within the lid so we've got the small pouring hole.'

Samuel watched as the doctor did as he said. The blades

were whizzing round at such a pace they looked like a grey blur. He felt uncomfortable, with the open hole in the lid, but repeated in his head, No poison.

Suddenly, the doctor leaned forward, placed his mouth over the hole and ostentatiously inhaled five times.

Samuel, who all the while had been nervously fiddling with the collar of his thick shirt, gasped.

'I'm absolutely fine, you see,' Dr Oak declared cheerfully.

Samuel held his hand to his chest and sighed with relief.

'Feel as right as rain,' the older man went on.

'Ah yes,' came Samuel's response, accompanied by a feeble smile. 'You do now, but just you wait a few moments,' he joked, 'and you'll keel over in a coma.' He tapped his nose and winked knowingly. 'Quick, give me Casualty's extension number.'

The doctor laughed, then pointed to the Kenwood. 'Do you want a go?' he asked.

Samuel shrugged, and moved tentatively towards the mixer.

'I don't know what you'll come up with next,' he said, a teasing note in his voice. 'Maybe it'll be a bit of careers advice? I wouldn't put it past you, if I ever said I was fed up with teaching, to suggest I apply for a job at the electricity board!'

Later that day as he was driving his family and Eddie to the cottage in Wales for Christmas, he repeated the remark to Liza and his friend, pleased that he could laugh at himself, and happy for them to laugh with him.

When Nell woke up in her single bed in Cillian's spare room she lay quite still for a while, procrastinating. The heavy bedclothes were irresistibly warm and soft. She stared up at the ceiling and, in the curious way people can be when only half-conscious, was content simply to think about its whiteness.

There was a knock on the door.

'Come in,' she said.

Cillian entered, shuffling. Both his old dressing-gown and his old face looked crumpled.

'Blinking Christmas,' he remarked. 'Couldn't find a big enough sock in my drawer.' He moved towards the bed, perched at the end of it, on the eiderdown, and held out a tatty plastic bag. 'Your very measly stocking,' he explained. 'Happy Christmas, angel.'

Nell sat up. 'What have you done?'

'Very little. There are only three or four things in it. And the paper's probably hideous. I didn't trust the patronising woman in the shop. I expect the silly bitch palmed me off with designs she couldn't sell to anybody who could actually see them. Silly bitch.'

Nell peered into the bag. 'It's perfectly all right,' she assured him. 'Gold with robins.'

'Ruddy robins. Anyway, she had halitosis. Serves her right. Can't stand robins. Smug buggers. Shall we go and have some coffee?'

Nell climbed out of bed and they went into the kitchen. She put the kettle on the stove and the bag of presents on the table.

'Why not open them now?' Cillian said, hearing the rustle, 'while we wait for it to boil?'

'I've got a few for you under the tree next door. I'm going to get a couple so we can undo them together.' A moment later she reappeared, dressed and bearing two parcels which she put in front of the old man.

He stretched out his arthritic hands and clutched them with his stiff fingers.

'You've wrapped them for me,' he cried delightedly.

'Of course,' Nell said, puzzled by his delight.

'My wives never bothered,' he explained. 'What's the point of doing up presents for a blind man?' they said, 'waste of paper. They had an odd sense of economy. By saving on Christmas paper they coud splash out on dresses. A very feminine sort of logic. Do I gather this one's a bottle?' he asked, clearly excited.

219

'Probably.'

'Ah ha! But what sort?' Cillian said, beginning to unwrap it. When he had done so, he fingered the label and the top. 'Jameson's Irish Whiskey,' he pronounced, giving Nell a kiss. 'You spoil me. Thank you, my angel.'

'How many brands can you tell by the feel of their label?' Nell laughed.

'Any number. You can test me one day. From Bells to Black Bush.'

'Not true. You know I know Irish whiskey's your favourite, lying old toad.'

'Well – ' Cillian said, 'I admit that might have helped, but I really can tell most of the different whiskies, I promise. Vodkas, too.'

Nell stood up to make the coffee, then opened one of her presents. It was a beautiful early edition of Chekhov's plays. She thanked Cillian profusely.

'I better make a start on lunch soon,' she said afterwards. 'What time is Jake coming?'

No answer.

'Cillian?'

'Lunchtime, I don't know, maybe a bit before. Drinks.'

Nell sploshed some milk into her coffee, and asked him what was the matter. 'You sound uneasy,' she commented.

'No, not really.' He rubbed his white eyebrows with the back of his liver-spotted hand, and nodded pensively, as if agreeing with a thought that had occurred to him not for the first time. 'I have a feel for things,' he remarked at last.

'I know,' Nell agreed, amused by his insistence. 'Whisky bottles.'

'I wasn't actually meaning that.'

'What then?'

'You're falling for him.'

'What?'

'Come on, you know what I mean.'

'Jake? Cillian, I'm not falling for Jake.' Nell opened the lid of her cigarette packet with a defiant flick of her forefinger.

'Oh, so I got that wrong then,' the old man murmured.

'I've only just split up with Conrad.'

'That doesn't mean anything. You weren't in love with the photographer.'

'All the same, I loved him. I don't fall in love with people. I don't believe in all of that.' Nell passed Cillian a cigarette and placed another between her lips. She watched as he took out his dull gold lighter from his pocket. The flame was tiny but he managed, as always, to locate the tip of her cigarette with a precision that appeared to belie his blindness. 'Far better to be on one's own,' she went on. 'Avoids endless misery.'

'And joy,' Cillian pointed out.

'Short term, perhaps. But ultimately we can only trust ourselves.' Nell looked out of the window, over the black rooftops. The sky was the colour of a canteen spoon. 'I want to be alone,' she said firmly.

'Nonsense,' Cillian dismissed the notion. 'Who do you think you are? Greta Garbo?'

Pause.

'Eh?' he said, prompting her to answer him.

'I barely know him,' Nell replied quietly.

'So what? As if that's ever stopped anyone in the past. For God's sake, let go.'

'No, I will not let go.'

'Well, then, you're a fool,' Cillian informed her, stubbing out his cigarette with emphatic stabs.

Nell stood up quickly. The backs of her knees pushed the chair. Its legs made a loud scraping noise on the floor. 'More coffee?' she asked abruptly.

'I said you're a fool,' he repeated.

She poured some into his cup anyway. 'Harsh words for Christmas morning.'

'Bugger Christmas. You're denying yourself happiness. I've got no sympathy for you.'

'You sound like Conrad.'

'Maybe photographers are wiser than I thought. I think you should relax your defences and do as your instinct tells you.'

'Which is?'

'To fall in love with Jake.' Cillian's voice sounded insistent, almost harsh.

Nell did not respond.

'Nellie?'

'I'm going to get dressed and go for a walk,' she announced, changing the subject. 'You can put the turkey in.'

'Can't you wait till this afternoon? Then we can all go,' he suggested cajolingly.

But Nell was uncompromising. 'I'll see you later,' she told him, and left the room.

Hyde Park was grey. The black trees appeared to be squirming in the wind, their branches naked and vulnerable, struggling against invisible assailants.

Nell wandered aimlessly across the damp ground. The balding winter grass was a mere patina on the smooth, sticky expanse of mud.

She zipped up her suede jacket and hunched her shoulders. In her haste to leave the flat, she had forgotten to take her yellow scarf. The cold wind was ruthless, indecent even, in its quest to invade exposed flesh.

Walking towards the Serpentine, Nell spotted a few other stray figures. There was one couple, far off, whose silhouettes were as black as the trees. An animated dog leapt around them, but they ignored it. They were holding hands.

A jogger with sinewy legs was coming towards her. As he drew closer, she could not help noticing that the colour of his flesh perfectly matched that of his T-shirt. Both were supposedly white, but in actual fact were greying, with sweat and with age. Not so his royal blue shorts, which dazzled amidst so much monotone. When the man passed, Nell heard the crunchy-new, sweat resistant nylon rasp between his thighs. Without stopping, he mouthed a breathy 'Happy Christmas', and carried on by.

Nell bent down to tighten the laces of her tatty, fig-purple Converse All-Stars. Then she plunged her hands into the pockets of her black jeans and continued walking. A little farther along, on one of the tarmac paths, a circle of pigeons had formed round a scattering of breadcrumbs. A pecking disorder, Nell thought, eyeing them as they fought with each other. She steered clear of them, but one flew up and flapped close to her ear. She ducked and ran a few steps but managed, only just, to avoid it. Her mind turned to Alfred Hitchcock, and Cillian's friend with the phobia. She shuddered a little, and tried to imagine instead the jogger's Christmas Day.

Had he unwrapped those shorts this morning? A present from his wife? Girlfriend? Would he return home to find she had laid the table specially with holly or crackers? Maybe there was no one at home, no holly and crackers? Perhaps he was alone, and had bought himself just one bottle of wine, for a treat, but nothing else? Very hard to pull a cracker with oneself. Virtually impossible.

In Hyde Park, on Christmas Day, a single jogger might well seem a little sad. But what about a solitary girl, with no companion, not even a dog, just wandering, directionless? She would appear pathetic in her loneliness.

But, Nell thought defiantly, she was not remotely pathetic, because she had chosen to be on her own.

Suddenly, an unwelcome image gatecrashed its way into her mind, as vivid as a frame on a video comatosed by the pause button: Marina's naked body astride Conrad's horizontal legs.

Best to be alone, Nell said in her head, taking her hands out of her pockets, and sucking her frozen fingers in an effort to warm them.

Don't let yourself be lured by the idea of romantic companionship. Folly.

That familiar expression of his, in profile, on the pillow, of blissful pleasure. My companion, accompanying someone else.

Nell, who was continuing along the path beside the Serpentine, skirted an ugly still-life posed in a shallow

223

puddle on the ground. It was made up of an empty polystyrene carton from McDonald's, one sodden wool glove and a crumpled Coke can.

Stand aside, she told herself, and watch everyone else kick each other in the face.

She looked down and swung back her foot. Then with the rubber toe of her sneaker, she struck the can, hard. It jumped quite high before landing back on the tarmac and scampering neurotically away. It ended up by a turning in the path, under a bush.

'Oi, do you mind?' an angry voice shouted. Nell had not seen the man with a dog a few feet ahead of her. They had turned the corner and appeared from around the other side of the bush. 'You stupid fucking idiot, that bloody thing nearly fucking hit me, you realise,' he railed. 'Fuck!'

Nell, alarmed by the outburst of fury, slowed down as the man strode towards her. His swagger was full of macho indignation and self-importance, but he was let down by his footsteps. They squeaked.

Loafers.

'Fucking hell, if it isn't Nell John,' Desmond Sprout exclaimed above Jagger's excruciating barks. 'Shut the fuck up,' Nell's ex-employer screamed at his dog before kicking its haunches. It yelped and went quiet. 'What are you doing,' he asked his former dog walker, 'in the park on Christmas day, kicking cans in people's faces?'

'Having a walk before lunch,' came the reply.

'What, voluntarily?' he questioned, wheezing.

'How do you mean?'

'Well, it seems odd to choose to go for a walk when you don't have to,' he gasped. 'Whatever for?'

'Why do you have Jagger, Desmond,' Nell began politely, 'if you're so lazy?'

Desmond laughed in that way of his that had mystified her in the past. It was a laugh utterly devoid of good humour.

'Because,' he explained, 'I can kick the fucker as much as I want and, unlike the wife, he can't get his own back and deny me sex.'

Desmond did not get any more charming, Nell noted. Even his smile lacked cheer. It was too slothful to make the effort to raise itself. Instead, his lips just moved back around his teeth as if they were stretched and tugged like a couple of resistant rubber bands.

'So, how's the acting career then, love? Got a job yet?' he asked patronisingly.

Nell nodded but felt disinclined to elaborate.

'Commercials,' he concluded by her silence. 'I can understand your reticence, but no need to be embarrassed. Plenty of dosh, after all, ha ha.'

'Belinsky,' Nell muttered.

'Is that a make of hi-fi?'

'No, Belinsky,' she repeated louder.

'Oh, him. I didn't hear you.' He paused to allow the information to sink in. 'What, you've got a part in *The Cherry Orchard*? Blimey, Nell, you've come up in the world.'

Nell might have supposed, by the expression on his face, that he was almost put out.

'I always knew you were a cracking little actress,' he told her. Was his tone grudging, or was it simply that he was still breathless? 'You'll be a star.'

'I don't want to be a star,' Nell said firmly.

'You almost certainly will be.'

'No, I certainly won't be. That is not the aim,' she hissed crushingly.

Alas, Desmond was not to be crushed. 'Oh, so what is the aim?' he rejoined.

'To work,' she answered simply, ostentatiously looking at her watch. 'I have to go now,' she added.

'You're on your own,' Desmond pointed out, ignoring her remark.

'Thank God.'

'No more Conrad?' His eyes widened, but not with innocence. 'Perhaps one day we can have that fuck that I proposed a couple of months back? Especially now you're going to be famous. I get a kick out of pleasuring starlets.'

225

This was Desmond's idea of humour.

'Shit, Nell, if looks could kill,' he went on. 'We are definitely not amused, are we? There must be someone else?'

'Possibly,' Nell sneered. She glowered at him with contempt, turned on her heel and walked away.

When Nell returned from her walk it was almost one o'clock. She found Jake in the sitting room with Cillian. They were drinking champagne.

Jake was leaning against the fireplace, his elbow resting on the mantelpiece, glass in hand. He looked dishevelled. The collar of his crumpled white shirt was undone and his aged, floppy tie knotted at chest level. The red of his classic cardigan matched that of the soft Marlboro packet in his hand.

He stepped forward to wish Nell Happy Christmas and to kiss her hello. 'You're frozen,' he commented. 'Here, come and stand by the fire.'

'Well, if she will go off for long walks on her own in the cold,' Cillian piped up. He was ensconced on the sofa. 'How was it?'

'Fine.' Nell omitted to mention her encounter with Desmond. It had ruined her walk. On the way back to the flat she had marched hurriedly, full of quivering anger and – to her intense annoyance – a little tearful. Now, though, safely back at home and in company, she preferred to forget it.

'Shall we open our presents before lunch?' Cillian suggested. 'It won't be ready for a while.'

He unwrapped another present from Nell. A pair of socks.

'Can I guess their colour?' he asked, holding them up. 'Yellow by any chance?'

'Not very original, I'm afraid,' she said apologetically.

'Perfect!' Cillian declared and thanked her.

Meanwhile, Jake quietly handed her a small brown-paper parcel. 'I'm sorry it's not very festively wrapped,' he said.

Nell untied the string. Inside was a shiny cardboard box, like a miniature shoebox. She lifted the lid to reveal a large, labelled insect, stuck in place by a pin. It was an *Aglae caerulea* or, rather, a beautiful metallic blue bee, from South America, like the ones he had shown her at the museum, and which she had especially admired. She kissed Jake and sat down beside Cillian in order to describe it to him.

'Does it look like a jewel?' he asked, in a put-on voice, like that of a bad, but earnest, Shakespearean actor.

Nell laughed, and told him it did.

'And is its arse blue like the rest of its body? Or, Jakey, is it only flies that are blue-arsed?'

'You're thinking of bluebottles,' his grandson said, smiling. 'I've told you their grand name.'

'I well remember it. I've been dashing around like a caerulean posteriored dipteran in the kitchen just now, trying to get lunch together.' Cillian, struggling somewhat, made to stand up. Nell gave him a hand. 'I'm going to check the sprouts, see if they're done,' the old man said. 'I hope I didn't light the wrong gas ring by mistake. I'm always forgetting which knob is which.'

'Do you want any help?' Nell and Jake asked simultaneously.

'Certainly not,' Cillian retorted. He felt his way to the door and left the room.

Jake shifted a log in the fire with his foot. The flames flowed up like orange chiffon in a wind. He refilled Nell's glass.

'Warmer now?' he asked.

'Much, thanks,' Nell said, sitting down on the leather-topped fender. She was watching the flames. Their heat began to sting her eyes, but the flickering patterns were compelling and she did not look away. 'What time did you arrive?'

'Not long before you. About half an hour.'

'Did you have a nice morning?'

'All right. I was working.'

'That's very conscientious, on Christmas Day,' Nell commented.

'I'm writing a book about bees,' Jake explained quietly. 'My publisher wants it by the end of January.'

Nell turned to look up at him. 'You never told me that.'

'Ah, well.' His kind smile reminded Nell of Cillian's.

'I know a manuscript is rather a private thing, but would you ever let me read it?'

'Oh,' he said surprised. 'I don't know, would you be interested? Nobody except people at the publisher's and a couple of colleagues has ever asked.' He sank his hands deep into his baggy grey trousers, confused but evidently flattered. 'I was planning to read it to Grandfather. Even though he's not a bee boffin, he makes a very good editor. Problem is, I'm so short of time.'

Nell laughed: the solution was so obvious.

'You really wouldn't mind?' he quizzed.

'Course not. I asked, didn't I? It makes no difference whether I read it myself or out loud. It'd be a pleasure to read it to him.'

A shout came from the kitchen: it was Cillian calling them for lunch.

The two of them, happy with their arrangement, went next door.

After lunch, still in paper hats, they returned to the sitting room for coffee and more wine. They were still one or two presents beneath the tree. They settled down to open them. Jake was pleased with the paperback Nell gave him.

The telephone rang. Cillian lifted the heavy bakelite receiver.

'Liza, my dear. Happy Christmas,' he said. 'Yes, we've had a wonderful day . . . Yellow socks . . . All plastered . . . How's Wales? I bet . . . We're all very jealous . . . Come for New Year? That's a lovely invitation, but I'm afraid I'm off to Dublin. If the bloody liver holds out another week, that is. But I'm sure Nell – hang on – ' Cillian put his hand over the mouthpiece. 'Your sister's asking you to Wales for New Year.'

228

'I thought there wasn't any room.'

'She says she'll somehow make room for any number who want to go.'

'Does that include me?' Jake asked in jest.

'Why not?' Nell replied with surprise as she took the receiver from Cillian.

'No, seriously, I don't think I can.'

'Shall I ask?'

'It's a nice idea,' Jake told her, smiling, 'but I'm meant to be working.'

Cillian was listening to them, head cocked intently, but he said nothing.

'D'you want me to say something to her?' Nell's hand was covering the mouthpiece.

Jake hesitated. 'Isn't it an intolerable imposition, particularly at this late notice, to ask myself for New Year?'

'You haven't asked yourself. I'm asking you.' Nell said hello to her sister on the other end of the line. 'Can Jake come?'

'Of course.' She and Nell then proceeded to make plans, exchange news. Then Nell spoke to Samuel for a while.

'Are you sure they didn't mind?' Jake quizzed when she replaced the receiver.

'Not in the least. Pleased. It'll be a squash, she said, but she'll work something out, and the more the merrier.'

'But we've never met. How d'you know she wasn't just being – '

'Liza doesn't do or say things,' Cillian interrupted, 'just to be polite.'

'I was intending to spend a solitary New Year working.'

'Well it's a good thing you aren't any longer,' the old man declared, taking a defiant swig of his wine. 'I can't be doing with such self-righteousness.'

'Please,' Nell urged, turning to Jake. 'Don't think you have to come. You can change your mind. Liza and Samuel are very relaxed.'

'No, I'd love to, but I am worried about this book – '

229

'You can do it there, you ass,' the old man told his grandson impatiently. 'Good God, you carry on as if you're constipated.'

Nell and Jake laughed. 'Oh, go on your walk,' the former said, 'before it gets dark.'

'What the fuck difference does it make to me if I walk in the light or the dark? I'll go later,' Cillian rejoined, kicking off his shoes and lifting up his legs to rest his feet on the fender. 'Give me a chocolate, Jake,' he ordered, ineffectually clicking his gnarled fingers. They made no sound so he clapped his hands instead. 'A rum truffle, please. Thanks. Now, keep your voices to a whisper because I'm going to go to sleep for a bit and it's important I'm not disturbed. I'm going to dream about New Year, you see, in Wales as it happens, with you lot all having a really nice time.'

So saying, Cillian dropped the chocolate into his mouth and, with a triumphant grin, leaned his head back on a cushion and closed his milky eyes.

# CHAPTER
# 10

The Welsh hills were black and mauve: beautiful bruises on the face of the earth.

It was raining. Just as a stocking across a camera's lens blurs the blemishes of an ageing actress's skin, so did the grey drizzle smudge the harshness of the bleak view.

Two or three small, dark houses could be seen dotted on the hillside, isolated and remote, smoke skimping from their chimneys. A few sheep were scattered about the valley. They were sodden and filthy, like paper handkerchiefs which had been scrumpled up and tossed in the gutter.

It was the day before New Year's Eve, and it was already dark. Samuel and Nell had been walking most of the afternoon. They were tramping up a hill together, heading home. With each of their steps mud splattered on to their ankles and calves, but neither of them noticed or cared.

'Shall we go to the pub?' Samuel suggested breathlessly. 'I think we deserve it. We must have been miles.'

'Where is it?'

'Not far,' he said. 'We pass the farm on the way. I promised Liza we'd get some milk.'

'Will we make it before it gets dark?'

'Should do,' Samuel quickened his pace. 'More to the point, will we get there before Eddie?' he laughed. 'What's the bet he's already at the bar, on his third triple whisky?'

The two of them hurried on.

When they arrived at the little pub half an hour or so later, they wiped their feet on a spherical brush which resembled a hedgehog and which was fixed outside the door. Samuel put his hand out to the wall of the building to balance himself.

'You know,' he began, battering his boots against the bristles, 'one of my things was to wipe my feet exactly four times each side before I went in anywhere. Lucky I'm less rigid about it now than I was – four times wouldn't be enough to rid this lot.' Clods of compact earth began to fall away from the jagged soles. 'God no wonder I was puffed: the extra weight!'

'What happens now when you don't do it four times?' Nell asked, unbuttoning the coat which Jake had lent her for the walk.

'Oh, I still feel slightly uneasy,' Samuel replied, following his sister-in-law inside. 'But at least I don't panic any more. The point is, I might not like doing it, but at least I can.'

'That's excellent,' Nell enthused, stepping towards the bar. 'Let me get you a drink quickly, to stamp out any current uneasiness.'

'I'm not sure Dr Oak would approve of your methods.' Samuel smiled mischievously. 'Still, make that a double whisky. I'm going to buy it, though, I insist. What would you like?'

Nell asked for beer. They went with their drinks to sit by the fire.

'Eddie's not here,' Nell observed, looking across the small room.

'Not yet,' her companion pointed out. 'He will be. Probably in a minute, with Jake.' Samuel was staring at his glass. His fingers were fiddling with it, turning it round on the table. 'He's nice, Jake.' Leading remark, accompanied by a raise of the eyebrows.

'Yes,' Nell agreed.

'You, well, you know?' Samuel ventured.

'Sleeping with him?' She took off her damp yellow scarf. 'No.'

'Not yet, anyway.'

'It's a possibility, I suppose. A casual thing,' Nell admitted, trying to sound insouciant. She even shrugged. 'This morning, in the car on the way here, we were talking and talking, and I thought, if it happens, well, that'd be nice.'

'Of course,' Samuel told her. 'You're in love with him.'

'Unlikely.'

'I forgot,' he teased, 'that would compromise those pessimistic principles of yours, wouldn't it? Love being the foolish pastime of the optimist?'

'Quite.'

Nell took a swig of her beer. The faint trace of froth left on the inside of her glass resembled a thin littoral spume left by the tide.

'Speaking of which – ' deadpan tone – 'Lucy Hardcastle?'

Samuel stopped turning his glass. He took a sip of whisky.

'Ah yes, that.' He rubbed his knees, and looked at the battered card lampshade on the mantelpiece. Was that dent a touch too close to the scorching bulb within? Just a passing thought. 'Over,' he said.

Nell saw that he was frowning. She followed his gaze to the lamp on the mantelpiece. Its old shade had a funny design: wagon wheels. Wagon wheels on a lampshade? Maybe that was why he was puzzled.

'The head tapping is on its way out.'

'I'm glad. Understatement,' she assured him. 'But is that significant?'

'Possibly,' Samuel answered. 'For the last few nights, after Liza and I – well – before we've gone to sleep, I've actually forgotten to check the plug downstairs: I don't know if that means anything. Dr Oak's sceptical about the significance of such simple cause and effect.' He broke off and folded his arms. 'But there must be something in the notion that the happier people are the less susceptible they are to irrational anxiety. Or perhaps it's just they're better able to control it, I don't know. Either way – ' He stopped abruptly.

'Things are working out,' Nell said, helpfully filling in for him.

'Yes, for the better. No, the best.'

233

'Marriage now completely perfect?'

'Without a doubt,' Samuel replied passionately. 'And you better believe it.' His voice was almost aggressively firm. Nell had never heard him like that before. She imagined it was a tone he usually reserved for his most recalcitrant pupils.

She did not answer his challenging remark, instead she put her glass to her lips. It half hid her face. Samuel's sincerity and conviction made her feel self-conscious, even a bit silly.

'The disapprobation,' Samuel reflected more softly, 'in your eyes, on the night of the play, made me feel ashamed, yes, for all the obvious reasons to do with Liza and myself. And I'd also made you angry and upset.'

'On her behalf,' Nell said.

'Understandably so. But it wasn't just that which got to me. You looked so bloody bleak. There was an air about you of irredeemable cynicism, and I realised it was me who had fuelled it. I was responsible.'

Nell remained silent, so Samuel went on.

'I was worried that, like it or not, what I'd done might confirm your whole dotty way of thinking, even influence the way you lead your life.'

'Like?' Nell asked.

'Like, I don't know, opting out. Like, if not exactly embracing solitude, then at least considering it or going into affairs doggedly determined to remain emotionally detached, and, another example . . . ' He hesitated.

'Go on.'

'Well, like,' he repeated, 'not allowing yourself to fall in love with Jake.'

'Oh?'

'Yes.' Samuel nodded emphatically.

'I see.'

'So, anyway, I thought: I'm buggered if I'm not going to prove her wrong, show her that despite my temporary lapse things have been for the best. In fact, they're even better than they were.'

234

'I'm glad,' Nell remarked distractedly.

The door opened behind her. Hearing it, she hastily turned round. It was a man with a drip on the end of his nose and bits of dust and straw on his jacket. The dairy farmer. He waved to them and they waved back. Then Nell turned to face Samuel again. He was staring at her. She emptied her glass and plonked it down on the table with a thud.

Samuel stood, picked up her glass and smiled at her. 'They'll be here in a minute,' he said, and went to the bar.

When Nell opened the door to the cottage, she kicked off her boots and padded over to the kitchen table in her thick socks. She sat down between Max and Nancy who were in their dressing-gowns eating bowls of Weetabix for their supper. They looked pink and warm. Nell sniffed and blew her red nose. The place smelt of wood smoke from the fires. And mothballs – unmistakably a bequest from Jake.

'Where's Mum?' she asked her nephew, stealing a sip of his hot Ribena.

'In the sitting room, putting up our camp beds.'

'We're sharing with Eddie tonight,' Nancy said. 'Now you and that man with curly lips – '

'Jake,' her brother interrupted.

' – have come, he's moved in with us.'

The children's eyes sparkled.

'Yeah,' said Max. 'He's sleeping on the sofa. He promised us if he wakes us when he comes to bed, he'll tell us a story. He's brilliant, Eddie is.'

'Your boyfriend's got funny teeth and smells weird,' Nancy observed.

'He's not my boyfriend,' Nell smiled.

Nancy, ignoring her, went on. 'But we do like him. He's got a soft voice, like our dentist who has rubber fingers and gives us water with a pink pill in it that's magic.'

Liza appeared in the doorway. She was wearing jeans and a plain grey sweatshirt. Her hair was tied back in a pony tail, and she wore huge hoop earrings.

235

'You're back,' she remarked, pleased. 'Did you have a nice walk?'

'Wonderful,' Nell replied. 'I feel completely exhausted. Legs like jelly.'

'Did you meet the others in the pub?'

'Yes.'

'They all still there?'

Yes again.

Liza smiled tolerantly. 'That's good. I'll get these two to bed, then we can have a bit of time on our own and catch up while I make a start on dinner.' Liza took her children's squishy hands and told them to kiss Nell goodnight. They went next door.

When Liza came back into the room a few minutes later, she settled down with her sister at the table. They opened a bottle of wine and started to cut up some vegetables.

'You're in the room you were in last time, with Conrad,' the elder of the two said. 'Sorry. Shouldn't have mentioned his name, should I?'

'It's fine,' Nell said, as unemotional as if someone had asked whether the milk was off.

'Jake's on a camp-bed in the passage. There wasn't any space for it in the sitting room. It was the only place. I haven't put it up yet. We can do it later. Think he'll mind being there, not having a room?'

'I expect he can cope.'

'Here, pass us a few carrots. You'll never get through those lot chopping at that rate. No, I couldn't think of another way round the lack of room. It was either him or Eddie, there, and the children were so keen to have Eddie in with them.' Liza paused, and carried on cutting up the vegetables. 'I do like Jake by the way. I must share your soft-spot for Irishmen.'

'Oh, what soft-spot, other than Cillian?'

'Didn't you get off with an Irish pop star at one time?'

'If you mean the ghastly fling I had when I was about eighteen with the lead singer of a band called the Banshees – '

236

'That's the one.'

'Liza, he was hardly a pop star. I think he might have once played one night in a pub in Finchley. Had he been half as tuneful as a banshee he might have got somewhere. Anyway, he wasn't even Irish: he came from Birmingham.'

Liza laughed. 'I got that wrong, then. Still, I thought you were like Samuel. He's always had a particular fondness for the Irish. The English teacher at his school is Irish.' Her thick knife continued slicing the carrots. Its sound on the wooden board was eerie.

Nell laid aside her knife and wiped her hands on her trousers which were still damp from the walk. She reached for her packet of cigarettes. Her cold pink fingers fumbled numbly to open its lid and draw one out.

'You met her, I think,' Liza continued. She tipped her head breezily from side to side as she watched herself chopping away. Nell noticed that her neck was as white as milk. 'On the night of his play.'

'Briefly.'

'She's got a lovely accent. Yes, very soft. Sad she's leaving, really.'

'Oh?'

'Well, she was one of his friends. Some of his colleagues are so awful. There was one called Ralph who he couldn't stand. Luckily, he left too, at the end of term: given the sack. It's all very hush-hush, but he got the woman who looks after the stationery cupboard pregnant, which in itself might have been all right, but for the fact a first-year caught them actually doing it in there, amongst the packets of new exercise books. The headmaster flipped.'

Nell giggled. 'It's like a soap opera.'

'It certainly is. I love all the staffroom gossip. Apparently, the head of the language department who was in love with this Ralph fellow, has taken to wearing black. But Samuel was thrilled to see the back of him.'

'What about Lu— ' Nell bit her tongue, and quickly lit her cigarette. Liza, concentrating on her task in hand, did not

237

spot that her sister's hand was shaking as she closed the flame in on the tip. 'What about the English teacher?'

'She's landed herself a new job, the head of the English department at a school back in Ireland. Samuel's fond of her. I imagined he'd be sad to see her go, but when he told me he seemed very pleased, excited for her that she was leaving so quickly and not having to stick out another whole term.'

'I can see that,' Nell ventured carefully. 'When you know you've got a new post, it must be frustrating to have to go through that thing of doing a term's notice at the old place.'

'Oh, I agree. I said it was sad, though. They shared break duty. I thought he'd miss her round the staffroom, but he told me he wouldn't. He said he still had Tim Crawford, the History Man, he calls him.' Liza threw the carrots into a waiting saucepan, and looked at Nell with a wide-eyed, puzzled expression. 'I said, yes of course, but you can still miss her all the same. Yet he swore not.' She broke off and glanced into a cupboard above the sink, 'Damn, I forgot to get more salt,' she mumbled to herself. Then, louder again, to Nell, 'Men are funny like that. Quite ruthless in a way.'

'Samuel's not ruthless. Unsentimental, that's all. Though he is sentimental about some things. Family.'

'Thank God,' Liza sighed fondly. 'Even if it does mean he has to tap his head however many times before he drinks coffee.'

'To stop the children being run over, isn't it, something daft like that?'

Liza nodded. 'I do love him, dotty though he is.'

'Not really dotty,' Nell said.

'Course not, and getting even less so.'

'Everyone has their little neuroses. Cillian told me he used to suffer from vertigo before he went blind. I remember once when he was in one of his rare self-pitying moods, he said he was glad he could no longer see because it meant he could no longer see down.'

Liza laughed. 'Typical Cillian remark.'

'His friend's got a thing about pigeons. Hates them. Can't go out during the day.'

'Eddie's constantly scratching himself,' Liza added. 'I wonder if Daniel's got anything?'

'His obsession is women,' Nell recalled, but not in the bitter voice she usually employed when referring to her brother and his girlfriends.

'Daniel!' Liza suddenly cheeped, getting up to jet water from the tap into the saucepan.

'What?'

'I barely dare tell you. It'll make you so cross.'

'No, I'm sure it won't,' Nell told her sincerely.

Liza hesitated as she sat down again to start work on the chicken. 'New girlfriend,' she said slowly, clumping the knife down through the pale yellow neck of the dead fowl. 'Ruth, she's called. Swears he's in love with her.'

Nell wrinkled up her nose, sceptical.

'I guessed you'd react like that. You never give him the benefit of the doubt. I know we've heard it all before, but when he rang on Christmas Day, he sounded genuinely ecstatic. Promise.'

Her sister smiled. 'If this is true, it's good news.'

'Wonderful. Will you tell Christabel? Poor thing, it's really quite soon after they split up.'

'Depends.'

'On what?'

'How she's feeling,' Nell replied. 'I expect she'll be pleased for him. She's happier herself at the moment.'

'Oh yes?'

'Much older man.'

'That's brilliant,' Liza said.

'No bad thing. Slightly more likely to stick around. Maybe this one'll last a little longer than the others.'

'Oh, come on, give her more credit than that. What's he like?'

'City, but I like him all the same. He's very funny, not pompous. Teases her a lot which is good, and seems to adore her.'

'Well I'm pleased. You?'

'Course. She deserves someone nice.' Nell paused for thought. 'Daniel, the sod. He never rang to tell me.' Indignant.

'Nell, can you blame him? Your cynicism. It's enough to put anyone off confiding that sort of thing to you.'

Nell shrugged, picked up the dismembered chicken's head, and threw it away.

Back at the table she poured herself some more wine. 'It's wonderful,' she said.

'What?'

'What do you think? Daniel.'

'Unlike you to say that,' Liza observed, buttering the bird and taking a sip of her drink. In the dim light, Nell could see greasy fingermarks on the side of Liza's glass.

'Well,' Nell sighed, rising from her chair again. She put her hands in the back pockets of her jeans, and walked jauntily to stand in front of the fire.

Silence while Liza gently punctured the pimply pink flesh of the chicken's thighs and breasts with sprigs of fresh rosemary. 'Do you suppose Jake has a funny neurosis?' she asked unexpectedly.

Pause while Nell considered the question. 'He might,' she replied, warming by the fire and to her subject. 'I wouldn't know – not yet anyway,' she added, with an uncharacteristic lack of caution which verged on the indiscreet. Followed by a small laugh.

'I wonder if he's got any phobias or obsessions? I mean, is he mad about anything?' she asked peering at Nell. Significantly.

Nell looked away from her sister's gaze with a degree of self-consciousness. She cast her eyes down towards the blaze of the fire.

'Oh yes. There's one very obvious thing,' she said airily.

'What?' her sister enquired in an indulgent tone, for once feigning innocence.

'He's mad about bees,' Nell said, and continued to stare at the fire in order that Liza could not see she was smiling.

'You know a bit about bugs then?' Eddie asked Jake a while later, when they had returned from the pub. The three of them were sitting in the kitchen with Liza and Nell, having supper. 'Funny line of work to be in, eh?' Eddie, who was wearing shoes but no socks, lifted his foot almost level with the table. Winking at Jake, he started vigorously scratching his ankle. 'Myself,' he continued, 'I hate the fuckers.'

Liza laughed and filled his glass. 'Jake's in bees,' she told him.

'Oh, bees,' Eddie said. 'Och, I've been stung by a few of them in my time. But the stings in their arses've got sweet FA on the teeth of my bugs. I can tell you, bees are goddamn soft in comparison.'

Jake put his fork down, leaned back in his chair and lit a cigarette. In the candlelight, his smile, as he looked askance at the Scotsman, reminded Nell of sepia photographs she had seen of Cillian as a young man. His full lips and unkempt teeth gave him the same beguilingly wicked air. 'You reckon?' he jokily challenged Eddie.

'You bet, mate,' Eddie said, tugging the collar of his jersey away from his neck and aiming a good slap at himself, just below the ear.

Jake took a puff of his cigarette. When he exhaled, smoke wafted about his face making him look like one of those romantic villains in a 1930s' movie; then it drifted away to dally with the candle flames. He kept the cigarette in his mouth as he began to roll back one of his sleeves. The others watched silently as he did so, 'Right, Ed,' he said at last, in a very serious voice, 'what's the bet my bee stings are worse than your bug bites?'

Samuel, Liza and Nell laughed. Eddie thumped on the table with his fists. 'Ten quid!' he cried. 'I'm as poor as pig shit – that's working for the Beeb for you – '

'And betting on the horses,' Samuel reminded him.

'Yeah. Okay,' he admitted, then turned to Jake. 'Still, ten quid. You haven't got a fart's chance in a hurricane, mate.'

'You're on,' Jake said, shaking his hand.

Nell noticed that Eddie's thick palm was calloused and his huge fingers were grimy and nicotine-stained. The tips had frayed plasters wrapped round them. By contrast, Jake's hand, accustomed as it was to the fiddly business of fingering entomological specimens, seemed almost delicate.

'Right, who wants to place bets and who wants to be the judge?' Eddie demanded. 'I'd better be honest: my friend here,' he declared, nudging Samuel, 'isn't allowed to bet.'

'Why?' Samuel asked.

'First, because it'd be unfair. You saw me at the hospital when my infestation was at its worst, so you know I'm going to win. Believe me, Jake, they're quite rife now, but they were rifer then, and I mean rife.' Another thump on the table to emphasise his point. A couple of plates and spoons jumped with fright. 'And, second, Samuel,' he resumed, 'because you're a loony git who has a suspect relationship with plug holes and people like you are automatically disqualified.'

'Objection,' Samuel protested, enjoying the mockery.

'Och, shut your face. Let's get on with it. Do you want to bet, girls?'

'Nellie can't bet,' Jake chipped in suddenly. 'She knows something about me that might influence her.'

Nell looked at Jake quizzically. She could not think what he was referring to.

'Och, don't tell me,' Eddie sighed wearily, disappointed, 'the pair of you were fucking in a field and attacked by a sodding swarm. In which case I admit defeat. You win.'

There was silence for a second or two. Samuel held his breath. Nell bit her lip and immediately fixed her eyes on one of the candles. She started to fiddle with its dripping wax, aware of a kind of discomfort which was perversely pleasurable. It was reminiscent of how she felt whenever a wasp hovered near her, threatening to sting. Hearing the insect's sinister hum close to her ear, she would remain completely still. Nonetheless, as she wondered whether or not it was going to strike, the adrenalin would be pumping inside her.

242

Then Jake broke the silence. 'Not exactly,' he laughed. 'It's just she knows I was working abroad recently, in rather hazardous circumstances.'

'Collecting bees?' Eddie asked.

Jake nodded.

'A field trip then,' the Scotsman commented, 'rather than a field fuck.'

'Yes,' Nell muttered. 'Eddie, we're not – ' she began timidly, anxious to explain she and Jake were just friends.

'You're sharing a room tonight, aren't you?' he interrupted breezily. While Samuel and Liza shook their heads, embarrassed, and explained that they were going to put a camp-bed up in the passage, Eddie turned to Jake who, Samuel saw, was watching Nell. But she was still rigidly gazing into the candle flame and so had not noticed that Jake was staring at her. There was a grin on her face. 'Come on, Jake,' Eddie said, 'we'd better be getting on with this so as to let you get to bed 'cos you won't be getting much sleep out there in the bleeding corridor. Roll back your other sleeve,' he ordered. 'No, in fact, take off your jersey. We'll get the girls to examine our backs to see who's got the worst sores.'

Jake laughed and obeyed. The Scotsman removed his own jacket and shirt. Samuel started to clear away the plates as Liza and Nell looked at the two men's backs and arms.

'Eddie, I can't see any bites,' Liza told him. 'Only patches of redness where you've scratched yourself.'

'It's hard to see in the candlelight,' Nell said, standing over Jake. He took her hand and ran her finger across his shoulders. His flesh was warm and soft, but she could feel a few bumps where he had been stung. 'God, Jake, how many are there?' Her fingers wandered over his bicep and encountered yet more stings.

'Where did you get them all?' Samuel enquired, filling the sink with water.

'Indonesia,' Jake replied.

'I think you win,' Nell said. She took her hand away from his arm.

243

'Indo-fucking-nesia!' Eddie exclaimed, shaking his head. 'Well, that makes me ten quid poorer.' He put his shirt and jacket back on, leaned back in his chair and pulled a crumpled note from his trouser pocket. 'No bloody wonder.'

'I think I could have predicted that,' Samuel remarked, washing-up brush in hand. He chuckled. 'Your bugs aren't exactly visible now, are they Eddie?'

'All right, all right. Delusory whatsit.'

'Parasitosis,' Jake corrected for him.

'Och, bloody 'ell, how do you know about that, then?' Eddie quizzed, good-humouredly.

'Working in entomology,' Jake replied.

'Right, you sneaky bastard,' he said, grinning and holding up the ten pound note. 'Because you cheated, you don't get this till you win another bet of my choosing. Okay?'

'Depends what it is,' Jake said sceptically.

'Oh God,' Samuel said with nervous anticipation. He pulled up the sleeves of his jersey with his teeth. Then he plunged them back into the sink.

'Right,' Eddie began, 'this time I reckon I'm on to the winner.' He took a sip of his wine and winked at his hostess before turning to Jake. 'Here's the condition then, and I trust you to be honest. If you can get a wink of sleep in that poxy camp-bed out there, you get the tenner back, but if you don't, I get to keep it. I bet you, mate, you won't stay the course.'

Later that night Nell awoke as Jake joined her in her small double bed, 'I'm sorry,' he whispered. 'Eddie was right, I couldn't sleep on that thing. Do you mind?'

'You'll lose your tenner,' Nell answered.

'He can keep his tenner,' Jake laughed, putting his arm round her. He smelt of red wine.

It was at that moment that Nell acknowledged to herself she had fallen in love with him.

Despite all her resolutions, it had happened at supper, about the time when she was examining his back for bee stings and he had taken her hand in his in order to guide her fingers across his shoulders. Then what Samuel had said in the pub earlier had come back to her; and she had also heard Cillian's voice in her head urging her to 'let go'.

More specifically, it was when Eddie had announced the conditions of the evening's second bet, and with it opened up in her mind certain possibilities.

Samuel who, when Eddie spoke, was at the kitchen sink with his back to everyone, had said nothing. Liza had laughed. Jake had puffed his cigarette nonchalantly and murmured, 'I can try.'

'You're going to have to,' Eddie told him, looking at Nell and laughing. 'You don't have much alternative.'

Then Jake had looked at her too, and smiled. Cillian's smile. It seemed to ask if her bed might not be an alternative if he failed?

The room with the redcurrant curtains was cold, but Jake, beside Nell in the creaky bed, was warm. They both lay completely still and nothing was said. In the dark she knew he was watching her, and under her arm she could feel his heart beating. Her muscles were tense.

After what seemed a long while he moved even closer and his lips touched hers.

# CHAPTER

# 11

On the morning of New Year's Eve, a whole year later, Nell woke up at about ten o'clock. Her eyes were bleared by a hangover. She tried to focus on the patterns covering the curtains, but the bunches of redcurrants seemed to move about of their own accord, as if they were real and wavering in a breeze.

Jake's forehead was buried in the nape of her neck. Nell was aware that he too had just opened her eyes. She felt his lashes judder a little against his skin.

'You awake?' he asked in a muffled voice. Only his jaw moved. His morning bristles tickled her. The sensation made her laugh. 'What's up, sweetie?'

'Your chin.'

'Sorry, I couldn't find my razor yesterday. Maybe Grandfather took mine from the flat by mistake, when he was packing to go to Dublin.' Jake, who had given up his flat in Bloomsbury, had been living with Cillian and Nell, in order to be with them both, for nearly nine months. 'Or maybe it's in the case somewhere? I must shave today. You didn't put it in by any chance, did you?'

'I don't think so. Samuel wouldn't mind if you borrowed his. I saw he left it on the windowsill above the kitchen sink. It's a snazzy new electric one.'

Jake, still in the nape of her neck, nodded. 'What would I do without you?'

'I can't imagine,' she mocked confidently. 'I'll have a look for yours, though, when I can be bothered to get up.'

'Don't get up,' he mumbled coaxingly, running his hands round her ribs.

'Uh huh.' She smiled with her bottom lip between her teeth. 'I know you so well, you're so predictable.'

'Please, you can't say that,' he protested, lifting his head.

'No, I know, you're not really predictable,' Nell said.

He leaned forward to kiss her.

It was after eleven when Nell and Jake emerged from the bedroom. Her hangover had improved considerably. They went into the kitchen and joined Samuel, Liza and Eddie at the table. It was covered with breakfast things.

'We've finished. Let me get rid of some of this stuff,' Liza said, stacking a couple of dirty cereal bowls and an eggcup, and peering into the red enamel coffee jug. 'I'll make some more coffee.' Heavily pregnant, she put her palm on the table to help heave herself up from the chair. Samuel hastily placed his hand on her shoulder and pushed her down again.

'Stay right there. I'm going to do it.' He took the forget-me-not blue pottery from her and kissed the top of her head. 'Right, you two, toast?' he asked, addressing Nell and Jake.

'It's not my pregnant state which makes him so willing to help, you understand,' Liza laughed, 'but the excuse to play with the new toaster. Max and Nancy gave it to him for Christmas. We reckon it must date from the early sixties.'

'It was their idea, wasn't it brilliant?' Samuel enthused. 'I can't stand people who boast about their children, but it really was inspired.' He put the plates in the sink and moved to the gleaming electric object on the sideboard. It was large and elegant, a great old Cadillac of a toaster. 'And so generous of them,' he added, glancing appreciatively at his wife, knowing it was she who had paid for it.

'Sam throw another slice in for me if you're making some for the lovers,' Eddie said, winking at Nell, who threw him a look of mock indignation.

247

'That's the joy of this thing,' Samuel explained, tapping his new toy, and putting in three slices of bread. 'It's got four slots!' He nonchalantly swept some crumbs from the toaster's surface. There was a lever at the side with which to turn the machine on. At its end was a shiny black knob. Samuel fingered it carelessly and, when he depressed it, the bread disappeared. He was like a magician completing an impressive conjuring trick.

'Right,' he said, when the toast had popped up a short time later. He delivered the three slices to the table with a triumphant flourish. 'Now,' he asked, 'who wants coffee?'

Jake helped Nell over a rickety stile. She leapt down and they continued walking along the muddy bank of the frozen stream.

'I think this was the way Samuel and I came last year,' she said.

'Are you lost, Nellie?'

'No, no,' she assured him confidently, pointing to a black hill in the distance. 'I remember that hill. The pub where we met you and Eddie is over the other side.'

'I can just picture us seeing the New Year in, shivering under a bush somewhere in the middle of nowhere.' Jake pulled the collar of his black coat up around his ears. 'That wouldn't be entirely without its attractions, but it might get a touch chilly.' He smiled.

The sky was cloudless and blue. The shrivelled leaves on the trees shimmered in the cold sunlight as if they had been aerosol-sprayed with Christmas gold paint.

'We'll have to cross this stream,' Jake remarked. 'Is there a bridge farther along?'

Nell looked blank.

'How did you and Samuel cross it last time?'

'I think there was a convenient piece of wood.' She glanced around. 'Oh dear.'

'No convenient piece of wood this time. It looks like I'm going to have to test the ice.'

248

'Jake, no.'

He laughed and rubbed her hand. 'Don't worry. I'm sure it's thick enough to take our weight.'

He trod his way carefully towards the glacial surface of the stream. At the edges the ice was white and appeared to have formed in overlapping lines like the hems of a number of organza petticoats. Jake tapped it with his toe and slowly inched the rest of his foot on to it. Then the other one.

'I can't bear to watch,' Nell said from the bank.

'Ssshh,' Jake told her gently, concentrating hard, listening out for the minutest sounds of any cracks.

Nell watched his back view as he made his tentative steps into the middle of the stream where the ice was black. Although he was tall and reasonably strong-looking, he seemed vulnerable with his arms outstretched in the optimistic hope that his weight would thus be more evenly distributed. His open coat flapped at his legs mockingly.

Suddenly there was a loud cracking noise, but the ice held.

'Oh shit,' he murmured shakily, without looking round at Nell. He remained completely immobile for a moment. 'I better take this off,' he added, thinking out loud.

'Be careful,' Nell urged.

Jake slowly removed his heavy coat, and chucked it on to the bank in front of him. Then, very carefully, he slid his feet across the remaining few yards of the ice to join it.

When he was safely on muddy ground he turned to Nell and held out his hands towards her by way of encouragement.

'Take it slowly,' he advised. 'It's all right as long as you don't decide to hopscotch over it.'

Nell laughed nervously and tiptoed on to the ice. 'I hate this.'

'If it breaks, I'm ready to save you,' Jake said, pushing up the sleeves of his jersey.

Nell held her breath.

'But it won't break,' he added.

'Are you sure?' she asked, taking another anxious step.

249

'Trust me. Do you trust me?'

She stopped and looked at him. He was standing at the edge of the ice, leaning towards her, ready to help. His bare arms and fingers beckoned in the cold breeze and his teeth held on to his bottom lip in suspense. His face, with its wide open eyes and curved dark brows, was sincere.

'Yes,' she answered firmly. 'I trust you.'

'Come on, then, you've only a little way to go.'

Nell carried on towards him. At last the tips of her fingers touched his, and she hastened her progress, perhaps a touch carelessly. Her final step broke the edge of the ice and she fell though it, up to her ankles in soupy mud. Jake quickly pulled her out of it on to the bank. She landed on one of his feet, and they both fell over, collapsing together on the slope.

'My God,' Nell exclaimed, as she lay on the hardened mud. 'I'm jittering inside. You were much braver than me.'

'Rubbish. I was terrified.'

Laughing with relief, they helped each other up. Jake put his coat on and took Nell's hand.

Samuel spent much of his afternoon chopping logs in the shed beside the cottage. When he had finished, Eddie insisted he joined him in front of the television. Later they went with Liza and the children to the pub to meet Jake and Nell, but they arrived first. Eddie bought a round of drinks. Shortly afterwards, the cold, exhausted pair of walkers appeared.

Samuel watched Nell as she told them how she and Jake had crossed the stream. As she spoke she rubbed her thighs with her hands to warm herself. Her brown hair which reached to beneath her shoulders had been blown about by the wind; her nose was red. With a childlike gesture, she wiped her watery eyes with the frayed sleeve of her jersey. She was still shivering, but despite her discomfort, she was in a good mood.

Samuel, sipping some whisky, felt warm inside. When he

looked at his sister-in-law he was aware of a not entirely unpleasant sensation of self-satisfaction. He glanced at her companion. Nancy had observed on more than one occasion that Jake's teeth weren't perfect (in fact she had put it less diplomatically than that) but he was nice looking and, anyway, imperfect teeth could be improved upon, if necessary. Unlike selfishness. That was less easily corrected.

Nell had had her fair share of selfish men. Perplexingly, she had fallen for one called Jerry. He would never let her smoke, so fanatical was he about the smell of cigarettes on her breath, yet he could not care less about his own bad breath, and ate garlic, whole cloves of the stuff, like other people eat cashew nuts. Another ex-lover, a failed musician, swore that the one and only place he could practise his singing was in her bedroom, more often than not, late at night. When she protested, he accused her of 'cramping' his 'artistic karma and creativity'.

But Jake did not strike Samuel as selfish or unkind. He was gentle. Samuel considered him to have integrity; and over the past year had grown more and more fond of him.

The two of them had had many conversations together, about politics and so forth, but they had also had a number about Nell. At Daniel's and Ruth's wedding, back in November, Jake had talked about living in his grandfather's flat, and helping Nell to look after the old man. As he spoke, though he did not say so specifically, he managed to convey how much he enjoyed being with her, how much in love with her he was. He hinted that he hoped it would last for a long, long time, perhaps even permanently.

Samuel had warmed to him, then, all the more. Later, Nell had approached them with an open smile, and the conversation had moved on. Jake had steered it towards a new topic in a manner that was neither alarmed nor neurotic, but simply discreet.

Naturally Samuel had never repeated the remarks to his sister-in-law or to his wife. He had remained an observer,

251

silently watching Nell and Jake, and he felt he had just cause to have faith that they would stay together.

'Don't take any notice of her,' Jake said. 'She was very brave.'

'Och,' Eddie piped up, 'that's all very well, crossing a bit of ice over some poxy stream in Wales! What about when you carry her off into the Indonesia sunset, or whatever place it is you decide to take the lass, what then?' The Scotsman turned to Nell. 'Are you going to be brave enough to stand the sting of his bleedin' bees, that's what I want to know.'

Eddie, Samuel told him in his head, you have this extraordinary knack for saying precisely the wrong thing.

'Where did you get the idea we were going to Indonesia?' Nell asked. 'Jake's already been.'

'I don't know! I just thought he might be planning to take you on holiday, or some such.'

'No such plans, I'm afraid,' Jake said. 'Brighton if she's lucky,' he added with a laugh.

'Really?' Eddie said. 'Nice place, Brighton. Samuel loves it, don't you, Samuel? Tell us if you decide to go, Jake.' He nudged his friend. 'We can recommend a great little bed and breakfast, can't we?'

As it happened, Samuel had never again mentioned the Brighton trip to his wife. For a moment he was anxious that Liza might mind about the reference, feel excluded.

He glanced at the dented lampshade with the wagon wheels on the mantelpiece. Then he heard Liza's voice. 'You wicked old bugger, Eddie,' she laughed.

'It's no good,' he sighed, 'whatever I say, I can't stir the shit between the two of you.'

Samuel turned round. The children, one on each of her knees, were quietly sipping Coca-Cola and talking among themselves. He saw the barely formed wrinkles beside Liza's coruscating eyes.

'Makes yer sick,' Eddie went on. 'The bastard loves you. He's got sweet FA to feel guilty about.'

'How do you know?' his hostess asked, humouring him.

252

'I'll tell you, darling Liza, exactly how I know. You remember where and how I met your old man: in a bin and in a state. Blimey,' Eddie said, pausing to take a swig of his drink. 'He was almost unable to look at an electric toothbrush. And what now? That same guy – your husband, my mate – is as happy as anything. How do I know? Well, it's obvious – you're eight months gone, and this very morning, I witnessed him in close contact with a socking great toaster of all things.' Eddie jangled the cubes of ice in his glass. 'In fact,' he added, 'close contact is an understatement. He was fondling its bloody knob.'

'We had a lovely time,' Nell told Cillian a week or so later when they were back in London and he asked after her stay in Wales. 'On New Year's Eve itself we just went for a walk, went to the pub and returned to the cottage for a quiet dinner, just us lot. None of that enforced festivity.'

It was a Tuesday afternoon. Jake was out at work but Nell and the old man were at home. Cillian had just arrived back from his annual pilgrimage to the bars of Dublin.

'The only concession to celebration was Samuel putting raisins in a bowl with brandy. He set fire to them and dipped his hands through the blue flames to retrieve them.'

'What? Is the fellow turning into a masochist?' Cillian asked. 'Wasn't that the sort of thing T. E. Lawrence enjoyed?'

'We all did it; it's some funny tradition,' Nell explained. 'They were delicious.'

Cillian leaned back against the cushions on his sofa. He seemed tired and, Nell guessed, in a certain amount of pain. 'How about you?' she enquired. 'I want to hear about Dublin.'

'Much the same as last year, and all the years before that. More dead, that's all.'

'Friends, Cillian? I'm sorry.'

'Friends, family. You name it.' He lit a cigarette. 'Ex-lovers. Ach, fuck it. I won't be going back, I doubt.'

'Why not?'

Cillian lifted his stiff hand and waved away her concern, like a bee that was bothering him. 'Ach,' he repeated.

'Get pissed?' Nell asked brightly, delicately.

'What d'you think? Not a minute went by . . .' Cillian's voice trailed off.

Nell was picturing his liver. She had an image in her mind of a yellow-green thing, shrunken and small, like one of those elastic slippers that shrivels and bends when the wearer takes it off.

'I don't go to Dublin and stay sober.'

'No, of course.'

'You sound like my fucking ex-wives, for fuck's sake.'

Nell said nothing.

'What?' he snapped.

'I didn't say anything.'

Cillian took a handkerchief out of the pocket of his old jacket, and dabbed his watery eyes.

They could hear the splatter of rain under the tyres of the car outside. Nell could see that the day was grey and bleak.

'I can't go back there,' Cillian announced again, crossly.

No response.

'Nell, are you still here? Where've you gone?'

'I haven't moved.'

'Well, why the hell aren't you talking to me, then?'

'You're in one of your self-pitying moods. I can't bear it. We've haven't seen each other for over a week.'

Silence.

'I don't think I'll be going back to Dublin,' Cillian said again, after some moments.

'I know,' Nell came back, 'and I've never heard anything so absurd.'

'I'm bloody old, probably won't make it to next year, and I don't give a shit.'

'That's all right, then,' Nell rejoined. 'But I'm afraid I think you will.'

'I admire your optimism.'

'And who do you suppose drummed that into me? Mm?'

The old man shrugged. 'Not just me,' he whispered. 'O'Neills generally.'

Nell smiled. 'Okay, and Jake too.'

'And Samuel Sorrell,' Cillian added.

'Him as well. But mainly you. And now you're being unspeakably pessimistic.'

There was a long pause. Then in a voice barely audible, Cillian said, 'I'm sorry, my bee.' He shook his head sadly. 'In my advanced geriatric state, I begin to wonder if perhaps you weren't right all along.'

'Nonsense,' Nell said. 'Look at me and Jake.'

'I concede an exception to my theory,' he told her, holding out his hand to indicate she should sit beside him. 'Allow me the luxury of being a grouchy old cynic in my old age, if I promise always to consider you two as scope for hope?'

Nell squeezed his hand. 'Let me think about that one. I'll tell you tomorrow.'

'When I kick the bucket . . .' he began, then stopped.

'When you eventually kick the bucket,' she corrected. 'What?'

'Promise not to be angry.'

'Yes.'

'I'll have one consolation – at least I'd given you a small helping hand down off the shelf.'

'I'm not off the shelf,' Nell protested, enjoying the conversation suddenly, and pleased she had managed to snap Cillian out of his mood.

'You wait, my bee,' he told her, tapping his nose knowingly with his finger. 'You just wait.'

# CHAPTER

## 12

'I think I fancy a bit of fresh air,' Cillian said a short while later. He finished the cup of tea Nell had brought him and put it down on the low table in front of the sofa. 'How about a walk, angel?'

'It's very cold and wet out there,' Nell said looking out of the window at the threatening sky. It was getting dark.

'No matter. We have coats and umbrellas. What are they for but to keep off the wind and the rain?' Cillian rose as hastily as his years would allow. 'I think we should wander along to the Natural History Museum, drop in on Jakey. He'll be leaving work soon. We can bring him back here in a cab.'

'I hope he won't mind us just turning up out of the blue.'

'Why on earth should he?' Cillian asked. 'I don't do it often. I think he secretly rather likes showing off his latest additions to the collection, describing all the new ones to me. He doesn't let any old Tom, Dick and Harry see his bees, you know, only the occasional bee type, and you and me. He hasn't got the time.'

'We're lucky, then,' Nell remarked, following the poet into the passage. They went along to the hall.

'He's fond of us, that's why,' Cillian chuckled. Nell helped him into his coat and gave him his black umbrella.

'Don't forget your scarf,' he reminded her. 'And none of that suede jacket lark. You must wear that old coat I gave you. It's bloody freezing out there.'

Nell laughed. 'If I said the same to you, you'd say I sounded like one of your bloody ex-wives!'

256

'That is as may be,' Cillian said, opening the front door and stepping into the lift. 'But I'm allowed to fuss about you. It's the privilege of the geriatric with one foot in the grave.' His tone had graduated from self-pity to humour.

Downstairs, they stepped out into the harsh street. The cold was uncompromising, but Cillian was not deterred. He slipped his arm through Nell's.

'I thought,' he said, ignoring the weather as they strolled along the pavement, 'we might embark on *Remembrance of Things Past* this year. Would you like that, angel?'

'Yes, now the *Cherry Orchard* run is over. That sounds like a very good idea. It's not as if I'm going to be pressed to find the time.'

'Ah, so you do think I might not have long? Are you worried we won't finish it before I go down the hatch?'

'No, silly. I meant the job offers haven't exactly been flooding in.'

'They will. The reviews were good for *The Cherry Orchard*.'

'For the production, yes. They weren't bad. But I only had a small part in it. I wasn't mentioned. I didn't expect to be.'

'You were marvellous.'

'How do you know? You could only hear me when you came with Jake, and I only had a few lines at that.'

'He said you were marvellous. Everyone did. You'll get another part.'

'This doesn't coincide with your new pessimism,' Nell told him triumphantly.

'Nor does your lack of hope coincide with your new optimism,' Cillian came back quickly.

Nell laughed. 'All right, all right. I've been thinking I might write off to a few repertory companies.'

'Have you? Well, you could, but there's no harm in doing a few auditions in London first. I know you can find work here. Working with Belinsky is a great point in your favour.'

They stopped beside Knightsbridge tube station. Nell, whose arm was through Cillian's, guided him across the small street by the entrance to Harrods.

'Besides, you can't go off touring round the country,' he said when they reached the other side, 'we've got the whole of Proust to read, and I'd miss you like hell.'

'Okay, I'll make a deal with you. How long do you think it'll take me to read you Proust at a rate of, say, a couple of hours or so a day?'

'A few weeks, I don't know, maybe months.'

'Fine. Over the next few months, then, or however long it takes. I'll spend the rest of my time going to as many auditions here as possible. If I haven't got anything by the time we finish the book, I'll try to get into rep.'

'Seems a good plan to me.'

'Ah, but meantime, you don't get off so lightly: you have to finish your collection.'

'Oh,' Cillian said, stopping at the kerb of Hans Road. Nell helped him cross.

'Oh what?'

'That might be slightly tricky. I can't force them.'

'I know that, but you can try.'

'Yes. I suppose I can try,' Cillian conceded.

'Of course it's different, but Jake wrote his bee book, and he found that very hard.'

'Completed it only with a lot of encouragement from you. He's very grateful for that, you know.'

Nell smiled. 'I had faith in him, like I have faith in you, and it was worth it.'

'Your brand of encouragement is so particularly encouraging: I promise at least to attempt to write whenever you are out at auditions.'

'I think our deal's a good one, don't you?' Nell enthused. Cillian did not reply immediately.

They carried on walking, and passed Yeoman's Row. Then, by a restaurant with a red awning which flapped violently in the wind, they crossed the Brompton Road. Between the Oratory and the Victoria and Albert Museum, the old man stopped for a moment to catch his breath, oblivious to the rain.

258

'What I like most,' he said, 'about our special deal, is that you sound so incredibly positive.'

'I am,' Nell told him. 'It's taken about twenty-eight years, but I really am. About everything.'

Although the old man's hand was weakened by arthritis, when he squeezed the thick sleeve of Nell's coat she could feel it. Under the umbrella she kissed his lined, hollow cheek, before they moved on.

A few minutes later they arrived at the entrance to the Natural History Museum.

Once they were inside, Nell clicked the umbrella shut. Drops of rain dripped from it, and from their clothes, darkening the surface of the stone floor like liver spots on the back of an old person's hand. She and Cillian shivered in the thick warmth peculiar to institutional buildings, and began to make their way to the Entomology Department. Their footsteps clattered on the hard stairs. By the time they reached the right floor, their noses were already tingling with the familiar smell of naphthalene crystals. Cillian was leading the way.

'How do you know where to go, it's so confusing in here?' Nell asked, following her blind companion.

'How do you think?' he sniffed jokily.

In the corridor they passed a man in a brown jersey, brown corduroy trousers and brown socks and sandals. He was carrying a glass case with various moths inside it. He nodded at them as he passed.

'It'd be a pity if you couldn't bear this smell,' Cillian remarked as they approached the doors to the department. 'You wouldn't be able to go anywhere near Jakey, let alone – '

'Cillian!'

He chuckled. 'You have extraordinary flashes of prudery,' he teased. 'I don't know where you get it from.'

'Not from you,' she laughed, pushing open the big door with her shoulder. 'Come on, through here.'

They entered the room with the maze of wooden cabinets

259

where Jake worked. The hushed voices of the scientists in their various little alcoves could be heard coming from a number of different directions. Cillian, sensing his way towards Jake's tiny study, passed the first two rows of cabinets, turned into the narrow passage between the third and fourth, and headed for the window. Nell was close on his heels.

Turning the corner, she spotted, against the fading light of the sky outside and a few yards away from them, the familiar silhouette of her boyfriend. His black trousers were wrinkled at the bottom of his legs, and she could see that the sleeves of his cardigan were rolled up. He was bending over an open drawer, his hands and bare forearms hidden as he fiddled with something inside. He was concentrating hard, someone was with him, and he did not hear the two figures coming towards him. The other person tapped his naked wrist to bring them to his attention. He looked up sharply.

'Oh, hello,' he said. 'What are you two doing here? How nice.'

'You sound as though we're disturbing you,' Cillian remarked.

'Not at all. Nell, hi.'

Nell smiled at him, and at the girl at his side.

'This is Melissa,' Jake explained.

Melissa was short. She had glossy red hair verging on the ginger, and a fringe. Her eyes were alarmingly bright. Their green colour, enhanced by tinted contact lenses, reminded Nell of a pool infested with algae. She had white, white skin which was so translucent that veins could be detected beneath it, in a subtle marbling effect.

'Melissa, my grandfather, Cillian O'Neill.'

'I apologise for interrupting your work. I didn't realise you were with somebody,' Cillian said jovially. Then he proffered his hand to the girl. 'How do you do, my dear.'

'Nice to meet you.'

Melissa was pretty. Early to mid twenties. Intelligent face, no make-up. She was wearing an old-fashioned jersey with a small collar in pale, thin wool like knitted lace.

'This is Nell,' Jake said.

Nell shook Melissa's hand and wondered if she was a research assistant, or a young scientist, perhaps.

Even through the powerful mothball atmosphere, she could smell the girl's delicious scent. Tuberose. Compared to the strong chemical odour of the crystals, it was so fresh and flowery it caused Nell to smile again.

'We'll go and sit in your little study,' Cillian suggested, 'till you and Melissa have finished.'

'Oh, no need,' Melissa assured the old man politely. She had a squeaky, warm-hearted voice. 'We weren't really working. We were just looking, weren't we, Jake?' She turned to him. He said nothing, so she carried on, obviously keen not to make his visitors feel awkward on her account. 'How do you know each other?' she asked Nell. Her smile was dimpled and wide with friendliness.

'Through Cillian,' Nell replied, still smiling, equally friendly.

'Oh, I see.' Melissa leaned over to peer in to the open drawer. 'Well, he's been showing me these green ones, I can't pronounce their name, but they're beautiful, aren't they?'

'Beautiful,' Nell nodded.

'You don't work here, then, Melissa?' Cillian's soft voice.

'No, no, Mr O'Neill. I'm in publishing.' Face still in the drawer.

'Ah.' The old man sounded pensive. 'I see.' Ever courteous.

Jake shot a glance at his grandfather; then at Nell.

'I think they're my favourites, the green ones,' Melissa continued brightly. 'Or perhaps the blues. They're really lovely too. Have you seen them before, Nell? Come and have a look. What do you think?'

Pause.

'I think the blues are very beautiful, too, yes, I agree,' she replied, staring doggedly at the carefully laid out specimens.

Cillian could not see his bee's expression, but he was able to sense that it had changed.

Taking her hand in his, he turned his head, very slowly, to face his grandson. 'Still with us, Jake?'

'Yes, he's still here, Mr O'Neill.'

'You know, Melissa,' said Cillian, 'play your cards right, and I dare say he'll give you a bee in a box for your birthday, maybe, or for Christmas.' His deadened eyes were still fixed, hard, on the younger man.

'Oh, really?' The girl grinned. 'That'd be nice. I don't know much, if anything, about them of course. But, like Jake, I am rather mad about bees.'